A Mt. Moriah Christmas

Kim Smith

MKB Books

A Mt. Moriah Christmas

First edition: 2021

Cover art Joe Therasakdhi at Self Pub Book Covers

Interior formatting Kim Smith, Author

Acknowledgements

Thanks to all the love and support I receive from my family and friends.

Thanks, also to these folks for their wonderful suggestions and editing advice. All writers need people in their life to be their first readers.

Angela Kay Austin

Linda Rettstatt

Ellen Holder

Michelle Fulmer

Maureen Bradford

ABOUT THE AUTHOR

♥

Kim Smith is the author of several genres. Her caper mystery series recently produced audiobooks, and there are young adult short novels. Her writing often stems from life in the Mid-South region of the US where she grew up and lived.

She recently celebrated twenty years as a published author and is so grateful to her readers.

Love Kim's books? Join her mailing list and be in on the latest of her work before anyone else gets to know.

CONNECT WITH KIM ON SOCIAL MEDIA!

Website: mkbrowning.com

Facebook: facebook.com/authormkbrowning

Chapter One

♥

J enny Jones hadn't been home to Mt. Moriah in almost six months. After an intense relationship with Brandon Daniels, the lead guitarist for *Sarcastix*, she'd been nursing her wounds in Nashville where he'd dumped her.

As she rode the Greyhound bus to Diago Springs, she thought about what her life had become. Six months of effort and minimal return in a relationship with a musician whose career was about to take off. Or so he'd told her.

She had been certain he was the man of her dreams when they'd met at the Collins' wedding this past summer. It didn't take long to see the fragility of her plan.

The Holiday Show, a five-city gig beginning just before Thanksgiving, booked Brandon and the band. He'd told her she could broaden her horizons, see a few places. She'd believed him and had been looking forward to it.

But that was before he got drunk. Every night. In his worst bout, he threw her out of the hotel room where they were staying. Alone in Nashville with limited funds, she'd looked up an old friend from high school who lived there. They reconnected on Facebook and Jenny pleaded her case.

"Gigi," she'd said over the phone. "I've gotten myself in a big mess. I need a place to stay for a few days until I can figure out what to do."

"You're welcome to stay here, Jenny," Gigi had replied.

And so, she had. For a short while. But in the end, Jenny swallowed the last of her pride and bought a one-way bus ticket home. Thank goodness she'd had the forethought to save some of the money Brandon had thrown her way instead of spending time with her.

She'd not heard a word from him in days. His drummer, Steve Nicholson, had called to see if she needed anything. Brandon had made no explanations to Steve and the others. Nothing except that Jenny was "out" and no explanation what that meant.

She thought it was an appropriate statement as she was truly out in the cold and out in the wide world with no hope of a future and no promises of help from her family.

And it was Christmas.

She stared out the bus window, and everything blurred. Family was another situation.

There'd be no fancy homecoming for her. The entire Jones clan had tried to warn her away from going with Brandon.

They'd told her, "He's trouble."

Every one of them.

She wiped her eyes with a corner of her hoodie.

Now they'd all sit looking at her across the breakfast table with *I told you so* faces.

Once she arrived at the bus station in Diago Springs, she considered calling her parents to ask them to come and get her, but it was late. Or early, depending on how you looked at it.

Instead, she called for an Uber to take her to her family's address in Mt. Moriah.

Later, as she watched her hometown drift by outside the window, she noted the decorations on Main Street. The theme was Christmas bells and there were big ones strung all along the street in red, yellow, and green. Even the co-op hosted a Santa and sleigh complete with bells strung along the side of it. Happy reindeers stood attached as if they waited to fly away on their once-a-year mission for all the good girls and boys.

Lights and tinsel glittered on a tree in the darkened shop windows of Pandora's Boutique and The Inn on Main Street looked inviting and friendly from lights draped across every part of the building even the walkway.

But to Jenny, it all rang hollow. The town looked dim beneath the lights and the decorations, and it had nothing to do with the lateness of the hour. It seemed like the town held its breath, like it was waiting for her to arrive, bearing bad news.

The car pulled close to the curb in front of her house, and she stepped out, pausing long enough to stare at the twinkling lights in the front bushes, and across the roofline. It looked so cheery, so normal. Like they had gone on with the holidays without her.

Defeat settled on her shoulders.

"Here I come to disrupt all their plans," she whispered.

She struggled to carry her bags to the porch where she dropped them like sacks of flour. She stood at the front door, wishing for a happier reason to be there. Maybe if things had been different, Brandon would be with her this first visit home. If things had been different, maybe she'd have a shining diamond on her ring finger and joyful news to relay. That would show her family she'd made the right choice.

But that was not how it turned out. Not at all.

She rang the doorbell and waited. Someone would wake up and stumble about in the dark to find out who was visiting at such an unpopular hour.

Now, she regretted giving her house key back to her dad. But she had been so certain she wouldn't need it. What a fool she'd been. Brandon had filled her head with so many unfulfilled promises, she'd lost count. And she'd believed every one of them.

She rang the bell again and heard someone fumbling inside. The light beside the door on the end table came on, and the curtains moved aside for a second, then the door opened, and her mother stood there, housecoat pulled closed in front, eyes wide with dread.

Fancy Jones flipped the lock on the security door and pushed it open. "Jenny!" she exclaimed, a little breathless. "Honey, what on earth are you doing here at this hour?"

Jenny dragged her suitcases from the front porch into the living room floor and paused, standing in front of her mother, trying to figure out what to tell her.

"Merry Christmas, Mom," was all that she could manage before bursting into tears.

~**~

Jeremiah Collins stood outside the next day, loading his pickup with a few trays of amaryllis bulbs he planned on taking into his market, Jere's Veggie Heaven. When he stood and straightened, he saw Jenny come out of her parent's house and get into their sedan. Mr. Jones was driving, he noted. They pulled out and took off down the street.

Jere clenched and unclenched his fists.

Was the man Jenny had left town with at her parent's house? Were they home for Christmas?

"Must be it," he muttered, slamming the tailgate a little harder than necessary.

He climbed into the truck, started the engine, and turned his music up as loud as he dared without waking anyone in the neighborhood. Nice angry music. Perfect for the mood he was in now.

He roared down the street, hoping to catch them to see where they were going. But they had already disappeared down the highway leading into town. They could have gone anywhere. If they were on Main, he'd likely see them as he drove through town.

What was Jenny doing home, if not for the holidays?

It was a week past Thanksgiving, and it wouldn't be a big stretch for her to come home for family time, except she'd told him she wouldn't return to Mt. Moriah, ever. She'd be thrilled to see her hometown disappear in her rearview mirror. And him too, he thought.

He tried to shake off feelings that flowed straight from his heart to his head. If Daniels came with her, he'd be sure to steer clear of them both. He didn't need that kind of disruption in his life right now.

When he arrived at the market, he unloaded the boxes of bulbs and situated them on a piece of plywood supported by two sawhorses out in front of the building.

His brother, Joe, arrived, jingling his keys and whistling. He walked up to assess the plant placement. "Looks good, little brother. Maria wants some of those to plant in the front flower bed."

Jere shrugged. "I guess."

Joe bent down a little to stare into his face. "Everything okay there?"

"Fine."

Joe didn't let it go, and asked more questions, digging.

Jere let out an aggrieved sigh. "Joe, it's nothing. I'll deal with it."

His tall brother crossed his arms and gave him a grin. Jere snapped, "Why do you think because I'm in a mood, you're entitled to know everything?"

"You're the kid who came after me. Mama and Daddy told me to look out for you. I'm just doing what they asked. God rest their souls." He made a sign over his chest and looked heavenward.

"Well, stop. I'm a grown man. I don't need you crouching over me with a worried face."

"Okay," Joe conceded. "But I'll lay a wager it's a girl."

Jere twisted around from where he'd bent to hide a watering hose. "What on earth makes you think that?"

"I had that same look on my face when Hope came back to Mt. Moriah."

Jere's mouth went dry. He didn't argue, remembering that time well. His brother had given them all fits while he and his love worked things out.

Jere unlocked the door and set about opening his store, ignoring his brother's smug nod at his silence. He wouldn't share with Joe that Jenny was back in town, or that his heart hadn't forgotten about her yet.

He dove into work to erase the image of Jenny's sparkling eyes and wide grin that threatened to spoil his day.

Later, Joe asked him for brown paper bags. "Had a run of customers buying minor stuff that needed bags this morning. We're running low up front."

"You know where they're at," Jere answered without looking up.

"Nope. Otherwise, I wouldn't ask."

Jere pushed back from the desk and went to the storeroom, pulled out a bundle and went to Joe at the counter to help him finish out the sale for the woman who needed a bag.

When she left, Joe turned on Jere again, arms crossed. "So, what's really going on?"

"What are you talking about, man?"

"Didn't you just see that? Are you even here today? You just cut old Mrs. Hastings off when she was trying to ask you something. She tore out of here like she'd been insulted. What's eating you?"

Jere stared out the front door and watched the woman cross the street, purse draped over her arm, face set in angry lines.

"Geez," Jere muttered. "I've got to get it together."

"You know you can tell me if it's a problem with Dana."

Dana Baker was the girl he'd been seeing ever since Jenny left with the guitarist. She worked over at the Pizza Emporium and had been his plus one for some time.

"No," Jere said, turning away. "Dana is not the problem."

He headed to his desk at the back of the store.

Joe followed him. He lounged in the doorway to the cramped space they used for an office. "Is it somebody else? Come on, man, you can tell me. Who's giving you such a sour face?"

Jere glanced up and noted the concern lining Joe's brow.

"Look, I saw Jenny this morning. It threw me a little is all. It's nothing. I'll figure it out."

Joe straightened and ran a hand through his hair. "Jenny? I should have known. What's she doing back in Mt. Moriah?"

"How should I know? I didn't speak to her. I assume she's here for the holidays. And before you ask, I don't know if that guy is with her. I didn't see him."

"Hiring that stupid band for our reception will haunt me forever," Joe said. "Okay, I'll let it go for now."

The front door opened, and a customer slid in. He added, over his shoulder, "But, we're not done with this."

Jere shook his head and focused on an order he wanted to place with a local grower. He needed more poinsettias, not more trouble. He needed to forget women, the whole lot of them, and plan on more stock for people wanting live plants. That's it, he thought. Forget them.

I need more small evergreen plants, and hardy winter veggies.

He sat back and chewed on the end of his pencil. He'd been considering buying some Christmas trees to sell out back of his place in the area used for parking. It was sort of an alley, but it was big enough. He figured he could place placards at the end of the building leading people to them.

The market had enough solid customers who would buy Christmas trees if he made them available. And sales from that would go a long way toward his reopening after the holidays. Snow had already threatened once, and he knew that if the weather went full-blown winter, he'd be closing the store for at least a couple of weeks.

He was used to it. Happened every year. But this time, he hoped selling Christmas trees would enable him a few extra sales days during December.

Jere bent over the order form, and time passed unnoticed.

~**~

Jenny sat across the dining table from her older brother, Sam. Her younger brother Dave sat next to her, and her parents sat at either end. The scent of fried bacon lingered in the air. The only sound was forks against dishes. Eyes peered at her every so often, quickly darting away. She buttered another waffle and waited.

Eventually, the talk began.

"So," Sam said. "Are you going to tell us what you're doing here on this bright and shining morning, like you never left?"

She dug her fork into the syrupy waffle and took a bite. While she chewed, she didn't answer, and it allowed her time to perfect her story.

When she could, she said, "It's the holidays. Am I not allowed to come home for the holidays?"

Dave laughed and shook a piece of bacon in her direction. "No way. You said you were never coming back home. Your home was wherever Brandon took you."

His mother frowned and motioned for him to stop waving his food around. "Jenny will tell us when she's ready to tell us," she said. "Stop badgering her."

Sam sipped coffee from a blue mug he'd created at his small pottery shop in town. He lifted it in a silent toast to Jenny before draining it. "Whatever you say," he told his mother. "I'm heading to work. I hope it's nothing too earth-shattering, Jen. I'm always here to listen if you want to talk." He said goodbye to everyone and excused himself from the table.

Gus Jones set his phone aside, and said, "I've heard the story, once in hushed whisperings in the wee hours and once in the car. I'm okay with letting the matter drop."

This made Dave frown. "Weren't you the one who said that if that *bleep* of a musician hurt her, you'd take some serious action?"

"Father's prerogative," Gus answered.

Fancy collected plates to take to the kitchen and Jenny decided that was a great idea. Anything to escape more probing for information about her life. Her mother washed, and she dried, neither saying much. It was a perfect opportunity to do some heavy soul-searching.

I need to get a job.

No way around that. She couldn't survive living at her parents' house, mooching off of them for long. But right now, during the long holiday period, jobs would be scarce. The ones that had been available were long gone with kids being off school wanting to make money for Christmas gifts.

She glanced at her mother's profile, wondering if she asked for a loan what would happen. Her cell phone bill would be ongoing. Brandon had paid it for her once and then given her enough money to take care of her responsibilities after that.

What would she do now? She didn't have a car. Her old Toyota had been handed down to Dave when she left. And he'd taken over her old room, as well, she'd noted unhappily.

"Mom," she started. "I've been wondering about something."

"What?"

"Dave's in my old room and driving my old car. If I'm going to stay here for a period of time, at least until I can get back on my feet, how will we work that out?"

"I guess the couch was not too comfy, huh?" her mother teased. "It's all fine. Sam is moving out soon, and we could fix up his room for you."

It surprised Jenny to hear this. "Really? When? And why?"

"Well, he *is* over twenty-one, you know. Way past time for him to move out. And his little art studio is doing well. He's been talking to the owner of the building who wants to rent out the loft over his place. He could move there and be living at his work."

Jenny snickered. Sam was over twenty-five to be exact. His love life suffered from the you-still-live-with-your-mother stigma. Who wanted a man still taking directions from his mom?

She finished drying the last plate and went back to sit at the table. Her father was looking at the news on his cellphone, and Dave had disappeared. Her mother joined them to drink a last cup of coffee before starting her day.

Gus Jones set the phone aside and quirked an eyebrow at Jenny. His openness to talk to her didn't go unnoticed.

"I need help, Dad."

He nodded. "I figured that much on my own. What are you planning to do with your life now? I assume you've had time to puzzle it out."

"I guess I'll take it one day at a time. I have to get a job. I need a car. I guess a little planning would be good."

"Where do you think you can get a job?" he asked. "It's the wrong time of the year to be looking, honey."

"I know, but I have to try. There has to be something. Anything."

"How are you on money?"

She scowled. "What money? I have none. Brandon gave me enough to keep my bills paid, and I budgeted it and saved some. I was going to use it for Christmas presents but ended up using it to get home on." She paused before asking, "Can I borrow some from y'all?"

Her parents looked from one to the other.

Her mother answered. "I don't know, sweetie. We have nothing extra right now. Dave got into some trouble in town, and we had a legal matter to settle. Ended up costing us a pretty penny."

Jenny's pulse quickened. "What kind of trouble?"

Her mother peered at her over her coffee cup. "Well, now, if Dave wants you to know his business, I guess he'll tell you. I can't tell him your situation any more than I can tell you about his. Just know that whatever extra funds we had, we don't have them anymore."

Jenny swallowed hard. This was not the additional trouble she needed today. What would she do now?

~**~

Jere always closed an hour for lunch on workdays. He needed the time away and figured Joe did as well. His brother went home to his

wife and her aunt, who was suffering from dementia. Pizza appealed
to his tastebuds, so he went to the Pizza Emporium around the corner
from his store.

When he got there, it was crowded. He waited in line to order his
pizza, looking over the heads of the crowd to find Dana, the girl he'd
been dating. She worked the checkout registers, and he relaxed. She
couldn't avoid him there.

Not that she'd try to, but she treated him like a second thought
sometimes. On one hand, she seemed to like him, but she didn't pass
up a chance to ditch a date with him. Still, Dana seemed a nice change
after Jenny ousted him from her life.

His mind returned to Joe's wedding reception. Jenny had stared
at the lead guitarist for the band, mesmerized. It was a group out
of Nashville called *Sarcastix*, and they weren't half-bad. They were
getting a lot of attention in the club scene anyway. Jenny became
star-struck overnight. He'd given up trying to sway her in his direction
that night. But then she'd dropped her bombshell a few days later.

She was leaving Mt. Moriah with the musician, Brandon Daniels.

In a week's time, Jere stood in the middle of the street between
their houses watching her load her scant belongings into the back of a
beat-up van. And she was gone.

He'd never admitted to having any serious feelings for Jenny. Maybe
he didn't even realize he had them, or maybe he didn't want to admit
to them. Either way, she'd left him flat, and he never got the chance to
tell her how he felt.

He'd lied to his family about why he went to Nashville weeks later,
saying it was for a trip to a farmer's market there. In reality, he'd gone
to find Jenny. He'd listened to her talk about Brandon's shortcomings.

"Maybe you should have figured out more about him before you
went all in on this situation," he'd told her.

She'd been told the same thing by her family she'd explained, but she wanted away from the small town. She felt like she needed so much more. Then they'd had an all-out battle royal, and he'd left Jenny there, puffed up like a gecko.

He moved up in line and placed his pizza order. "Pepperoni, light sauce, thin crust."

He grabbed napkins, placed them on a tray, added an empty cup, and some silverware before inching through the line to the checkout. Dana looked over assessing the line's length and saw him.

She grinned, and a sparkle lit her eyes before she turned back to the customer in front of her. Once he had thrown in the towel on Jenny, he did just what he knew she wouldn't want him to do. He called Dana Baker and asked her out.

When he made it to where she stood waiting to ring him up, he grinned at her.

"Small pizza, soda, as usual." Then, added in a low voice, "Are you taking your lunch soon?"

She shrugged. "I hadn't planned on it, but I guess I can. That's $11.98."

Jere swiped his debit card. "Well, I'll get a table for two, and you can come over when you get free. I don't have to rush back to the store. Not a lot of business today. Think everyone is at home digesting their turkey dinner, not planning their Christmas decorations."

"It'll be better this weekend," she assured him, doing a finger wave as he took his tray and moved away.

He thought about what she'd said. Maybe this afternoon when he left, he'd hunt up Will at the co-op and talk to him about Christmas trees. The two of them could split the profit selling them together. Joe wouldn't be interested in helping now that he had a wife and a home to go to. Hope would likely have him working the holidays at her dress shop.

That thought made him laugh out loud.

He munched on his pizza and scrolled social media. He finished his food and looked around for Dana, spying her, laughing, and carrying on with someone seated at the table closest to the check-out stand.

Jere sipped his cola and waited for Dana to finish chatting. But instead, she slid into the table with the man and ate from his pizza.

Angry, Jere took his trash to the receptacle and stopped by their table on his way out.

He studied the man. Dark hair, dark eyes, expensive suit, smirk on his face at something Dana had said. Dana glanced up at Jere, annoyance registering on her face. She excused herself, stood, and walked with him a few feet away.

"I'm sorry, Jere," she said. "I got involved with Simon and forgot you were waiting for me. I'm trying to get a lead on a job where he works."

Jere played it cool. This wasn't the first time she'd blown him off for someone else. "No worries, Dana. I'll see you around."

On the way to the car, he decided he wouldn't call her for a while. Let her see how it felt to be *forgotten*.

Jenny had forgotten about him the same way when she'd met Daniels. What was it about him that made women think he wouldn't mind that kind of treatment?

He jetted out of the parking lot, squealing his tires.

Chapter Two

♥

J enny zipped her jacket against the chill wind that blew when she stepped outside. It wasn't a perfect day to take a walk, but Jenny had to clear her head and think. Seeing the worried faces of her parents and the inquisitive faces of her brothers had only muddled her thoughts even more. Not one of them would understand how she felt. Defeat wasn't in her bloodline.

She set out on foot for a nice long walk around the park in Mt. Moriah. It wasn't far, only a few blocks, and she didn't mind walking in the cold. It gave her a chance to admire the neighborhood decorations.

Christmas was her favorite time of year. Everyone smiled and said "hello" and "Merry Christmas" whenever you encountered them. And they focused on giving gifts to their loved ones. The whole give-instead-of-receive ideology struck her hard.

She'd never been a beggar before now.

But it would take money to buy gifts, and that would require a job. She would need to find one fast. After realizing that her parents would not be forthcoming with any extra money to help her, she'd wandered through a few sites online.

But nothing showed up. Jobs in Mt. Moriah didn't exist. The town had no position open for any business. It depressed her. Everyone else found jobs online these days, but not here.

Instead, she would have to go face-to-face with people she knew in town and ask if they had any positions available. If the gossip mill weren't already in full swing, it would be when she showed up on the doorstep of every business.

Why did you make such a big deal about leaving home for Nashville?

She entered the park, cut across the grass and the paved road, and stepped through the trees where a walking trail crisscrossed the area. With the added shady overhang of trees, the temperature fell even more. She slid her gloves on and pulled her hood up.

As she walked along, she noted how many of the trees hadn't yet dropped all of their leaves. The winter winds of December still hadn't arrived to shake them free. It wouldn't be long before the woods would be bare and foreboding in their starkness.

Wintry woods would fit my mood right now.

She strode down the dirt path until she made it to a small arena situated for Sunday in the woods church services. It was Thursday and no one was around. She decided this place was perfect for sitting and thinking.

The sun broke through the golden leaves on the tree arching overhead, and she smiled at the warmth and brushed off a bench to sit on.

Then, she focused on her life and what she needed to do. There was nothing more to be said about Brandon. That chapter was finished. Time now to forge ahead and make a new life for herself. She could return to school to learn a trade at some point, but right now being able to pay her own way and not have to rely on her parents came first.

When she'd lived at home before, she'd never had to worry about such things. Her parents made certain she'd always had a car, a place to lay her head, and money. She'd worked odd jobs ever since she'd graduated from high school. Her parents had filled in with everything else. Or Jere had by paying her way at movies and on dates out to eat.

Jere Collins had been on the periphery of her mind all day, but she'd shoved it away over and over. She dreaded seeing him again. He had made it plain when he'd seen her in Nashville that he thought she'd made a mistake and that she would regret it.

And now, here she sat in a patch of sunlight on a park bench, agreeing with him. At least silently. She would never admit it to his face.

On the heels of that thought came another one.

Jere. He was someone she could start with.

He might have a job she could do. He owned a business in town if he was still open at this time of year. He usually closed it down due to lack of customers or maybe it was the lack of fresh fruits and veggies in the winter. He hated greenhouse grown veggies, he said once.

If he was open, maybe he would let her run it for him a few days a week? She'd entertained the thought of working there over the summer, but her life took a different turn.

Normally, asking Jere about a job wouldn't trouble her. They'd been neighbors and friends all her life. But since taking their friendship to a new level last summer, she felt that asking him now seemed a fools' game. If he still held a grudge against her because of Brandon, asking Jere could be a big mistake.

He wouldn't spare her feelings. He never had.

She straightened, decision made.

She had to start somewhere. Jere seemed like the most likely place to begin with. If he wanted to berate her every day for her poor decisions, then so be it. As long as he gave her a job.

Then, dark thoughts intruded on her day.

What if he said no? What if he couldn't forgive her for her recent defection? She'd seen the hurt in his eyes when she'd told him she was leaving.

She stood from the wooden bench, brushed herself off, and headed back down the trail the same way she'd come. Jere Collins would never refuse her. They had too much history.

She hurried along, shoving aside thoughts of how pathetic this visit to the market stand would be.

~**~

Jere returned to work, a scowl on his face. Joe hadn't gotten back yet, and he relished the quiet. He needed time to process his emotions. He thumped a large bag of potatoes onto the ground and shoved it under the table where he kept stock.

Dana and her nonchalant way of treating him had to stop. Either she was in this thing, or she was out. He didn't want to end up watching her disappear with a musician one day. Or a swarthy looking man that even he admitted was better looking than him.

Joe came in about that time. "Do we have any winter squash? The stock looks a little thin," he added, shoving his thumb over his shoulder.

Jere stalked to the stockroom and waved at him to enter. "It's in here, Joe. You shouldn't even have to ask these things now. You've been here long enough to know."

"Whoa," his brother answered, shock registering on his face. "What's with the attitude?"

Jere had to stop his fidgeting and face his brother. "I'm just sick of people today. You ever have a day when you just couldn't understand people? Well, that's me."

"Did you have a run-in with Jenny?"

"No. This time it's Dana."

"What did she do?"

Jere shrugged and headed back into the market area. "Nothing. I'm done talking."

Joe collected a basket of squash and headed back outside.

After a bit of alone time in the office, Jere stood and stretched, and went to find Joe.

"Hey, bro," he said, walking up to Joe who was sweeping the floor in the market.

Joe stopped and quirked an eyebrow. "Speaking to me again, huh?"

"Yeah, sorry about that. Listen, I've been thinking of buying some Christmas trees and selling them out in the back lot. What do you think? Would you be interested in working through the holidays? We could keep them up for sale through Christmas week."

"A little late to the party, aren't you?"

"Yeah, as usual. But what do you think?"

"I wasn't planning on working. Figured you'd be closed. I sort of agreed to work at Pandora's so that Diana could celebrate Christmas in her new home with Will."

"Ha," Jere said. "If you don't help me, then I'll ask Will. She won't be celebrating with him."

"Ah. Well, I don't want to be shivering in the winter weather to make a few bucks. Not worth it to me."

Jere nodded. "Okay, old man. I'll ask Will."

Joe went back to sweeping, and Jere pulled his phone out to dial Will Birmingham.

"Yo," Will said when he answered.

"Yo yourself."

This was usual banter for them when calling, which they rarely did these days.

"I would have texted you, but you never answer them, seeing as how you have a girlfriend now," Jere said.

"Do too. Eventually."

"Well, this couldn't wait, hence why I'm calling. Do you want to go get a beer this evening and talk about Christmas trees?"

"Christmas trees?"

"Yeah, I'm about to order some and sell them for extra income. You want to get a slice of the pie?"

"Sure, man. Always up for cash."

"Meet me at Carl's. I'm feeling like crawfish and brew."

"Sounds good. What time?"

"Seven?"

"I got you, man," Will said, and they disconnected.

Jere went back to the stockroom and pulled out a carton or two of cucumbers. Hot house grown, but always a big purchase. He felt much better now than he had earlier. Women would not rule his day. Past, or present.

He and Joe were preparing to close the market for the day when Jenny entered. Jere felt all the air in the place evaporate and it became hard to breathe.

She nodded to Joe who turned to look at Jere.

"Hey, Jere," Joe said, goading. "Look who's here."

Jere didn't know what to do. Should he shake her hand, give her a hug, or ask her to leave? He stood there, like a deer caught in headlights.

Joe left, headed to the stockroom.

"What's up?" Jenny asked, an attempt to be friendly.

"What are you doing here?" He didn't mean to sound so hateful, but the words came out in a rush, and he was powerless to stop them.

"I came to see you. To let you know I'm—"

"What? Married? Pregnant? Thanks, I feel so much better now."

A hurt look crossed her face, only to be smothered by a different one. A light sprang in her eyes, and he almost feared she intended to slap him.

~**~

Jenny had walked all the way home from the park, begged her brother to let her drive the car that she once owned, and came to see Jere. Now he stood before her, saying hurtful, hateful things.

Her anger flared. "Jeremiah Collins. What a horrible thing to say."

He fiddled with a tag on a bag of oranges. "Why? Are you ashamed of something? What are you doing in Mt. Moriah? I thought you'd die before you came back here."

She considered walking out, but the need to ask about a job kept her planted where she stood. "I'm home for good. It's over between Brandon and I, for your information. And no, I'm neither pregnant nor married. Are you happy now that you're informed about my personal life? Can you say invasive?"

He walked away, standing near the front door. "I don't care, Jenny. I don't care about your personal life. We said all we needed to say in Nashville."

A resigned air descended about him, scaring her.

"I came here for another reason," she said, hoping to get to the real reason before one or both of them said something that couldn't be unsaid. "I'm looking for a job. I'll be happy to work through the holidays if you have anything I can do."

He turned and glared at her. "Oh, so you broke up with the musician and came home with your tail between your legs and think I'm supposed to just forgive and forget and help you out?"

She nodded. That was exactly what she wanted. "Despite our recent differences, I can be objective. Can you? I'll work hard, Jere. I need a job."

"Get out," he said, softly, turning away again.

She moved to touch his arm but pulled away at the last minute. He wasn't ready. The timing for this was all wrong.

"I'll go, but you have to at least tell me if you'll think about it. I swear Jere, I'll do anything. I'm desperate."

His shoulders lowered, tension expelled. "I'll think about it. Now just go."

She nodded and turned to leave, but a grinning young woman with raven hair stood in the doorway blocking her way.

Dana Baker. Jere's sometime date. Jenny had never understood what he saw in her. She was attractive, but rude. In a matter of moments, Jenny remembered the days before she'd met Brandon Daniels. She had asked Jere to stop seeing Dana and when he did so; she gave him all of her time. They'd gone everywhere together, from picnics to parties. But then, she'd met Brandon at the wedding and that was the end of that.

When Jenny left town, she must have driven Jere right back into Dana's arms.

Jere glanced from one to the other. "Hey, Dana, come on in."

She entered and paused a moment to glare at Jenny. Then she draped her arms around Jere's neck and planted a long kiss on his lips. "Hey, I sure did miss you."

Jenny looked at her feet to avoid seeing the scene play out. It was an obvious attempt to show ownership. Dana wanted Jenny to know that territorial lines had been drawn.

She took a deep breath and strolled through the door to Veggie Heaven, holding her head as high as she could.

When she got to her car, she glanced back at the little market and thought about all the good times she'd had with Jere. What she had done to hurt him might never be fixed now. Dana was vindictive, and she would make sure of it.

Jenny eased through the town she'd grown up in, decorated for her favorite time of year, and wondered how on earth she would ever make her life normal again when even her old allies were her enemies.

~**~

Jere disentangled himself from Dana's embrace and moved a few feet away. "What're you doing here?" he asked. His voice sounded far more strangled than he wanted it to.

"I came by to see if we were on for dinner. Lunch was a bit of a bust. What was *she* doing here?"

Bitterness, like bile, rose in his throat. "Never mind Jenny. Your lunch was a bust after you ditched me for someone else. How terrible for you."

Dana looked out the window where Jenny had gone. "No. She's the one who ditched you. I explained what happened at lunch. I'm talking to people trying to get an office job. I'm sick of going home every night smelling like pizza. Do you know how much I make per hour? It's ridiculous. I'm better than that."

He tried not to smirk. She had no office skills that he knew of. If she was serious about getting an office job, she should try different tactics.

"You were obviously flirting with that guy."

She shrugged and perused the vegetables near her. "Whatever. He said he'd see about getting me an interview. That's all I want."

Her detachment from her behavior and how it affected him made him ready for her to leave. "Look, I have some stuff to do. I'm meeting someone tonight for a drink and dinner. We'll have to catch up later."

She stared at him. "Who is it?"

He crossed his arms. "Why do you care? It's not a date or anything."

She moved toward him, a pleading look on her face. "Jere, is it Jenny? You know she's no good for you. I'm sorry about lunch. I'll make it up to you. Come over tonight. You know you want to."

Her obvious offer of an intimate encounter turned him off. She was too much sometimes.

"Can't," he told her, sweeping past her to the door. "Come on, get on out of here. I've got work to do."

She looked as though she wanted to argue. She stood on tiptoe to get a kiss from him which he gave her, lips barely touching. There was no heat in that kiss, and he intended for it to be that way for a while.

Joe came from the stockroom when she left. "Whew. Man, you've got problems in your life. Glad mine are all fixed now."

"No problems. Jenny will find a job somewhere else, and Dana will have to find another boy toy."

"Not the way I saw it. You got it bad."

"What are you talking about?"

"You're still in love with Jenny. You haven't fully addressed that entire relationship. That's why you're pushing Dana away."

"Well, thanks, *Dr.* Collins. I'm awful glad not to have to pay for that assessment."

Joe stepped closer. "Listen, I'm not telling you what to do or anything, but if Jenny is home for good and that other guy is off her list, then why don't you see where it goes?"

Jere wanted to punch Joe in the gut. "And then what? Let her tromp all over me again?"

"Well, the other choice is make up with Dana. I'm sure she's easy to...manipulate," Joe said, a grin crossing his face.

"Dude," Jere said, moving past his brother. "You're making this so much worse with every word you utter."

"It's my job, little bro. It's my job."

Jere glared at him over a pile of carrots. "Well, find a new line of work, will you?"

"Speaking of which," Joe added. "You going to hire Jenny?"

"I don't know. She sounded desperate."

Joe thrust a hand on his hip. "Just remember she's been our neighbor for a lot of years. You know her better than anyone. If you need help through Christmas, especially with those trees you're talking about, you could hire her."

Jere headed to the office. "I'll think about it. I have to talk to Will first. He's got a connection to a tree farm around Diago Springs. This may all be a pipe dream."

Joe went out the front door, leaving Jere to his thoughts.

What if he hired Jenny? He'd have to see her every day. He'd have to have conversations with her, maybe even hear things about her life he didn't want to know.

But then again, working for him, she wouldn't have to fret over money. He could pay her decent wages and give her a hand with getting back on her feet. He shook his head at these thoughts. Did she even deserve such treatment? Joe's reminder of how long they'd known her returned to echo through his brain. He was so conflicted.

~**~

Jenny made it back home and sat in the car for a few minutes. What would she do for a job if Jere didn't hire her? Would she even be able to find anything else? She could ask Diana if the boutique needed any help, but she already knew the answer. They wouldn't have any work. The co-op wouldn't have anything either. So, that left restaurants, and the one theater or the library, or maybe the grocery store out on the highway.

She let out a long sigh.

"You're in a real pickle, Jenny," she said out loud, collecting her purse and cell phone. She got out of the car and saw Dave jogging down the driveway.

"Keys, please." He held out a hand and she dropped the keys into it. "Hope you left some gas in it."

"Nope. Ran it all out. Trips into town take so much of it, you know," she answered, a bored note in her voice.

He ignored her comment, climbed in the car, backed out, and raced down the street. She didn't even wonder where he was off to. With Dave it could be anywhere.

She looked up at the sky and assessed the weather. It wasn't freezing but it was getting cloudy. She strode into the house and called for her mother.

"Kitchen," came the reply.

The house was a split-floor plan, divided by the big family room in the middle. Jenny skirted the back of the couch and went into the kitchen where her mother stood at an island looking in a cookbook.

"What's up?" Fancy asked.

"My blood pressure," Jenny answered. "Dave can be so rude."

Her mother looked surprised. "How so?"

Jenny waved her hand. "Never mind. I went to see Jere about a job. He was noncommittal so I don't know if that will go anywhere. Do you know anyone in this entire region that's looking for help?"

Fancy placed the thin strip of ribbon that she used to mark her place in the cookbook and closed it. "Haven't heard anything lately. Did you check with Sarah over at the beauty shop? She hires part-time help to run the reception desk sometimes."

Jenny shook her head. "No, I haven't, but to be honest, I need full-time. I need to make money. I have bills to pay."

Her mother tilted her head and gave her a long stare. "Honey, you're trying to make a quilt out of a tarpaulin. There's never anything here at the holidays. You know that. Right now, most folks are gearing up for family gatherings. They're not interested in hiring."

Jenny knew that. She knew it in ways she wished she didn't. Jere Collins looked to be her best bet, and she dreaded the thought of working with him. He would never let her forget how she'd dumped him for Brandon, and ditched Mt. Moriah for the bright lights of Nashville. And there was the matter of running into the loathesome Dana.

"If you hear of anything at all, aside from part-time at Sarah's shop, let me know. I think I'm going to hit the Internet and see what I find. I may have to go farther out, like Diago Springs."

Her mother nodded. "Let me know how I can help. I'm sorry you have to deal with this right here at the holidays."

"Me too," Jenny replied.

She crossed her fingers hoping Jere would come through. Their history of friendship for so many years had to count for something. She'd swallowed her pride and gone to him. Couldn't he have a little sympathy? She stiffened her back and decided if she ever got back on solid ground, she would never rely on a man again.

As she scrolled through listings, some in Nashville, she realized it was worse than she'd thought. There were no jobs she could apply for in the entire county around Mt. Moriah. Her mother had the whole situation nailed.

If Jere failed to hire her, she had little else to pick from, aside from maybe a few hours a week at Sarah's place.

She ran her hands through her hair and clutched her face. "Oh, my goodness. What am I going to do?"

~**~

Jere slid into the seat across from Will Birmingham at Carl's Craw-fish. "'Sup?" he asked Will.

"The sky," Will replied, bumping fists with Jere across the table.

Jere pulled a menu over and perused it. The restaurant had good Cajun food. And a lively crowd for the week after Thanksgiving, he thought, setting the menu aside.

"So, let's talk trees," Will said.

"Yeah, I mean didn't you say you knew someone over at Diago Springs with a tree farm? I thought we could get some from them and sell them off the back lot."

"You got money to buy them with?" Will asked. "They ain't sold on consignment."

Jere considered his words. He hadn't worked out the plan that far. "I...um...no. I guess I could ask John for a loan, depending on how much it would cost."

"We can get good deals by buying in bulk. I'll call Bobby over at Christmas Forever Farms and get you a quote. You got a way to transport them?"

Jere nodded. "Yeah, I have my truck."

A server interrupted their conversation by asking for their drink orders.

"I'll have sweet tea and your jambalaya," Will said.

Jere handed his menu to the young man. "Yeah, me too, only bring me a beer before dinner, maybe two."

When the server left, Will gave Jere an inquisitive look. "Two beers? Must be Dana. Are you okay?"

"Not really. Had some trouble with her at lunch and then she came to the shop and interrupted something there. Something I will *not* tell you about so don't ask."

Will held up his hands. "Far be it from me to force anything out of you."

"Now about this tree business. Do you have any idea how much money we could make?"

Will shrugged. "In this small town, likely not much."

Jere shook his head. "No, man. Even here, if we start early enough, we can clear over ten grand."

Will leaned forward. "Now you have my full attention."

"So, I figured we could buy trees to resell, and also, wreaths, and any other evergreen stuff that the tree people could offer. Businesses in town are always looking to hang fresh evergreens through the holidays."

"Some shops have decorated their place. Not much need."

"I know, but not everyone. Just some on Main Street. That's the Chamber of Commerce's doing."

"How will you advertise?"

"Signs out front of the stand, online, newspaper."

Will nodded. "Okay, maybe word of mouth would work, too. What are you thinking for pricing?"

Jere leaned back and allowed the server to deliver their drinks. Once he left, Jere took his glass and slugged back the beer. Will raised an eyebrow.

"Man, that girl has got you in a bad way."

Jere took a deep breath. "It isn't just Dana, although she's becoming more and more of a headache."

"I tried to tell you so," Will said. "But if it isn't her, what is it?"

Jere fiddled with his paper napkin, using it to wipe down the condensation on the sides of the glass. "Not sure I want to talk about this yet."

"Okay," Will said. "I'm not asking again." He drank some of his sweet tea and waited on Jere to relent.

Jere sighed. "It's Jenny."

"Jenny?" Will asked, incredulous. "Jenny I'm-a-celebrity's-girl-friend Jones?"

Jere nodded and looked around for the server. "I'm going to need another beer."

Will shook his head. "Me, too, after that breaking news."

Later, when they had finished eating, and Jere felt more relaxed, Will asked his question about pricing again.

"I don't know, dude. What do you think is a good price?" Jere asked.

"Lower than retail."

"Like?"

"Try fifty for the small ones, sixty for the medium-sized ones and eighty for the big ones."

Jere tilted his head. "Really? That sounds too low."

"You want to sell them, right?"

He nodded and held out his glass of tea to clink with Will's. "To Christmas."

"And the wild women of Mt. Moriah," Will added.

"Jenny's not wild," Jere said. "Dana's wild. Jenny's just confused."

Will laughed. "Confused? She seemed to know what she was doing when she left town with that guy from *Sarcastix*. She was the envy of every girl in this town, I think."

"How so?"

"It's every woman's dream to be a rock star's groupie. They think it gives them street cred or something."

It was Jere's turn to laugh. "Then she's about to ruin all their hopes and dreams, isn't she? It didn't turn out to be such a grand play after all, I understand."

"Just don't let her tell that story to Diana," Will said, pulling out his wallet. "We're heading to the unknown territory of matrimony one day. I don't want to have to live up to any musician's standards."

Jere retrieved his wallet also, and they waved to the server to come ring them up. While they waited, Jere and Will continued to discuss logistics of a tree sale on the lot behind Jere's Veggie Heaven. When they parted later, Jere felt much better.

He could handle Dana and her drama, and he might have an answer for Jenny as well. If she wanted to be in sales, that is. He would need someone to work in the market while he and Will sold trees on the lot.

The thought of being in Jenny's presence every day gave him indigestion. Their history was long, and recent enough to have vivid memories. Her glowing face as she swayed to a love song by Brandon Daniels returned to smite him. He yanked the truck off to the side of the road and rolled his window down. The chill of the near December air wafted in to cool his face before he succumbed to retching.

Chapter Three

The next day, Jenny put her fuzzy slippers on and dropped a long tee shirt over her gown before padding out to the kitchen. When she was almost to the doorway, she heard low voices talking and slowed down to listen.

Eavesdroppers often hear informative things.

"Be quiet, man, she's going to hear you."

"No, she won't, she's still asleep. Besides, I'm done talking."

"Not yet, you ain't. I'm not finished trying to stop you."

"Shut your pie hole, Sam. Jenny's my only sister. I'm not going to allow her to be treated like some second-class citizen around here."

"She's my only sister, too, idiot. What? You think I want her to be hurt by gossip around town?"

A pause. Then, "No, of course not. So, maybe we should work together?"

Jenny had heard enough. She wheeled around the corner into the kitchen and strolled to the coffeepot. The two heads that had been leaning together, conspiring, moved apart, and the men looked at her innocently from the kitchen table.

She poured a cup of coffee, added flavored creamer to it, and then a dollop of sugar. The spoon clattered against the China cup as she stirred it. When she had sipped for taste and found it perfect, she swirled into the dining room and sat with her brothers.

"What's going on?" she asked, looking at each of them, one from the other.

"Not much," Dave answered, shoving a big bite of bagel into his mouth.

"Yeah, not much." Sam shrugged and looked away.

She sipped from her cup and set it down, leaning toward them, elbows on the table. "You're both terrible liars. I heard some of the conversation as I was eavesdropping from the living room. What sort of gossip mill has started in town about me and why are you trying to stop it?"

"I guess some folks saw you out in town yesterday, and they started jabbing each other with their elbows and making assumptions," Dave said.

"That's to be expected, I guess," she said. "Why do you feel like it's your duty to stop it? And who is doing it, anyway?"

Sam sat back and gave her a serious stare. "You can't mean you don't know who would do that?"

"No," she answered, returning his stare with her own. "I don't. And also, I don't want to know. People in Mt. Moriah talk. They're going to talk about me and about my situation. Then, hopefully, Christmas will take center stage, and I won't be the star on their holiday tree any longer. Move on."

Dave sighed. "Sis, it's not just you anymore. Sam and I have a stake in this, too. He more than me, actually, because of his little business. So do Mom and Dad. Everyone wants to know what happened. The questions are: Is she pregnant? Is she married? Is she single? Is she broke? Is she..."

Jenny interrupted him. "Stop. Just stop. It's no one's business in this town what I am or am not. No one. They can just keep on wondering. What do you want me to do? Take out an article in The Chronicle explaining the situation?"

"We were going to go to Jere and have a word," Dave said, looking at his plate.

"You most certainly will not," she replied, leaning farther across the table. "Absolutely not. He's not the source of the gossip. I can promise you that."

Sam put his hand out to calm the pair. "You're getting above intervention level here. Mom and Dad don't need to know all this. They've got it hard enough."

"Yeah," Jenny said. "And what about that? Dave, what on earth happened to you while I was gone? They won't give me details other than you cost them a lot of money."

He played with the silverware on his plate. "It's nothing. We've settled it."

"I understand that, but what happened? Listen, I'm bound to find out sooner or later. Someone will feel it their duty to fill me in." She sipped her coffee and waited for him to tell her. He had never been one to keep secrets.

"I got arrested."

Now she sat up straighter and pinned him with her glare. "What? What did you do?"

"I was at the park and fooling around with some friends. A guy got a little wasted and started a fight. I was just trying to stop him. The cops thought I was the one that started it and slapped cuffs on. The problem really got bad though when they found some weed and a weapon in my car."

Jenny's heart sank. "Oh no. What kind of weapon?"

"Just a baseball bat. But because I was involved in a brawl, they called it a weapon."

"What about the weed?"

"Mom and Dad got a lawyer, and we had it all taken care of. Stop with the worry. All good."

His reassurances fell on deaf ears. "So, do you have a record now?"

"Expunged. First offense. Had to do community service."

Jenny sat back and took a deep breath. Her younger brother had always been a hothead. She was certain getting him off hadn't been easy ... or cheap. No wonder her parents' savings account had been emptied. She shook her head as she internalized this news.

"Listen," Sam said. "I'm going to get out of here. If you think Jere Collins is not the stink-stirrer about your situation, then fine. We'll let it go. But don't be surprised when heads turn as you walk about Main Street."

She shrugged. "It's fine, Sam. I'll figure it out."

He patted her shoulder as he walked by.

"Yeah," Dave added. "You should be turning heads for a better reason."

~**~

Jere entered the kitchen at the Collins' household to find John and Maria already up and having coffee.

"What day is it, anyway?" he muttered as he helped himself to a cup of coffee.

"It's a nice, sunny, Friday." Maria injected her own brand of sunshine into her words. His older brother, John, had been married to her for almost thirteen years. They had two kids, Trey, age eleven, and Susie, age ten, both very grownup and well-behaved.

Maria had pulled the three Collins men together into an entire family, especially when Joe had returned home after a fire burned him out of a living and a life. She didn't allow a lot of nonsense when they put up a fuss with her and usually got her way.

Jere liked her immensely and did his best to stay on her good side. If she wanted him to bring home food for dinner, he did it. If she asked for her car to be washed, no problem.

This morning, he seated himself at the table and noted she was staring at him. Not a good sign.

"What?" he asked.

"Did you brush your hair before coming to the table?"

He ran his hand over his hair and did his best to smooth it down. "I guess I didn't."

"Joe says you are planning on adding on to the market stand for Christmas. What is this plan?"

He sipped his coffee and thought about what all he and Will had discussed.

"Yeah, well, about that. I'm thinking of buying some Christmas trees from a farm over by Diago Springs. Buy it in bulk and resell." He glanced in John's direction. The intention was not lost on his brother.

Maria asked, "You have money for all that?"

John moved the morning dishes away, a sure-fire sign he was interested.

Cashing in on that interest, Jere continued. "I might. I did a little research, and we can clear at least ten grand and maybe more by doing this. It would really keep me going through the cold weather months when business is slower. Also, as a test, might be something that I want to do every year."

John nodded. "How much to get in?"

Maria fiddled with a napkin, listening.

Jere sipped his cooling coffee and made his brother wait. "Not sure exactly yet, but Will says if we buy in bulk—and that's what I'm looking to do—we can get a better price."

"You want to borrow this money from your account?"

There it was. The question that had been nagging him since last night. Each of the brothers had an account set up in their name after their parents had died. They had no access to it without approval from the other two. Jere had hit his to buy Veggie Heaven five years ago, though he hadn't touched it since.

"Yeah, maybe," he answered, avoiding looking at John.

"Do you know your balance?" Maria asked.

"No. I haven't even looked at it since getting my store."

"I think I hear the kids. John, eat something with that coffee. You know how it gives you stomach aches." She left the table and went to check on the kids.

John stood with his coffee cup in hand. "Maria made some turnovers, Jere. They're in the little toaster oven. Good with coffee. Get you one."

Jere nodded and followed him into the kitchen. "Do you know our balances, John?" he whispered.

"Yes."

"What's the verdict?"

"You might have enough for this venture, but I think it's fair to warn you, if you bomb with this, you won't have any more for another one."

Jere felt his heart turn to stone. "Really? I didn't realize I used almost all of my money with the purchase of the store. Hm. Maybe I should think a minute before committing."

John lifted his cup in a toast. "Don't fret over it. I'm going to talk to Maria about maybe putting in some of our money as an investment in this. If the return is as good as you say, we all might have a merry Christmas. You can always take your return and put it into the fund when it's all done. Then next year, there will be the money for it then."

His brother's wisdom made him smile. "That's true, big brother. Absolutely true. And how will you convince Maria to allow you to do that?"

He blew across the top of the hot liquid and cast a grin in Jere's direction. "I won't have to. I think you just did it for me."

~**~

Jenny dressed in a warm sweater over a long skirt and her fur-lined boots for a trip into town. She wanted to visit with Sarah at her beauty shop. If there was a chance of even a part-time position there, she needed to move on it. The main reason, she thought, was to avoid working with Jere. Especially since Dana had shown up on his doorstep and flung herself into his arms.

Dana and Jere together like that made her head swim. The potential to see them every day, or almost every day, made her cringe.

If Sarah doesn't have anything, you may have no choice... She shook off the negative thoughts and tried to think of something else. She collected her purse and went to find Dave for car keys.

It didn't take long to discover he had left. She hunted for her mother and finally found her on the front porch, rocking back and forth on a wicker swing.

"Isn't it too cold to be out here?" Jenny asked, holding the door open to speak to her mother. The air that flowed past her into the house was chilly.

"Not for me," Fancy answered. "I'm feeling a bit warm."

Jenny eased out and sat with her mother, who seemed angry.

"You're mad about something. I can see it in your eyes."

"Yes," Fancy answered, letting out a breath. "I guess I am."

"What's up?"

"Not one of my children's lives has turned out as I had hoped. A mother wants so much more for her kids. I had hoped you would find love and a happy home, and the boys, good solid paying jobs to secure their future so your father and I could live quietly in our retirement years. It's been anything but that."

Guilt smote Jenny right in the gut.

"Mom, I'm so sorry that I brought all this trouble back home. I promise as soon as I can, I'll be back on my feet and self-supporting. Don't worry about me."

Fancy patted her leg. "Not you I'm worried about, honey." Then she looked at how Jenny was dressed for the first time. "Where are you going? Too dressy for sitting around here."

"Thought I'd try the hair shop. I guess working part-time there now might turn into full-time after the holidays. Worth a shot anyway."

Her mother smiled at her and said, "Oh, I'm glad. Would be much better than slinging hamburgers somewhere."

Jenny didn't bother letting her know that she'd also spoken to Jere Collins about working at the market. She felt sure her mother would have plenty to say about that.

Once assured that her mother was in a mood over one of her brothers and nothing more serious than that, Jenny stood and took a step off the porch before her mother stopped her.

"Jenny? How're you going to get there?"

"I'm walking today, it looks like. Good thing we don't live too far away. I could actually walk to work every day. How cool is that?"

Her mother shook her head. "Can't you wait until one of the boys comes back? It's too cold to walk." She pulled her jacket tighter around her. "I'm going in for hot tea. Come and join me."

"I would, Mom, but it's Friday, and if Sarah will hire me I could be working this afternoon. So I'm just going to go." Jenny motioned toward the end of the street. "If I see Dave or Sam in town, I'll get a ride back with them."

Fancy nodded and stood to go inside. Jenny could feel her eyes on her back as she picked her way across the yard to the street.

It didn't take all that long to make it to Main Street. Jenny had cut across a few side streets and came out close to Pandora's Boutique. She strolled past, looking into the window at the decorations. On impulse, she went inside the dress shop to see what was new.

The fact was that she wanted to get the gossip mill going as soon as possible and couldn't think of any better way than by visiting some of the women who would start it for her.

The doorbell jangled as she stepped inside. Pandora's décor had been updated recently, and she approved of every single change. There was more glass, more chrome, and more mirrors. Twinkle lights on the tree in the front window glimmered like a prism around her as she blinked at her reflection in a three-sided mirror.

She looked like microwaved death. So bad, in fact, that she darted right back out the door.

~**~

Jere stood in the back of the market's lot, appraising the space and how many trees he thought would fit. When Will had said, "bulk" he wasn't sure whether that was fifty or five hundred.

"Five hundred trees won't fit, that's for sure," he said aloud, walking the distance from his back door to the end of his property line, which fell smack in the middle of the alley. From that point across the alley stood the back of Abe's Absinthe, an upscale men's care store. The dumpsters for those businesses were lined up like little brown boxes.

He held his hand cupped over his eyes to block the bright sun shining from a robin-egg-blue sky. The area was longer than it was wide. He could use some of the area belonging to the shop next to him because they were closed for renovations. Or he might be able to talk to Abe to see if he could use some of his back lot for the venture.

As he stood there contemplating his choices, with his back to the door of Veggie Heaven, Joe shuffled his feet against the sand on the paved road to get his attention.

"Sorry to bother you, Jere, but there's a few folks inside. Looks like we're going to have a busy day."

Jere allowed his eyes to sweep the area once more. "Yeah, okay. I'm coming."

Joe disappeared back inside, and Jere peered across the alley again.

When Joe takes his holiday break, I really will need someone to help me out if I'm going to stay open.

It was a good problem to have, he had to admit, but the only person he'd even considered was Jenny. Chagrined, he considered how he might have to call on her before long if the Christmas tree idea took off.

Then, as if he had magically summoned her, Jenny strolled out into the sunlight, blinking at him.

"Hey," Jenny said. "Joe said you were out here."

He swallowed hard. Was she the reason Joe had come out to get him? Why hadn't he just said it was Jenny who was gracing them with her presence?

He mumbled a hello and turned back to the lot, trying to collect himself. It was a shame she could still turn him into a pile of pudding, even now. He pulled his cell phone out and checked the time. All he needed was for Dana to show up again. But it was almost lunch, and she would be at work, so he breathed a little easier.

"What are you doing out here? Sunbathing?" she asked, a joking note in her voice.

He closed his eyes, crossed his arms, and tried not to give in to the hot words bubbling up on his lips. He walked off twenty steps using the heel to toe method, then half-turned and did it again to figure a square of space. When he came to the end of this procedure, he stood too close to Jenny for comfort.

He glared at her. "What do you want?"

"I-I'm..." she stuttered. "I'm wondering about the job thing."

He moved past her and stood just outside the doorway to the market, arms crossed, scowling. "I haven't decided yet."

Her entire body deflated. She looked sad and exhausted all at the same time. He couldn't believe how terrible that small action made him feel.

"Okay, thanks." She took off down the alley toward the side street and around the end of the building. He stood there staring, heart in his shoes.

Why did he feel so guilty? Hadn't she done worse to him when she'd dumped him and gone to Nashville? Then, when he'd found her there, she told him that she had never loved him, and she had found her true soul mate in Daniels—wasn't this just retribution for that?

He stared down the alleyway, the memory of her straight back and the determined set to her shoulders haunting him. Frustrated, he shoved the entire Jenny situation behind a door in his mind that was reserved for her and what she wrought in him. Pushing memories away and locking them behind a mental door had gotten easier with time.

But as he strode into the building, he heard words from his soul.

"Two wrongs don't make a right."

Chapter Four

♥

J enny fumed as she strode down the side street to get back out on Main. She'd walked from Pandora's to Jere's in the hopes she could convince him to hire her. *What a mess that turned out to be!* Jere was determined to make her suffer for what had transpired between them in the past. He intended to make life in Mt. Moriah as difficult as possible. She'd hoped he would move along and get over it since he had a new girlfriend, but no, he refused to move along at all.

The thought of Dana returned to mind, and she cringed. *How could he take up with such an awful person?* He used to have some taste and class. Now he was like every other man she'd encountered, bewitched by a bustline. Her resolve to avoid ever being in another relationship stiffened her spine. *Such a waste.*

Deep in thought, she nearly tromped past Sarah's Head Shop. When she looked up and saw the striped barber pole, she stopped. *Get it together, Jenny.*

Sarah Greene, the owner of the style shop, greeted her from a booth situated beside the receptionist's area. Jenny stopped in front of the desk and smiled at her.

"Well, hey there, Jenny. I heard you were back in town," Sarah said. "You in here for a cut or color? I can fit you in for a cut, but a color might be a minute. Got a few ahead of you."

"Actually, I'm in here for a more or less business reason. My mama told me you might be looking to hire someone for your reception desk."

Sarah's face changed from welcoming to apologetic. She laid her comb aside, patted her customer on the shoulder and moved to stand behind the front desk. "Oh yeah, honey. I think I mentioned that to her when I saw her in here last. But gosh, that's been a little while ago. I've already hired out that position."

Jenny shivered, fighting the tears that built behind her eyes. "Oh, okay then. Thanks anyway," she said, moving out the door and back onto the street. *I have to find a place to sit down. I have to sit down. I have to...*

The salon's door opened, and someone came out. Jenny, already awash in tears, turned to see it was Sarah. The older woman eased up to Jenny and put an arm around her.

"I heard some of what happened to you. I'm real sorry things turned out that way. And I'm sorry about the job. If anything opens, I'll call you first thing, okay?"

Jenny nodded.

Sarah pulled away and peered into her face. "Until then, for now, go over to the Pizza Emporium and ask to speak to Blaine. I heard he's always hiring. It won't close over the holidays and will be respectable work. You listening to me?"

Jenny nodded again and smiled at the woman through her tears. "Thanks, Sarah. Really."

"Go on, honey. No woman deserves the treatment you got. I'm always here for you."

Jenny turned away and headed back down the street. She was cold and tired and utterly miserable. She'd have to check out the Pizza Emporium later. She moved onto the side street where Sam's little studio was said to be. She hadn't ever been there, but if she had any luck at all today, maybe she'd see Dave's car parked in front of one of the places and catch a ride home.

Fortunately, she did find exactly that. She noted a hand-painted sign that simply said "Studio" and made a quick assumption that her brothers would be found there. She opened the door and the smell of paint and oil assaulted her.

"Dave, look who the cat dragged in," Sam said, nodding in her direction. He was wiping off a brush and stood in front of a large canvas, still in the process of being created.

Dave sat on a forlorn couch at the side of the room and stood when he saw Jenny.

"What's up, Jen-Jen?" he asked, using her name from childhood.

"I need a ride home. I've been to hell and back and honestly, if I have to walk any farther out in this cold air, I think I'll die."

Her brothers both took inventory with a sweeping stare.

"Have you had anything to eat?" Sam asked, setting the brush aside and walking toward her.

"Yeah, you look a little wiped out," Dave agreed, joining him.

Those were the last words she remembered hearing just before everything went black.

~**~

Jere had worked steadily ever since Jenny's quick departure. Guilt gutted him every time he remembered how she'd looked as she turned the corner. If he ever treated her that way again, she wouldn't take it lying down.

When no customer appeared for over an hour, he decided to go home. Joe had already left, and the early nightfall made staying open past four almost pointless.

He locked up and strode to his truck. A chill wind blew against him making him look skyward. Gray clouds towered over the mountains around Mt. Moriah. Maybe snow tomorrow? He had never really been much of a weather watcher, but Maria was. She kept them all informed about what to expect.

He figured it must come from being a mom. She had to know when the schools would be closed, as they oftentimes did close in the winter months when snows blew in. Mt. Moriah, unlike the bigger towns, housed no snow removal equipment aside from what the townsfolk had for personal use.

He got into his truck and revved the engine, rubbing his hands together as he waited for it to warm up. His mind went back to Jenny and the dilemma they faced. It appeared that he would have to concede the battle.

She wanted a job, and he needed her.

Well, he needed someone to run the place for him while he engaged in the Christmas tree situation. She was a townie, and people knew her. They would do business with her the same as they would do for him.

He pulled away from the market and headed home, his headlights illuminating the evergreen trees all decorated for the holidays on the corner of Main and Court. He would have to come up with something for decorations for his place soon. Maybe if Jenny came to work there, she would like to do that.

He realized that her set shoulders and the determined jut of her chin meant he had to forgive her. Just a little. It was for the good of both of them.

"But so ... help me God," he said aloud. "If she ever brings up the name of that arrogant jerk she left town with, I'll clobber her." It felt good to get that off his chest, even if it was to the silence in his truck.

He turned on the local country music radio station, and in a few moments, hummed along to a popular tune. When he turned on his street, he looked first to the Jenny's house. Looked like everyone was at home.

He parked the truck, slammed the door, clicked the clicker to lock it, and headed straight for Jenny's house. *Might as well get this over with.* When he knocked on the front door, he expected someone to answer fairly quickly, but they didn't. He rang the bell in case they hadn't heard his knock.

Sam answered the door, blinked a moment, and then greeted Jere. "Hey, Jere. What's up?"

"Not much, man. How are you?"

"Doing good. What's brought you over at the neighbor's house?"

Jere laughed. It had been an ongoing joke between Jenny's brothers and him for a long time. "Oh, you know ... a girl."

Sam stepped out onto the porch and let the door close behind him. "Jenny isn't taking any callers tonight, Jere."

Something in the way he said it made Jere really stare at him. "What? Why?"

Sam's face was an open book. He looked worried. "She's sick. Fainted at the studio this afternoon. We don't know what's up. Mama called the doctor, and they recommended a clinic visit."

"Oh, wow. Well, no biggie. I'll try to talk to her later, or tomorrow or something. But would you let her know I came by? I hope she's okay." He stuck his hand out and Sam took it, shaking on the promise.

"That I *will* do, Mr. Collins."

Not knowing what else to say, Jere stepped off the porch and headed to his house. He could feel Sam's eyes on his back briefly before the
porch light went on behind him, lighting his way home.

When he was about to close the front door to his house, he looked
one last time across the street and thought he could make out Jenny
sitting wrapped in a blanket on the sofa. He wondered what she was
thinking and if it was about him. He closed the door and leaned against
it for a moment, allowing dread to fill every fiber of his being.

~**~

Jenny sat bundled in the blanket, watching a dull British movie, and
praying for sleep to take her out of consciousness soon. Her brothers
had made her drink orange juice and had taken her home. Her mother
seemed to think it was low blood sugar due to the fact that she hadn't
eaten more than a plateful of food since she'd landed back at home.
Mama's probably right.

But she'd agreed to go to see the doctor tomorrow, anyway. She
didn't feel bad anymore, but she wasn't known to be a fainting type,
so it scared her a little.

Her mother had made her some herbal tea and a plate of homemade
spaghetti. She'd eaten all of that and realized she'd been ravenous.
Then, with so many carbs inside her stomach, she'd curled up on the
couch.

Sleep was coming soon. She could feel it. But she wanted to think
about what she was going to do before she drifted off. She turned the
television volume down and took a deep breath. No work at Sarah's,
no answer from Jere, even though she'd heard him at the door earlier.
The only option left was the Pizza Emporium.

She was less than thrilled.

But it was a paying job. It would keep her bills paid and help her get
a start on life again. Then when the holidays were over and the kids all

back in school, she'd try to get on at a legal office or a bank. Anywhere but a restaurant.

Jenny had sworn to herself once she graduated high school, she would not work at a restaurant. It was not her style. She didn't care to be face-to-face with rowdy teens and drunk hipsters every day or night. And the Pizza Emporium sold booze. That would be the norm, she was sure.

How many kids would she have to ask for ID from every day? How many drunken brawls would she have to bust up every night? She shivered at the thought of it. This was not her life. It couldn't be. Her life was one where she was a musician's girlfriend, like Nicole Kidman, married to a singer, living in Nashville. Her future secure and bright.

What had happened?

Brandon Daniels was what had happened. He had been the beginning and the end of all her troubles. She clicked the off button on the remote and watched the screen go black. In movies and in real life, in songs and poems, it was always a heartbreak, always a devastated romance, that ruined a life.

And it hurt more than anything that Jere had shunned her, as well. She couldn't get over how her former best friend had been so harsh, so dismissive of her not once, but twice. Didn't he at least want to be friends? True, she had said some difficult things to him when he'd seen her in Nashville, but didn't he know she didn't mean it?

She had been talking through her problems, trying to make out like she didn't have any. *No, he doesn't. He was flat out in love with you, and you broke his heart.*

"But I didn't mean to," she whispered to the empty room as she turned out the light. "I didn't want him to know how much I was hurting."

The reality of her words struck her in the heart. If he would ever listen to her, she'd make him understand. She'd explain how admitting defeat to him, when he tried telling her she was going to lose, was more than she could stand at the time. She didn't want him to know how she'd failed before she'd even gotten started.

And she didn't want him to ride in on his white horse and save the day, either.

~**~

That night over dinner at the Collins' house, talk around the table centered on Christmas and what was on everyone's list. Maria always wanted a written list from each family member with sizes so she could decide what was to be purchased and what was just a wish-list.

Trey and Susie had no trouble coming up with a list and promised to produce it tomorrow. Jere looked at Joe's empty seat and wondered what he would say. Since his marriage to Hope and the move to her aunt's house in the holler, Joe hadn't been around much for meals. Jere hoped he would be around for at least a holiday brunch, which they always had on the day before Christmas.

"Has anyone heard anything from Joe?" Jere asked. "Wondering what he and Hope might like for a Christmas gift since they got all those wedding gifts. Might have been all they needed."

"You don't worry so much about Joseph, and worry more about you," Maria said, wagging a finger at him. "This year is about us, here." She waved a circle that included the members at the table. "Joseph and Hope will take care of themselves."

"Oh, I know," he said. "I just wondered."

John grinned. "You can use that extra money you're going to get from Christmas trees to buy me a big fat riding lawn mower."

"Shoot, dude," Jere said, sharing the grin. "Buy it yourself. You're in on this gig."

The kids excused themselves and headed to the family room.

Maria scooped the remaining mashed potatoes from a bowl and dumped it on Jere's plate. "You eat more and talk less."

He gaped at her. "Maria. I can't eat all that."

"Try," she answered, as she headed to the kitchen with the bowl.

He shook his head and dug into the mass. When she came back, she carried two fresh pieces of meatloaf, which she dumped on his plate as well. "Makes good sandwiches. That's what I do."

Jere wanted to laugh, but he was too full. He didn't like to disappoint his fiery sister-in-law, but she was going to keep feeding him until he begged her to stop.

"Okay, but this is all, please. I can't move already." He turned the best sad-eyed look he could muster on her.

She relented. "Okay. Just don't want you passing out like Jenny did."

This raised Jere's antennae. "What happened?"

John watched his wife disappear back into the kitchen and answered for her. "Apparently, she didn't eat much, took a long walk into town, and then around town, and when she got to Sam's studio, she fainted. Her mama came over asking for ginger ale. Something made her sick to her stomach after the fainting episode."

Jere nodded. "I heard she was sick. Going to a clinic tomorrow, Sam said. Didn't know the whole story, so thanks for filling me in. Terrible shame."

"What is?" John asked.

"Well, I mean," Jere replied, a little hesitantly. "She only just got home. I mean, that's terrible to get here for the holidays and then come down sick."

John gave him a long look. "Don't think it's that kind of sick, bro."

"Huh? What kind of sick are you talking about?"

"She could be pregnant, Jere."

Fainting ... upset stomach ... Suddenly, the picture became clearer in his mind. So clear, he wished he could turn the images off.

"She said she wasn't," he muttered out loud, looking at the cooling meat on his plate. Food became obnoxious to him, and he shoved it away.

"She might not know yet," John whispered.

Jere stood and pushed his chair back with his legs. "God, I hope not. I was going to hire her for the market while we sold trees out back. I need someone to be inside, handling transactions at the register. If she's ..." He let the unspoken thought drift away. *She can't be pregnant. She just can't be.* He looked around the room before saying, "I'll figure it out."

John nodded and Jere tore out of the dining room.

Chapter Five

♥

"Now Miss Jones," the nurse said, "just keep taking those pills until they're gone. And go easy on the heavy, spicy food. And do follow up with your family doctor, won't you?"

Jenny nodded at all the advice and glanced out into the hallway. Her mother sat ramrod straight with her purse clutched in her lap.

"Thanks." She took the prescription and headed out of the door. Fancy greeted her and stood.

"I'm fine, Mother, just like I said I was." She hated the snarky way the words sounded but her mother's fear that she was pregnant was obnoxious to her. She would die if she had to bear Brandon's baby.

"Oh, well, thank goodness for that," Fancy answered as she followed Jenny. They went to the pharmacy counter and left the script to be picked up later. Jenny was mostly certain that she wouldn't need to take the pills to settle her stomach. She didn't have a virus. She had something worse.

Stress and anxiety over finding a job was giving her an ulcer.

They got back into the car and drove home. Jenny didn't speak to her mother again, and when she got home, she went straight to the couch and plopped down.

"Do you want your mother to make you a sandwich?" Gus asked. He stood just outside the living room, wiping his hands on a dishtowel. "She said you needed to eat."

"I had oatmeal before we left. I'm fine, thanks."

He left her alone, and she dove into trying to figure out what she could do. If working at the Pizza Emporium was her only choice, then she would just have to deal with it. She looked at the clock on her cell phone. They would just be opening, and she didn't want to get there during lunch rush. It would be too busy to get an interview.

She looked at her clothes. Too casual for an interview, anyway. She would get a shower, change into something more appropriate, and leave in about an hour. That would put her there at almost one. Just in time to wait out the crowd. But it was Saturday. What if Blaine didn't work on Saturday?

She looked up the number to the restaurant and called.

"Yes," she said to the voice that answered, "is Blaine there?"

"Comes in at two," the voice told her.

"Okay, thanks," she said, disconnecting.

She had an extra hour to wait. She wandered into the kitchen.

"Is Dave around? I'm going to need a ride into town."

Fancy looked up from the cookbook she was reading. "Haven't seen him."

Gus poured a glass of tea from a pitcher in the fridge. "Gone to talk to Jere Collins, but I think the car is here."

At the mention of Jere's name, Jenny cringed. "Okay. If you wouldn't mind, ask him to wait if he has to go anywhere. I need him to give me a lift."

They both nodded. She strolled through the house until she came back to the living room and looked out the front window, hoping to see her brother with Jere. She hoped he wasn't gossiping about her. That would be the worst insult, but Dave was not above doing something like that. He and Jere had been close in school and gotten even closer during the time she dated Jere.

If Jere wanted to know what was going on with her, all he had to do was ask Dave. Her brother would not hesitate to fill him in. It was like a conspiracy with those two.

Frustrated, she headed upstairs to find clothes and take a shower. Maybe the pounding of the shower jets would knock some sense into her.

She was almost finished drying her hair when she heard her mother call up the stairs to get her attention. She draped a towel around her body, stepped out of the bathroom, and strode to look down at where her mother stood waiting.

"What? Did you call me?"

"Yes. Dave just got home, and he said if you want a ride into town, you have to come on soon. He's threatening to leave you."

"Okay, I'm almost ready."

She frowned as she pulled the towel off and tugged underclothes on, then dropped a long-sleeved dress over her head. Why couldn't Dave just be kind and wait and not complain? Why did she get stuck with surly man-babies for brothers?

Finally, she hurried downstairs.

Dave sat on a hassock in the living room, hands between his legs, coat beside him. He looked at her when she finally arrived. "About time," he muttered, standing. He bunched up the coat to carry it.

"What's the rush?" she asked, scooping up her purse and phone, and tugging a jacket on.

"I've got business to take care of."

He held the door for her, and she hurried out. When she told him where she wanted to go, he made a gagging sound. "Ugh. Not there."

"Why are you making that sound?"

"That's the last place you want to work, Jen-Jen."

"Why?"

He shrugged and didn't answer.

She gave up and stared out the window. Soon, he pulled into the parking lot at the pizza place. "I'll be back in about an hour to get you. Be ready."

She got out and slammed the door, imagining the rant he'd give her when he returned.

~**~

Jere watched Dave pull away with Jenny in the car. He felt a little smug now that he knew that she wasn't pregnant. She hadn't lied to him, after all. In fact, the family had been in an uproar as none of them knew the truth either. At least that's what Dave had said.

Jere went back into the side yard and through the garage door. It wasn't too late. He could still hire Jenny. She hadn't found anything yet, and Dave was certain she wouldn't either. Not much was available. Jere mentioned to him that he was considering hiring her. His friend thought that was a good plan.

"Lord yes, hire her. She's driving us all nuts about a job," Dave had said.

Jere had also mentioned to Dave that if he wanted in on the Christmas tree plan, it wasn't too late. Jere was certain Dave was heading to the bank when he drove away. But why had Jenny been with him?

He shrugged. Not his concern.

With John, Joe, Dave, and Will in on his tree buying venture, his holiday plan was as good as set. The money had been easier to collect than he had imagined. But since it was a new endeavor, it was not unexpected that his closest friends and family would be supportive. If they all pitched in their time too, there was no way it would fail.

He skirted the kitchen and headed straight upstairs for a shower. He had to meet Dana in an hour. She'd called and begged and pleaded while he was trying to talk to Dave. He finally gave in to hush her up. He figured having a meal with her couldn't lead to any trouble, and if she acted up, he'd take her home.

Simple.

An hour later, he stood outside the Pizza Emporium, waiting for Dana to get off work. She'd said she would get off at two, but so far, she hadn't come out and he worried that she'd decided to work over or worse had gotten a ride with a friend. He paced a moment before pulling on the door handle and stepping inside the restaurant.

Very few people were inside. He quickly saw Jenny with Blaine, the manager. They were seated at a table off to the side of the dining room, their heads bent in a deep discussion.

She was trying to get a job here. She wanted to work at the place where his current girlfriend worked? This was a disaster in the making. Dana would never allow Jenny any peace.

His heart dipped, and he walked up to the counter, looking for Dana. She was nowhere to be seen. When another girl strolled out from the back to wait on him, he asked her in a low voice where Dana was.

"Oh, she left about thirty minutes ago."

"Did she say where she was going?" He tried to control his anger. The girl was utterly unreliable.

"Um, home I think."

He nodded and thanked her, turning to go. Blaine came up the aisle toward him, and Jenny had stepped outside.

"Hey Blaine, I was looking for Dana. They say she's left so I'm out too," he told the manager as he passed.

Blaine murmured a quiet okay.

When he stepped outside, Jenny sat at a table, looking for someone. "Miss your ride?" he asked.

She gazed at him. "No. He just hasn't made it back yet."

"I'll be glad to give you a lift home. I'm headed there myself."

She looked at her cell phone and sighed. "Okay. I guess he forgot about me."

She followed him to his truck, and he opened the passenger side door for her. His truck was tall, and she was fairly short. She had to climb up into it. Once she was inside, he shut the door and got in on the driver's side. They were pulling out when Dave came roaring into the parking lot. He paused beside them, and his window opened a crack.

Jere let his window down. "I've got Jenny. Headed home now."

"I'll let you have her. I've got that package you wanted."

"See you at the house."

They left at the same time, but Dave went west, and Jere went east.

"What package?" Jenny asked.

Jere glanced at her and answered, "Business."

She fell silent, and he searched for something to change the subject. "Did you get the job?"

"How did you know I was applying for a job? Did Dave tell you?"

"No," Jere explained. "Blaine's the manager. Nobody sits with him unless they're applying for a job."

"Oh," she said. "Well, I don't know yet, in answer to the question."

Jere got a text or two and glanced at his phone, lying in the cup holder.

Dana. Let her wait.

He remained silent for the rest of the trip, not knowing what to say or how to even say it. Why was asking Jenny to work for him so hard?

She got out and left him sitting in his truck in the driveway.

~**~

Jenny went upstairs and changed into her most comfortable clothes, a tee shirt, and pajama pants. She didn't intend to go out anywhere else that day. She was zonked. The manager, Blaine, had promised to call her in a few days to let her know what he was going to do. She felt like if he wanted to hire her, he would have done so on the spot, not opted to call her back.

She could feel depression lingering over her like a bad smell. Was she never going to get things going in her direction? Why hadn't Jere even mentioned a job? The door to that conversation had been wide open when he asked about the job at the Pizza Emporium, but he didn't walk through it, or talk about it, either.

And she'd seen his phone screen light up with text messages. Four had pinged through on the way home. It had to be Dana. She wondered why he didn't answer them and then flaunt it in her face. That seemed more his style these days.

She plopped down on the couch, anger lining her body. She grabbed the copy of the local paper that someone had left lying on the coffee table. She hoped to bury herself in something to take her mind off her current situation. If the paper didn't do it, there were plenty of books on the bookshelves in the family room.

She turned the pages and saw a big announcement flash by. She flipped back to it.

"Come all ye faithful, to the Christmas Celebration being held on Court Square on December 17th noon until! There will be food, music, and fireworks as well as a dance party and free giveaways!"

Her jaw dropped. Who was putting on this big event? She sought out names, but there were only sponsors like the Inn on Main Street, and Pandora's Boutique. She wondered if Sam's Studio would be interested in such an event. Sam could display his wares on easels along the sidewalk.

She took the paper with her into the kitchen, hoping to find her siblings or parents there. No one sat at the table. She decided to make a cup of hot tea and wait to see who showed up. Her mother had a rather good collection of teas. Everything from chamomile to green tea with lemon. She opted for the latter.

While the water heated in the microwave, she looked at the paper again. A Christmas celebration. It sounded like fun. She would plan to go if she had someone to go with. She was certain her brothers would go solo or with dates but going with their sister wasn't going to be in the program.

She had just dropped her used tea bag into the garbage when she heard someone ringing the front doorbell. She padded to the living room and looked out to see who was there.

Jere?

Frowning, she opened the security door and gave him a questioning look.

"Hey," he said. "I was wondering if Dave had made it back yet?"

She shook her head and opened the door wider. "I haven't seen him. In fact, I haven't seen anyone since I got back. Come on in."

He stepped inside and shook off the chill. "Thanks. It's getting colder by the day."

"Do you want some tea? I just made a cup if you'd like some."

He smiled. "That would be great."

She led the way to the kitchen, but Jere had been to their house and through all the rooms, on many occasions. She poured more water in the measuring cup and stuck it into the microwave. "It'll just be a sec to get more hot water."

He nodded and strolled to the table, where he seated himself. She took her cup of tea and joined him.

"Looks like a nice, quiet Saturday here," he commented.

She looked down at her clothes. "Yep. I'm not going out any more today. It's getting colder as you mentioned, and I really have nowhere to be."

He rubbed his hands together to warm them and studied her. "Nowhere to be? That sounds sad."

"It is, and it isn't. I need some down time. Time to reassess what I'm going to do now."

The microwave dinged, and she went to make his tea. He followed her and ended up standing far too close to be comfortable. She moved away, and poured a cup of the boiling water, then dunked a tea bag into it.

"Here you go," she told him, handing him the tea.

He took the cup and set it on the counter, then grabbed her hand again.

"Jenny," he said, pulling her close to him.

"Jere," she answered, a note of panic in her voice.

He kissed her. It was a simple thing, really. His lips over hers, hers responding to his. She melted into his arms. For a few unforgettable moments, they were back where they'd been six months ago.

Chapter Six

When he lifted his lips from hers, he couldn't believe the look of passion in her eyes. They were half-closed and sexy. It terrified him. He took three quick steps backwards and fled. He heard her calling him, but he didn't stop moving until he was safely in his own house. He peered out the front window to make sure she didn't follow him. There was no way he would survive another encounter like that.

"What on earth are you doing, man?" he asked himself out loud, shoving his hand through his hair, moving away from the window.

He shivered from more than the chilly air he'd just rushed through. He had a girlfriend. Although she wasn't the best woman he'd ever been with, it wasn't his habit to play women like they had no value. That was not something he did. How did he allow that kiss to happen?

The fight with Dana returned to mind. He was mad at her and had gone to the Jenny's to see Dave. He was only going to have a cup of tea and wait for Jenny's brother to show up. Totally innocent.

So—what was that kiss all about?

He could pass it off as needing a thrill because Dana flatlined his ego. But he could see now that it was more than that. Jenny had seemed hurt and alone, and he couldn't stop himself from trying to comfort her. She had been more than just a friend to him at one time. Maybe unconsciously he still considered her a part of his life.

But a kiss?

He needed an intervention. He walked through the house into the kitchen. Maria stirred something at the stove. The aroma of roasting vegetables filled the room, and his stomach grumbled.

"Are you hungry?" she asked without turning around.

"Yes. What's cooking?"

"Right now, leeks. Soon, mushrooms. I'm making a risotto."

He felt the pull of comfort food. "When will it be ready?"

"When do we eat dinner at this house?"

He looked at his cell phone. It was three-thirty. They usually ate around five. Wintertime meant the sun went down sooner and everyone looked forward to getting dinner and lounging in front of the television.

"Okay," he said, retreating.

As he contemplated the remote and a mindless show to watch, the front doorbell rang. He stopped all forward movement. What if Jenny had come to demand an explanation? What if a good old-fashioned face slap was in order?

He made a quick right and headed upstairs, pretending not to hear the bell. When it rang again, Maria yelled at him from downstairs, and following that, he heard her open the door.

It was Dave. Jere heard him greet Maria.

"Where's Jere?" Dave asked.

Jere jogged back down the stairs. Maria shot him her meanest frown and left in a huff.

He greeted his friend. "Hey, Dave. You got the money?"

Dave handed him an envelope from the bank. "Yep. You buy the trees and tell me when to be there and I'll help you sell them."

"Might need help loading them into people's cars more than sell-ing."

"Whatever. Happy to help."

Jere smiled. "Thanks. It's going to be a great Christmas for all of us."

"Uh huh, and most especially Jenny." He crossed his arms.

Jere hesitated in the process of shoving the envelope into his back jeans pocket. "What do you mean? Why Jenny?"

"You hired her, right?"

Jere looked at his feet. "Oh. No, not yet."

Dave punched him in the arm. "Dude. You're killing me here. Get over there and ask her to come work for you. Do it right now."

"Oh, no. I ... I can't right now."

Now Dave gave him a curious stare and waited for an explanation.

"We sort of had a fight."

"A fight?" Dave seemed a tad worried about Jere's confession. "About what?"

"Well, it wasn't a real fight. More like a disagreement."

Dave shook his head. "Jere. Dude. Go over there and make up. I mean it. She has to have a job and get money or she's going to get everything I've worked for. My bed, my car, you name it. Mom and Dad will give me the boot and give her the gold."

"I'll do it tomorrow. Right after church."

"Jere, I swear, man, if you don't get her on your payroll this week-end, I'm going to move into your room over here. See how you like it."

The thought of sharing a bed with Dave made Jere laugh out loud.

Dave opened the front door and made to leave. "Seriously though, she needs something to go her way. She's making herself all kinds of sick over her life right now. I feel bad for her."

Jere remembered the feel of her lips under his. "Me too, Dave. Me too."

~**~

Jenny tried to stop Jere, but it was obvious he was as shaken by the kiss as she was. She went upstairs and looked at herself in the mirror. Her thoughts while lip-locked with Jere made her want to examine herself from inside out.

That kiss only brought to the surface what she'd been afraid of all this time. They were not finished. Their relationship might have verbally ended, but physically? It was as alive as it had ever been.

The mirror showed no sign of the turmoil she felt inside. She wanted that to continue. No one needed to know about this.

Because this would be an impossible situation to explain. She could hardly explain to herself what had happened and what it meant.

Could she work for Jere, knowing how she really felt? Could he? Because the love on his face, that ... *I'll-take-care-of-you-forever* look ... refused to leave her memory.

In fact, it was the first indication that Jere held anything but contempt for her and she wasn't likely to forget that anytime soon.

She wandered into the bedroom that used to be hers. Dave had made it uniquely his. Band posters on the walls; sporty, speedy car magazines on the floor; and piles of clothes everywhere. She really didn't want to go backwards and have the girly room that she'd once had. Let Dave have this room. She would find a way to get a place of her own.

Maybe Sam would have a spot in his loft that she could curl up in. She flipped off the bathroom light on her way back downstairs, and as she reached the bottom, Dave came in.

He glanced at her as he shut the front door. She turned the corner and darted in front of him on her way to the kitchen. She had a bit more spring in her step than before the kiss. She hoped no one else realized it and asked questions.

Too late. Dave started in on her as soon as she put the water pitcher into the microwave to make more tea.

"What did you and Jere fight about?"

She turned to face him. "What? What fight?"

"Jere said ... oh, I get it now. It wasn't a fight at all, was it?"

She shrugged. "We might have had a few words. Not a fight in my book, anyway."

"He said it was a disagreement."

She refused to meet his gaze and made herself busy pulling a tea bag out and setting her cup up with her favorite condiments.

"No matter what he said, or you said, y'all need to make up. He's going to ask you to go to work at the market stand. I think that's a good plan. I hope you'll say yes."

At this she stared at him, her brain in instant overdrive. "How do you know that? Have you been over there discussing me and my need for a job? David Jones, if you have been gossiping about me—"

"Stop," he interrupted her. "It wasn't like that. He was abrasive to you when you came to see him, he said. He also told me that you were really the only person he knew he could trust to work his registers and all that during Christmas. He's going to be selling trees this year, and he's going to have his hands full. He needs you." He took the water out of the microwave and poured it into her cup. "But you did not hear any of that from me, understand?"

She stood there mute, not knowing what to think. What on earth did Jere think he was doing, kissing her silly one minute, and offering her a job the next?

Jenny took the cup Dave handed to her, and while he made a cup for himself, allowed all the emotions to flow through her. Was Jere offering a job as an olive branch and the kiss had been unexpected for him? Was he coming over to ask her about the job and the kiss just happened? It sure shoved him right back out the door.

She sipped the hot tea and wondered whether she should get dressed and head across the street or not. He needed to explain a few things.

Dave waved a hand in front of her face to get her attention. "Hello, Shuttle Discovery. Are you coming back to earth now?"

She nodded. "Why didn't Jere ask me when he was over here a little while ago? If I'd known that he wanted to hire me I could have ... avoided some things."

Dave shrugged and headed for the table. "Don't know. But Mom and Dad should be home with the groceries soon and hopefully a plan for dinner. I suggest you get all your ducks in a row, or they'll be asking questions."

~**~

Jere's argument with Dana precluded any chance of a date. He wanted to go over to Jenny's and apologize and ask her to come to work for him, but they needed time from the kiss before the next encounter. It was like he took advantage of her in a low moment, and she would have something to say about that.

But he'd come to realize in those brief few moments that she was still the woman he knew. Still the same Jenny. No matter what else had happened in her life, she was the same underneath. Her vulnerable side got to him in ways nothing else did.

He found the remote to the television and flipped it on. The local news flashed on screen and the anchors were making small talk before they dove into the news of the day. When their first segment ended, a commercial came on. It was all about the Christmas Celebration being held on the court square.

Jere had heard rumors about it. The town council was trying to create a sense of family in the small community and sought something that could be done year after year. He didn't have a problem with it. His business was close enough to the site where they wanted to hold the event that it might actually bring in some business.

He grabbed his cell phone and called Will.

"Yo," his friend answered.

"Yo, yourself," Jere returned. "Hey, did you talk to the tree people yet?"

"No. They're closed on the weekends right now. Going to be seven days a week soon. Hope to get over there on Monday. You want to come along?"

"Yeah," Jere said, pacing the floor. "Yeah, I think I do. We have a few investors in this venture already. I think this is going to go over really well."

"Cool," Will said.

"All right. Give me a call on Monday and let's plan this."

"I'm going to set up an appointment. Likely afternoon."

"I'm in."

They disconnected, and Jere finally sank onto the plush recliner and relaxed. Jenny wasn't coming to get him, Dana wasn't calling to fight with him, and his dinner would be ready in a little while. If his luck held, his business would be exploding.

What else could a guy want?

When Maria called them all to come to dinner, John had joined Jere in front of the television, and the kids draped across the couch on either side of him. There was a sense of peace in the family at this time of day, and Jere smiled.

"Food, at last!" John said at his wife's call.

"I'll race you," Trey called, shoving himself off the couch.

"No," John told him. "No racing in the house."

Susie stuck her tongue out at her brother. "Nah, nah, nah, nah, nah."

Everyone headed for the dining room. The smells of roasted vegetables, grilled meat, and spices filled the room. Jere's stomach twisted with hunger.

"Man, this smells so good!"

They sat and allowed John to say grace before digging in.

During dinner, talk was limited. But when most of the food had been consumed, John reminded his children to lay out clothes for church the next day. They reluctantly left the table to do evening ablutions and get ready for Sunday services.

Maria turned to Jere. "You are going to church with us tomorrow, right?"

Jere hemmed and hawed for a moment. Finally, he said, "Sis, I just don't know. I mean, Jenny's back in town and well, I don't think I can face her in church right now."

"Why not?"

"We have issues to work out. It will be hard to have compassion and brotherly love for each other right now."

John wiped his mouth and set his napkin aside. "Isn't it a wonderful thing that God doesn't feel that way about us when we have issues?"

Jere squirmed and Maria grinned at her husband as she rose to take away plates.

"Okay," Jere said, ducking his head. "I'll go. But please don't sit us with the Jones."

"Might be like ripping off a bandage," John told him.

Maria replied from the kitchen above the clattering of dishes. "Can't start the healing until you acknowledge the wound."

Jere really hated when his family was on opposite sides from him. And he really hated when their side made more sense than his.

~**~

Jenny woke up early. Too early, she'd decided as she lay about in bed on her phone. She intended to go to church this morning if she failed at everything else. Why she wanted to go was just her depth of desire for reconciliation. She wanted forgiveness for her wanton disregard for family and the ties that bound her to them. The relationship with Brandon had taken away so much from her, but it had given her one thing back.

Faith.

She believed in the providence of a higher power, and she had the faith that no matter what happened to her, she was going to prevail.

With that in mind, she rolled off the couch and began digging through her clothes to find something worthwhile to wear. Eventually, she settled on a scarlet dress made from sweater material that hugged her curves. She stood in front of the long mirror in the hallway and considered the dress held in front of her. Maybe it was a bit too much for a church outing.

Suddenly, she didn't care. Let the gossips go to their gossip. She was wearing it with her favorite Christmas earrings and necklace. She wanted to begin living again. She wanted to celebrate the coming holiday. If it meant suffering long looks from the old ladies seated nearby, so be it.

Deep inside her mind, she heard the tiny voice whisper, "Jere always loved this dress."

She hoped this would be one Sunday that the Collins' would decide to skip church. She would feel so self-conscious with the memory of that kiss etched in her mind. Every time she turned his way, she'd catch his eye, and she knew he'd be remembering too.

Her mother was up stirring around in the kitchen, so Jenny set the dress aside, tied her robe tighter around her middle, and went to see if coffee was brewing. The scent of it struck her as she turned into the kitchen.

"Mm..." she murmured.

"Almost ready," her mother told her.

They had been through this routine a lot of times over the course of her life. It was comforting to settle back into something normal with her family.

"So," Jenny said. "Going to church today ... will be interesting."

"What do you mean?"

"Well. The first time for me to be back...people wanting to talk about why I'm back ... you know the drill."

"I wouldn't worry about it that much, dear."

"Oh, I'm not worried about it. I'm just hoping that it hurries up and passes through the crowd. And then heads out the door so we can all just forget how I left in a tizzy and came back in the dead of night like a criminal."

Her mother tilted her head and crossed her arms. "It wasn't like that, and you know it."

She shrugged. "Maybe so, but the point is, they don't know it."

"None of their business," her mother pointed out. "And besides, it's a place of worship. If they spend more time doing what they're supposed to and less time minding business that isn't theirs to mind, everything will be right in the world."

"From your lips to God's ears," Jenny said. "Is that pot one of those that allows you to take a cup before it finishes dripping?"

"Yes. It has interrupt-a-cup."

"Oh good. I need it now, and I need to get upstairs and get in the shower before the men get up." She grabbed a mug from the mug tree and proceeded to make a cup of coffee.

Her mother smiled and shook her head. "Some things never change."

Jenny didn't argue, but only took her cup with her as she collected her clothes and went for a shower. It wasn't long before she heard grumbling from the male sector about women in bathrooms taking so long to do their business.

She put on a slash of lipstick and observed herself one more time before opening the door to smirk at Dave. He shook his head and stepped aside with his arms crossed to allow her to exit. When she was halfway down the stairs she heard, "Look out, men. She's back!"

The fact that her brother had even noticed her in a way that other guys would made her laugh. But the words he uttered sent her into a bout of anxiety.

Chapter Seven

♥

J ere followed the family to church in his own vehicle. At some point today, he would have to address the situation with Jenny, and he might need a quick escape if things didn't go well. He also intended on paying a visit to Dana unless she showed up to church. But if she gave him another ration of nonsense as to why she couldn't spend time with him, he would wash his hands of her for good.

The thought of Dana and what she had destroyed in the time they'd been together made Jere frown. She always tried to make him feel like she was interested, especially if it was a hook-up. But on a daily basis, he was treated much differently by her. And the worst part of it was that Jenny had warned him.

He remembered the time Jenny had begged him to quit seeing Dana. Her answer to that arrangement was for him to start seeing her. Jenny had said she would be his plus one. His only one. That thought made him frown even more. Why had she done such a thing only to dump him when the first guy came along that gave her a little attention.

Why wasn't I enough?

These thoughts followed him into the sanctuary at the First Baptist Church. He nodded to a few folks he knew from Veggie Heaven. He hadn't been much of a regular attender until Joe came home. Maria had made it known that Joe needed spiritual guidance, and they all were going to help him get it.

When he saw Will Birmingham, he made a shocked, then strangled face so that Will would know he was stunned to see him. Will hadn't been to church in a long time, either. Diana sat beside him, looking happy.

"Hey, you two," he said in a whisper, bending over Diana's shoulder to bump fists with Will. "Good to see you here."

"You too," Will said with a smile.

"Hi, Diana," Jere said to her. "Y'all doing okay?"

She nodded and smiled at him. "Doing fine, Jere. Just fine."

"We still on for tomorrow?" he asked Will.

"Yep, I'll let you know when. Likely afternoon. I'll call or text you."

Jere patted their shoulders and moved away. He looked around to find where his family had gone. They were seated in the front of the congregation. No back row seating for them. He took a deep breath and walked down the aisle. As he got to the row where Maria and John and the kids were sitting, he noted that Joe was missing. He didn't like to put anything in the mix, but hoped that Hope's aunt, Maddie, was not ill or any of that. Hope was missing, too.

But on the other side of the aisle, Mr. and Mrs. Jones and Dave and Jenny were seated in their regular spots. He took another deep breath and moved to the far end of his pew. As far from them as he could get. He tried hard not to look down the row to see if Jenny was looking at him.

That succeeded up until Brother Bill began preaching. Their pastor was a fire-and-brimstone man of God. He held his Bible for the entire sermon and lifted it up to punctuate his points. Jere heard the message today, all the way through to his soul. When he talked about forgiveness, Jere looked over to see how Jenny was receiving the words being spoken.

She stared at him with tears in her eyes, silently begging. That was almost his undoing. He nodded at her to let her know he was harboring no grudges today.

Maybe never again. He wasn't a monster.

He looked away and stared at his worn Bible. The pages open to the passage that Brother Bill was illustrating. The words blurred, and he wiped his eyes. Everyone deserved forgiveness. He did. Jenny did. Dana could use some forgiveness for sure. Maybe even that Daniels guy did too.

He lifted his head and stared at the baptismal font glittering behind the minister. Above it, planted in the wall, stood a massive stained-glass rendition of the Last Supper.

Jesus even broke bread with his enemies. Seemed such a simple thing to do. Forgive and forget. Could he do that?

Jere decided no matter what, he had to try.

~**~

Jenny had never been so moved as when the preacher talked from the pulpit this day. She was moved to tears. Then, when Jere looked at her, it was like divine intervention. He and she had come to some unspoken agreement in one glance. She waited until the altar call to slip out of the sanctuary.

She hurried to the ladies' room to check her makeup and dab her eyes. She was going to have to face Jere after church, and she didn't want to look like a raccoon when she did so.

While she stood in the stall, trying to calm her ragged nerves, she heard someone come into the bathroom. Then it became obvious it was more than one when they began speaking.

"Well, I heard she came back after he got tired of using her for his plaything. When he got booked for a record deal, that was it."

"I was at that wedding, and she was hanging all over him in between sets. It was pitiful in a way."

Jenny held her breath. They were talking about her! She killed the urge to open the door and confront them. Who was that, anyway? She listened carefully, trying to place the voices.

"She came into the shop and talked to Sarah about a job," the first voice said. Jenny closed her eyes and could see the busty brunette who worked across from Sarah's stall. She had a rather loud voice that carried over all the noise of the hairdryers and other hair instruments.

"Guess she can't expect her music man to foot her bills now, huh?" the other voice replied. She couldn't figure out who that was. The voice was so familiar.

"Well, you better just hang on to your man, is all I'm saying," the brunette added.

"Oh, don't worry," the other girl said. "She'll never get him back. Jere is so wrapped around my finger."

Dana? It had to be. Jenny shook her head, vowing to let Jere know how his girlfriend was manipulating him.

"Wrapped, or whipped?" the hairstylist asked, giggling.

"Oh, honey, it's both. Wait until he gets a load of me now. He won't know whether to sit or stand."

"What are you up to now?"

The pair of gossips lowered their voices. Jenny could hear little of what was said, but then the girl from the shop guffawed and they shared a conspiratorial whisper. The bathroom door opened, and their voices were swallowed into the hush of the church.

Jenny eased the stall door open and looked out. They were gone. She smoothed down her dress and thought about what she'd heard.

"I didn't even know Dana went to church," she muttered out loud as she pulled the door open and stepped out of the bathroom. She looked around hoping to see the women for final identification, but they were gone and the crowd from the congregation mulled everywhere. No one left church directly after services. They usually gathered in groups and talked for a while.

She found her parents laughing with some people they knew, but Dave was missing.

Jenny strolled to stand at her mother's elbow. She waited patiently for them to finish their chat, but her mind was anything but patient. She wanted to have a word with Jere, but not if he was with Dana. She casually looked around and saw the two of them standing outside one of the doors that led into the building.

Jere wore a frown, and a thunder cloud couldn't be any bleaker. She'd seen that face before. It was his look that said he had reached his dead-level end with a situation and wasn't going any further with it. Then, just as Dave strode up to encourage the parents to finish so they could go, she saw Jere thrust his hands on his hips and shake his head.

Dana struck a pose like she was a movie star caught in a lie on the red carpet. She wagged her finger in his face, and when the door opened Jenny could almost hear what she said. Her voice was above a normal tone. Jere waved her off and stormed away, leaving her in his wake. She didn't wait long to follow.

So much for talking to him after church.

Her parents finally took the hint from Dave and wrapped up the stories that they were swapping. The family said goodbye and turned to go. They headed out of the building and toward their car. Jenny looked around to see if she could find Jere's truck and maybe see more of the heated conversation going on with him and Dana, but she was a few moments too late.

Jere's truck roared out of the parking lot and a pale, unhappy look-ing Dana sat in the passenger seat.

~**~

Jere had barely recovered from the sermon's admonitions when his forgiveness plan was tested. Once again, he was waiting for Dana to appear.

She volunteered to work in the childcare center during Sunday services a few times a month. He thought it was generous of her, but he wished she would spend more time with him at church. He'd been encouraged a number of times to join a couples Sunday school class, but she always declined saying she didn't want to get to church that early.

He sighed as he walked toward the reception area to wait for her. He hadn't seen Jenny leave, but she didn't come out with her folks, so he figured she must have gotten a ride home with someone else. He hated that they didn't get a chance to speak. He really needed to talk to her and try to work something out. He had a job for her, and she needed a job. It sounded so simple when you looked at it that way.

I'll just catch her at home, I guess.

The women's room door opened, and Dana and Lori Kitchens came out. Lori was one of the stylists at the beauty shop in town, and he personally didn't care for her. She was loud and rude and made off-color jokes that were sometimes embarrassing. The two were laughing and acting silly.

He crossed his arms and waited for the onslaught. Lori said hello to him and goodbye to Dana all in the same breath.

At last.

They strolled to the doors leading outside and paused to talk. Dana started with her whining about how he should have come to her place and picked her up.

"You get up early, go to Sunday school, and you can't even come by and get me? What is that all about?" she griped.

"You told me you didn't want to get to church that early. I took that to mean you were fine with catching a ride some other way when you were ready to go."

"Jere Collins. Have you ever heard of a cell phone? What do you use that for?"

Her tone was insulting. She had picked the wrong day to start a fight with him.

"Look, Dana, we've had no time to be together in days. You ditch me at your work, either when I'm sitting there, or before I even get there. Then you show up today at church and act like I should be bowing and scraping because you deigned to grace me with your presence," he said, frowning. "Well, I'm a little tired of this game to be honest."

"What game, Jere? What are you talking about? I'm in the childcare center. You know where I am. Why can't you come to me for a change? How come you act like it's my duty in life to be at your beck and call?"

"What? You've got to be kidding me? Since when were you ever at my beck and call?" Jere asked, his blood pressure skyrocketing. "That's never happened."

"Okay, let's just go. This conversation is going nowhere fast." She flipped her hair back over her shoulder and gave him a nasty look. "We can finish this discussion in the truck."

"Nope. You can find another way home. I'm leaving." And he turned and stormed away, but she followed him all the way to the truck, begging him to wait.

He relented finally and allowed her to get in. He didn't bother to help her up into the cab, although it was a steep climb on a good day.

She wore heels too, making it even more difficult. He got a bit of sick satisfaction watching her struggles.

She managed to get into the pickup and when she slammed the door, he said, "Dana, I just don't know what to do about us. I don't think this is working out."

"Don't say that, Jere. Please don't say that," she pleaded, putting a hand on his arm. He started the truck and shook off her hand.

"I'm fairly sure this is the last time we'll see each other." He gunned the truck and squealed tires when he hit Main Street.

~**~

When Jenny got home, she changed into more comfortable clothes and shoes. And once that was done, she went to the kitchen to help her mother prepare an early dinner. Sunday dinners at home were always her favorite. During the winter months, dinner sometimes consisted of beef roast, root vegetables, and some delicious salad or fruit. As she approached the kitchen, she could smell ham baking.

"Yay! Oh, man," she said, inhaling loudly. "Does that ham have pineapple rings on it?"

"Yes," her mother answered. "And cloves."

This made Jenny's mouth water. "What can I do?"

"How would you like to make some biscuits?"

"Sure," she said, nodding. "Where is the flour?"

Soon, she and her mother were chatting like old friends while she mixed up flour and buttermilk and the other ingredients. Then, when she finished kneading the dough and put it in the fridge to keep the butter in it from getting warm, she heard Dave calling her to come to the living room.

She washed her hands free of dough, wiped them off on a striped kitchen towel, and went to where her brother held court on the couch.

"Jere just got home," he told her, pointing at the front window. "You should go over there and talk to him about a job."

"I think he should come to me about a job. I already went to him."

"Jenny. Don't be an idiot. Do you want a job or not?"

"Don't be name-calling, David."

He shook his head and said under his breath, "I swear you and he are the most difficult people in the world to deal with."

"Are not," she told him, turning to grab her sneakers off the floor. "But maybe I will, just to show him that he can't hide from me."

"Yes," Dave said, pumping his fist into the air. "Go, please go."

She sat in the recliner and slipped on socks and shoes, then went to tell her mother that she had to run over to the Collins' house. "I'll be back in a few minutes. You might want to go ahead and stick the biscuits in if I'm not back soon, though."

Her mother nodded and waved her away. "No worries, but you get back here soon. We're going to be ready to eat in another thirty minutes or so."

Jenny agreed. She grabbed her coat and shrugged it on. The air outside had turned chilly even before they'd gotten home from church. She trekked over the front lawn and across the street and into Jere's yard.

He must have been waiting for her because he opened the front door before she ever climbed the first step on his front porch.

"Hey, Jenny," he greeted her. "Come on in."

She did as he instructed, and he asked if she wanted to take off her coat. She declined and explained that dinner was waiting for her.

"I mostly came over to talk to you about a job. I know you're still thinking about it, but I don't want you to lose sight of the fact that I really need to work."

He nodded. "Yeah, I ... um ... I've been meaning to talk to you."

"So, Dave says."

"Yeah, I guess he and I did talk about it for a minute."

"And they say women are the worst for gossip."

He grinned at that and looked at his shoes. "I guess I'm willing to hire you at the market if you still want to work there."

"You know I do," she said.

He looked at her, tilting his head. "Are you sure? You know we have some past history. We're going to have to work through that."

"I'm willing to drop any grudges if you are."

"I don't think that you should have any grudges. I mean, you left me—us—the town here." He waved his hand to indicate the world.

"Yeah, but if I had been very happy here, I would've stayed, don't you think?"

"Sometimes you have to find happiness inside of yourself, Jenny."

She thrust her hands into her pockets and tried not to sound snarky. "I'm working on it."

He smiled. "Okay. Well, when can you start?"

"How about tomorrow? Not trying to sound desperate or anything but I kind of am."

"That'll be fine. I have to go out to look at Christmas trees in the afternoon, so come in about nine a.m. and I can show you how to run the register."

She felt her entire face blush. This was really going to happen.

"Thanks Jere. I won't let you down."

He nodded and opened the door for her.

She grinned all the way across the lawn and into the street. She realized when she got home that they hadn't even mentioned the kiss.

Chapter Eight

♥

Jere closed the front door and walked to the side table in the hallway to pick up his phone. Twelve missed calls from Dana, five texts, and two voicemails. He shook his head and went into the living room to read everything.

"Jere, please answer your phone!"

"Why won't you talk to me?"

"Whatever I did, I'm sorry and I won't do it again."

"Everything was fine until Jenny Jones showed up again."

"I'm going to keep calling until you answer."

And she had. The voicemails were more of the same, only tearfully said. He decided that, for once, he was going to turn his phone off. And he did, knowing that tomorrow she'd just keep trying. He sighed. Jenny hadn't mentioned the kiss, and he didn't encourage conversation on the subject. Anything was better right now than hashing over his impulsiveness.

His nephew, Trey, strolled in and joined him on the couch. They turned on a documentary about national parks and soon he forgot about his troubles with Dana and his kiss with Jenny.

When Maria called everyone together for dinner, Jere reluctantly joined the family. He really wanted to just go to bed but going to bed so early would bring Maria around with a thermometer for a fever check.

She watched him closely throughout dinner. "What's wrong? You don't like the chicken?"

He glanced at her. "It's not that. The chicken is good."

"What is it? You sick?"

He shook his head. "No. It's nothing."

She pointed at John with her fork. "If you all bring a cold into this house, I will stick you all in the bed with some medicine. You hear me?"

"It's not a cold, Maria," Jere told her. "I've got a lot on my mind, is all. Think I'm going to go up to bed."

He left the table and heard Maria speaking in low tones, rapid-fire Spanish. He could hear John trying to explain the whole Dana situation to her, but it all was lost as soon as he went upstairs.

He knew what she'd say. She'd say that Dana was not right for him. She was too loose and too loud. He knew Maria would say that because she had always said it. Maria was a fairly good judge of character, and she had always found Dana lacking. Too bad he hadn't listened to his sister-in-law before he'd gotten so tangled in Dana's web, he was choking to get out of it.

After he undressed, he lay on his back and stared at the ceiling. His life had been on the way to being a good thing. He had a business he enjoyed, a girl that made him happy, and a family that loved him. Who could ask for more? But then, Jenny had left in such a rush, and he'd felt so lost without her that he had settled for whoever could give him comfort.

Funny how Dana hadn't been slow to fill in that role. He considered her reasoning. If she was the gold-digger that Maria always made her out to be, then she was definitely mining in the wrong place. Or was she?

He could be considered a catch to some girls. He had a business. No matter that it had struggled for a long time before finally seeing black instead of red in his books. Maybe Dana thought if she hooked him into marriage she'd live an easy life. He laughed out loud at that thought. She always looked for someone else to boost her into a better job. Maybe she thought he'd boost her into a better life.

He turned over onto his side. She was wrong if that was what she thought. And he didn't want a bond like that. Relationships these days required both persons to work hard and bring home funds to keep things afloat. There was *no* easy street. That was a certainty.

Then, like he had summoned her, Jenny's face floated into his mind. He tossed over to the other side. Why did she always come to mind during his weakest moments?

Simple. She'd been in his life a long time. She had an easy way about her, and she always had the right answers. Well, at least she did when it came to everyone else.

Why didn't she have the right answers when it came to her own life?

~**~

When Jenny got home, she bravely told Dave he was right, and she got the job. He congratulated her, but it sounded a little hollow. He wanted her to get a job as much as anyone, but it was because he wanted her to be able to sustain herself and move out. He as much as said so.

She thought about that after sending him out of the living room so she could pick out clothes to wear to work on Monday. Why couldn't her brothers be happy for her to succeed? Why was it always self-motivated with them?

Guilt assailed her when she realized that Sam had never acted self-serving. He always seemed genuine when it came to her. He tried to help her. He didn't make her feel less of a person for her failings. The difference between her siblings was amazing. Maybe she should talk to Sam and see what he thought about her life and what she should do now.

And really listen to him this time.

She selected knit pants, a long-sleeved shirt, and low-heeled boots, and then made up the sofa bed. When she finally dropped down on it, she pulled the blanket up to her chin, and went over the afternoon again in her mind.

Going to Jere to ask for a job had been easier than she thought it would be, but since Dave had hounded him about it, maybe she should have expected that. Dave was nothing if not convincing. Knowing him, he might have even told Jere he was going to send her over to his house to live, unless she got a job soon.

Her imagination went wild with images of living with Jere. She giggled a little, and then she laughed out loud. What a weird thing that would be. But if she were being honest, she couldn't help but think about renewing a relationship with Jere. She knew him inside and out. She could no more imagine him kissing her for no reason than she could fly to the moon. He felt it, too. There was unfinished business between them.

The look that had gone on at church sealed it for her. He still cared. And after hearing the gossip from Dana in the ladies' room, she felt like he needed her now more than ever. Dana was planning something devious for Jere, and she wanted to stop it before it got started.

But how?

She wasn't friends with Dana. She didn't have any mutual friends with Dana, aside from Jere. She wished she could get into Dana's inner circle. She'd flesh out the situation quickly if she could do that.

She curled up on her side and planned on how she wanted the day to go tomorrow. A new job was always stressful, but Jere would help her. And she would make it worth the effort. Maybe she'd take him a bagel and coffee in the morning. She even knew how he liked it. Black with a teaspoon of sugar.

~**~

Jere got up later than he wanted to. He took a quick shower and dressed, leaving home without even drying his hair.

He wanted to get to the market before Jenny so he could think about things to show her how to do. There was so much to be done on a daily basis. Joe mostly handled sales and keeping things stocked so she didn't have much of that to do. Running the register and helping him stay organized would be a good start.

When he got the place open and had time to look at his phone, he saw a call from Joe.

"Hey bro, what's up?" he asked when he called Joe back.

"Dude, we all have the crud. I'm calling out sick."

"What crud?"

"Sinuses, throat, cough, you name it. Feel like a big fat tub of you know what."

"Aww, man. Yeah, keep that stuff at your house. Get better soon. Let us know if you need anything. Y'all got plenty of soup?"

"Yeah. That's about all any of us feels like eating."

"Okay then. Keep me posted. No worries about coming in, though. Jenny is starting today. I went ahead and hired her. I'll need her when this tree business gets underway."

Joe started coughing and had to let Jere go. He sounded horrible.

Jere looked at the clock. It wasn't even eight yet. His heart felt lighter when he thought of Jenny coming to work. She was the right choice. He could trust her with his business, even if he hadn't been able to trust her with his heart.

He went into the storeroom and began making a pile of things that needed to go out to the garbage out back. Some potatoes had gone bad, and the smell was killing him. He didn't want everyone else in the building to wrinkle their nose at it either.

While he was engrossed in restocking bins and carrying trash out, the front door opened and closed. He stood from his stooped position to see Jenny walking toward him. Something about her made his blood rush. Why did he still get so excited when he saw her? They were past history, not even in the books anymore.

"Hey, Jere," she greeted him, smiling. "You doing okay?"

He smiled back. "Good over here. How about you?"

"Fine. So, what have you got for me to do?"

He moved a bin back into the storeroom and closed the door. "Let's go into the office for a minute. Nobody is up and moving our way just yet."

She nodded and followed him. When they got to the small office, he noticed she had brought a lunch. "Oh, I forgot to tell you. I usually close down for an hour in the middle of the day for a lunch break. Is that okay? You can always just sit in here and eat if that's what you want to do."

She handed the bag to him. "No worries. This isn't my lunch, it's for you." She also handed him the coffee that she carried. "Got it just the way you like it."

He didn't know what to say. He opened the bag and saw two big fat bagels from the Inn on Main Street, and his stomach did a somersault.

"Oh, man. Thank you so much. I actually ran out of the house with nothing more than a shower this morning."

"I figured as much. Your truck was gone when I got up."

"You didn't have to do this you know." He bit into the blueberry bagel and closed his eyes at the taste. After he chewed a few moments, he said, "But I sure am glad you did."

She pulled a spare chair over to the side of the desk and sat down. "It was no problem at all."

He sipped the coffee and stared at her for a moment. "Before we get started, I think we need to address the heifer in the room."

She tilted her head. "Okay."

"I didn't mean to shock or upset you the other day. That kiss was just an impulsive act on my part. I apologize if it has made you feel some certain way about me."

She shrugged. "The only way it made me feel was that maybe you and I are still close. I want that. You have always been my best friend."

He smiled at that. "That's what I want too."

Just before he could tell her a few things about the register and how to run the front counter, the door to Veggie Heaven opened and closed. Jere leaned out from where he sat and saw Dana headed their way.

Her face looked like she hadn't slept much, and she wasn't going to be nice.

~**~

Jenny knew before she even saw Dana that she was approaching. Jere's face went from placid and happy to angry and tight in a matter of moments. Jenny steeled herself for an onslaught.

"Well, what have we here?" Dana sneered.

"Dana, don't start." Jere stood and moved to lead her back out of the office.

She yanked away from him. "You're not going to treat me like this, Jere Collins. I knew something was up. You can't just ditch me one day and not expect me to track you down for an explanation. Why aren't you even taking my calls?"

He stopped trying to herd her. "Because I don't have to, Dana. You're not my mother. I don't answer to you."

"No, but I'm supposed to be your girlfriend."

"Yeah? Well, maybe you'll be interested to know that people who are in a relationship don't act the way you do."

"Newsflash. People in relationships don't sit around drinking coffee and goofing off with their exes either."

Jere glanced at Jenny. "Would you excuse us for a minute?"

She nodded, moved out of the office, went past the bins of food, and stepped outside in the morning sun. She could hear their raised voices from her place outside.

Apparently, Dana had not been keeping her word to Jere about their dates, and she was calling him out about Jenny's presence in the office. He told her he had hired Jenny. Now she was screaming at him about his incessant need to keep Jenny in his life.

They lowered their voices, and Jenny couldn't hear anymore.

She picked an apple from the bin out front and rolled it around in her hand. She felt terrible about being the cause of an argument between Jere and Dana, but even from her vantage point she could tell Dana was just being super possessive and jealous.

I wonder if she would have been that upset if he had hired someone else that was a female.

A few more minutes passed, and presently, Dana flung the door open and stormed out, giving her a shoulder shove as she passed. Jenny controlled her quick temper and gave Jere a few moments before she re-entered the market.

He was in the men's room when she finally went inside. She went to the register and looked at all the buttons and screen. It didn't look that complicated. She should be able to manage alone.

Finally, Jere came back to the counter and apologized for Dana. "She's just bought herself a one-way ticket to lonely town," he told her. "But I'm sorry if she said anything that upset you. You're not the problem. She is."

Jenny nodded and let him go on with a bit of a rant.

"She really believes she treats me well. She doesn't ever give me any consideration at all. Not like ..." He stammered and swallowed the word 'you.'

"It's fine, Jere. I'm not upset, and she didn't say anything that matters to me."

He crossed his arms and moved around the end of the counter until he stood beside her. "That's good. I hope you don't ever take anything she says seriously. That girl has issues."

"Some folks say the same about me." The admission came out easily. Jenny laughed, and Jere joined her.

"You're all right. No sweat."

She pointed at the cash register. "So, show me what I'll be doing with this machine."

He nodded and started tapping buttons and giving her information a little rapid fire.

"Whoa," she said, finally putting out a hand to stop him. "I don't think I'll have any trouble, but I might forget something because you're going through it a little fast."

Someone came into the market about that time and Jere said, "Here, let's wait on this man and you can ring it up. I'll walk you through it."

After a short walk around, the man came up to the counter and gave Jenny his purchases. He had a basket with a handle and had piled the food into it. Jere showed her how to take each item out and to look up the sticker on it on the register. Then she had to ring it in. It was fairly easy. Much easier than she had anticipated.

When the man produced his debit card, Jere showed her how to direct the customer to insert the card into the machine and what to watch for after that. In just a few moments, the customer had his receipt and his bagged goods and was on his way.

Jenny grinned at Jere, and he gave her a high-five. Nothing had felt this good in a long time.

~**~

Jere was rather pleased with how the day progressed after Dana had left. Jenny got the hang of the register right away, and he felt confident about leaving her alone. He went back to the office and finished up some paperwork before getting ready to head out for lunch. Will still hadn't called him, so he decided he would head over to the co-op while he was out.

He joined Jenny out front and told her they were going to knock off for at least an hour. She gathered her belongings and waited for him to go out. He turned the sign over to 'closed' and locked up.

"Listen, Joe isn't coming in today. They are all sick at his house. And I have a meeting with Will to go talk to the Christmas tree folks today. How about you go on home and call it a day? I may not make it back until late this afternoon and if business is slow, I may go home early too."

She nodded. "Okay, no worries. I'll be back here tomorrow at eight o'clock sharp. Right?"

"Yep. I'll see you then."

She smiled at him and strolled down the street, heading toward Main. He called to her, and she turned around and went back.

"Listen, I'm going over to the co-op. Why don't you let me give you a lift somewhere?"

"Oh," she said. "Um ... I was just going to walk to Sam's studio and see if he would drive me home. It's not a bad day to walk, though. Could you just let me out when you stop at the co-op? I can walk the rest of the way, no problem."

"Sure," he said, waving for her to get in the truck. "Get up in here." He helped her up into the cab. "All right there?"

She smiled and nodded, pulling the seat belt across herself.

He slammed her door and went around to the other side. Soon they were heading down Main toward the co-op. Jenny felt like she had always felt with Jere. Safe. It was a much-needed emotion.

When they passed Sarah's Head Shop, the brunette who had gossiped with Dana stood outside the shop, a cigarette to her lips. Jenny didn't try to hide. She hoped she ran inside and called Dana to tell her who was with her boyfriend. She also hoped Dana called her out about it. She had a few things she wanted to tell Miss Dana Baker. And Lori Kitchens had better watch herself too. Jenny wouldn't hold back on either of them if it came down to it.

Jere pulled into the slot at the co-op and Jenny jumped down from the truck and waved goodbye to him with a smile. She could almost feel his eyes on her back as she went down the side street, across from the co-op and toward the studio.

The sun beamed down on her, and she enjoyed the warmth. Work today had been great. Jere was sweet and patient and she had no problems. It felt wonderful to be able to say she had a job. It was going to feel even better when she got a paycheck.

As she opened the door to Sam's studio, she realized that she had never asked Jere about her hourly pay. She didn't even know how much she would be making.

Beggars really can't be choosers, I guess.

Sam greeted her from behind a mountain of canvasses. "Jen-Jen. What brings you here? I thought you were working?"

"I was. I am. We took a lunch break, but Jere has business this afternoon and wasn't sure how long it would take, so he let me go early."

Sam nodded. "Oh, I see. Well, what can I do for you?"

"Drive me home?"

"Ah. I knew there would be a catch."

"I would walk but these boots ..."

"Fine, fine," he laughed. "Let me get these brushes into cleaning stuff. Be right there."

She relaxed. Maybe for the first time since she'd been back to Mt. Moriah.

Chapter Nine

♥

J ere waited for Will to finish up his business at the co-op and then the two of them climbed into Jere's truck to drive over to the tree farm. It wasn't a long way, and GPS found it easily. The two friends chatted amicably while they went along.

"How's Diana?" Jere asked.

"Busy. The shop has been inundated with customers ever since the word went out about the Christmas dance. Seems every girl in the county is planning on attending that one."

This made Jere pause. He had forgotten about the dance. He was confident that Dana wouldn't want to go, and he really didn't want to take her either. The way things stood right now, they might be broken up.

As if reading his mind, Will asked, "You and Dana going?"

"Don't know. Things are a little tense right now."

Will cast a sidelong stare in his direction. "How so?"

Jere shrugged. He wasn't sure who was at fault anymore. If he admitted he had a role in the situation, he would have to look at why and that would bring out a whole world of things he didn't want to think about right now.

"Dana and I have had a difference of opinion as to who should be the attention-seeker at the moment."

"What is that in English? Attention-seeker?"

"Let's just say that when I want a date, I can't ever seem to find her. And when I decided to let things cool, she felt slighted."

Will sat back in his seat. "Oh. One of those."

"Yeah. Let's just say it hasn't been a good week."

"I'll change the subject then. What have you planned for this event with the trees?"

Jere turned into the lot. "Nothing yet. I'm still trying to figure out the whole tree thing. How many, where they'll go, what price I should sell them for. Everything."

Will nodded. "Fair enough. Just hope the Dana situation doesn't cramp your style or plans."

Jere laughed. "She may not be my plus one anymore, man. Hold that thought."

They got out of the truck and approached the building. People walked around, selecting their trees. A man who had been standing off to the side saw them. He wore a quilted vest over a flannel shirt and jeans. He hurried up to them, hand out.

"Hey now," he said, shaking each man's hand. "Y'all looking for a tree?"

Will shook his head. "Well, sir, we have an appointment with Jake. He around?"

"I'm Stan," he told them. "You must be Will."

Will nodded. "This is Jere Collins. He's the man with the plan."

Jere pointed out at the lot. "I'm interested in buying a bunch of your trees for resale over at my place. Is that a doable thing?"

"Sure," Stan answered. "How many are you looking to buy."

"My first time to do this, Stan. Can you let me know what others do?"

"Come on, let's take a walk and I'll illustrate what I tell you with the trees. Jake is on a business call at the moment, but I can help y'all."

They followed him out into the rows. There were several varieties of trees and each one had different prices. Each type had varying sizes, so Jere had to decide on the type he wanted and what size.

"Now," Stan said. "Most people pick a fir because they have fullness. That can be good, but that can be bad too. Come December 25th when they really want their tree to shine, it can be so dry that all they see is a pile of needles."

Jere snickered. He had that problem every year, no matter what tree they brought home.

"But that can happen with all of them if they aren't kept hydrated," Stan explained. "The second favorite is the spruce. And then, of course, good old pine."

Jere looked at each type as Stan pointed them out. He wasn't upset that there were only three main types. He could get some of each kind and cover all his bases.

"How many of each type does a reseller usually buy?"

"We sell in lots of ten, at thirty a piece for small to medium ones. Now, that's a buyer slash reseller price. The general public doesn't get them for that," Stan said. "The larger ones are more expensive, but to be honest, not a lot of folks want one of these big honking trees. They have to cut the top out."

"Three hundred for ten of these?" Jere asked, touching the nearest one.

Stan nodded. "Yes. You can resell them for more. Seventy for the medium ones is not a bad price."

Jere was convinced. He thought he could sell the smaller ones for sixty and the larger for seventy and come out ahead. First year to do such a thing and turn a profit? He was happy.

"Where do I sign?" he laughed.

Stan motioned for them to follow him to the building, where he would work up a contract for them.

~**~

Jenny decided to wash a load of clothes and plan out what to wear tomorrow to work. It hadn't been terribly cold at the market. Not like she had anticipated. Maybe she could wear comfortable shoes instead of boots.

Dave was out running errands for her father, and Sam had dropped her off and gone back to the studio. She and her mother were alone in the house, and she was trying to allow her mother a bit of free time.

She wished she had a car. It would be great to be able to drive herself places at will instead of waiting for someone to come along to take her.

All in good time.

She wandered back into the kitchen, boredom taking over. Her mother had a list on the counter where she was preparing to go to the grocery.

"Hey, Mom," Jenny said. "I'd be happy to go to the store for you."

"Oh, thanks honey, but it's sort of my outing for the week. You can come along if you want though."

Jenny thought for a moment. What was the harm? "Okay, sure. I might find some foods to try for lunches."

She went to collect her coat and debated even wearing one. It was the warmest part of the day, and it hadn't been very cold to begin with. She opted for just wearing long sleeves. She did pull off the boots and tug on sneakers, though.

Her mother decided at the last minute to allow her to drive her car. "I don't really feel like fighting traffic and finding a parking spot. You drive us," she said.

Jenny was only too happy to comply. There was something about driving that made you feel in control. Once they arrived, she pushed the basket through the store a few steps behind her mother. She was in no hurry and allowed her mother time to shop.

She found a few packages of pasta dinners that she could make in advance and heat up the next day. She made a mental note to look at frozen dinners as well. She didn't even know if the market had a microwave.

Just as they made it to the middle of the coffee aisle, Jenny looked up and saw Dana pass by the other end of the aisle. She cringed, hoping not to run into her. She didn't want a big scene in the middle of the grocery store.

Fancy Jones would be the first one to comment on the way low-class folks acted if Dana started anything. Her mother had a sincere, yet direct way to her southern charm. Biting and stinging words were her specialty when the occasion called for it.

That would do nothing for her attempt to re-assemble into Mt. Moriah society, Jenny decided. *Better to just lie low and say nothing to Dana at all.*

But the next time they entered the next aisle, she saw Dana on the far end of it, practically clinging to the arm of a man. This was no fatherly type of connection. The woman was all over him, pecking his cheek and pinching his butt playfully.

Jenny felt her stomach turn to jelly. Her mother seemed oblivious to any of the goings on and kept on walking straight toward the couple.

When they got close enough for Dana to look up and recognize who was watching her, she pulled the man away from them and hauled him toward the frozen food section, talking to him in a hurried whisper.

Fancy turned to Jenny and frowned. "Wasn't that—"

"Yes, yes it was."

"Isn't she—"

"Yes, yes she is."

"Well, I declare. What on earth is she going on about? They seemed a little too familiar with each other to me."

"Yep. And I'll bet Jere doesn't know it either."

Fancy pulled her purse higher on her shoulder. "Best not tell him in front of Maria. That girl has true Hispanic blood with a fiery temper to go with it. But I must say..."

Jenny nodded, and they went on. Her mother didn't even have to finish her thought aloud. Jenny heard it loud and clear.

She watched for Dana the rest of the trip, seeing her with the swarthy dark man jetting out of the store before she and her mother got to the checkout.

I'm telling Jere. He deserves so much better than that cheating so and so.

Chapter Ten

♥

J ere couldn't wait to get home to tell John about his dealings with the tree farm. He was certain this would be the best thing to happen to Jere's Veggie Heaven since he'd opened it. But when he pulled into the driveway, John wasn't home. He climbed out of the truck, walked to the front door, put his key in, and went inside. He yelled for Maria, but she didn't answer either. Neither of the kids were home.

He wandered through the house looking for a note, and finally saw it propped up on the coffeemaker.

"Gone to Joe and Hope's to take soup. All the family is sick. Be back soon. Us"

"Wow," he said aloud. "Must be bad for Maria to make soup."

He wondered if he should get back in the car and drive out to the holler and check on things, but then decided it would be better to wait for the others to get home and get the information from them.

"I can't get sick now," he muttered. And as if to fight off any bugs he might encounter, he shook out two vitamins and chewed them up. They were gummies but of adult variety. They were good too, which made him mind less about taking them.

He peered out at the driveway across the street and saw Jenny and her mother get home. They pulled bags of groceries from the back of the car and hauled them inside. He felt a twinge of guilt for not going over to help, but he wanted to let Jenny breathe a little. She had to be around him all day, as it was.

Things would really kick in tomorrow. The Christmas tree people had offered delivery of trees to the shop at no charge. They had a nice, big flatbed that they could haul them over on. This had been a major sticking point for him, and now it was settled. He wanted to run through the house screaming yippee but refrained.

Instead, he went to the kitchen, made himself a bowl of what was left of the chicken soup that Maria had whipped up for Joe and his family. It was still warm, so he pulled crackers from the pantry and sat at the table to eat. He pulled his phone out to scroll social media while he ate and found that there were a couple of missed calls.

First one was from Maria telling him where they were going and why.

Second one was from Jenny. She sounded mysterious. He looked at the time. She'd just called a few moments ago. He dialed her up and waited while it rang.

"Hello?"

"Jenny? It's Jere. I got your voice mail. I'm at home if you want to slide over."

"Oh okay. Yeah, maybe it's better if I tell you this in person."

"Door's open. I'm in the kitchen slurping soup."

"You sick?"

"No. I'll explain when you get here."

"See you."

They disconnected, and he got up to grab some milk from the fridge. He was sitting at the table sipping it when Jenny strolled in.

"Oh, that smells great," she said, sniffing his bowl.

"Maria made some for Joe and family. They're all sick. It's still warm, get you a bowl."

She shook her head. "Can't stay long. Mama's about to start on our dinner and I need to get back. But, um ..."

Jere lifted his eyebrows. "What's on your mind? You sounded weird on the phone."

"Yeah, about that ... Did you know Dana was seeing someone else?"

He set the spoon down gently in the bowl. "Well, I didn't have any proof until now."

"I swear I'm not trying to start anything here, but she was practically making out with this guy she was with in the grocery store. I mean, out where anyone and everyone could see them. I'm shocked someone else hasn't told you."

He nodded. "I have been getting this vibe from her that she just wants to use me for times when she can't get the interest of anyone else. That's what the blow-up was about at the market."

"Looks like there's a reason for it." Jenny's eyes were kind and concerned.

He smiled at her. "Don't worry about me or her. We're toast, it seems, anyway."

"Not until she says so, apparently. Listen, she's the sort of person who will bounce back to you when her current plan doesn't play out like she wants it to. Don't be available when she does."

He stared at her.

Why? Do you want to bounce back to me now?

~**~

Jenny was mostly silent while helping her mother fix dinner. She washed and sliced cucumbers, tomatoes, and carrots for a salad. The two of them rarely got into each other's way from years of doing chores together. It was soothing to Jenny's soul.

Jere had taken what she'd said about Dana too well. He didn't seem surprised to begin with, but he just *accepted* it. That told her he wasn't that crazy about Dana after all. But then again, what man would be? The image of the dark man Dana had been clinging to came to mind.

It was like some bad romance movie where the ex-girlfriend discovers the mess the current girlfriend is walking in and tells the man. Usually in the movies, though, the person relaying the info was made out to be a liar, or even worse, accused of trying to hurt the man who had left her for the other.

Jenny didn't want to be that person. As she moved from task to task, she made up her mind not to run to Jere with everything she heard and saw out of Dana from that point forward. It was none of her business. If he wanted to know more, he would have to ask her directly.

Dave wandered into the kitchen, looking hot and disheveled. "What's for dinner? I'm starved."

Jenny gave him a quick once over. "Spaghetti and salad. What have you been doing?" Then she sniffed at him. "You stink."

"Humph. Thanks. Hard work is what I've been doing. Shower here I come." And he spun around and disappeared.

"What on earth?" Jenny muttered, staring after him.

Her mother leaned close to her and said, "He had to start his community service. Been likely picking up trash off the highway."

Jenny giggled. "Oh. I thought prisoners were the ones who did that."

"Close enough," her mother answered.

Later, when Sam arrived, the women were putting the garlic bread in the oven and declaring dinner was almost ready. Sam leaned onto

Jenny's shoulder and said, "I'm going into the studio tomorrow rather early. You need a ride to work?"

"Yes, I do, if it's not a bother."

"No bother at all," he told her, smiling. Then he scooped up the bowl of salad and took it to the table. Sam joined their dad, who had slipped in and seated himself at the table, for the usual dinner table discussion about the news of the day. Soon, Fancy brought a massive stockpot full of spaghetti to the table, and Jenny followed with the basket of bread.

Dave joined them all, hair still wet, yawning.

After a moment of prayer over the food, Fancy began serving everyone's plate. Dave yawned again, bringing a frown of consternation from his dad.

"A little hard work would kill you, Son," Gus said.

Dave grinned. "Almost did today."

"Well, you get all that business finished up. Don't miss any days, and you might find a resolution to this problem." Fancy gave him a stern look.

"Don't worry," he replied, digging into the steaming pasta. "I don't want to ever do this again."

"I'd say you learned your lesson, then," Gus said.

Silence followed this statement as everyone savored the dinner.

Sam spoke next, pausing to sip his tea and allow his dinner to settle. "So, I have news."

All eyes turned to him.

"Yes, I am going to rent the loft above the studio. I signed the papers today. I'll be moving this weekend."

Fancy patted his arm. "Really? Oh, I'm a little sad at that."

"Mom, we've been over this."

"I know, but still."

Gus said, "Fancy, let it go. The boy's got to get out and get a life. He can't stay under this roof for his whole life."

Jenny thought furiously about what this meant. Was she going to get Sam's room? She looked back and forth at her parents.

"Jenny, having you come back home really sealed the deal for me. I wanted to move out, and you were the catalyst to shoving me out the door," Sam said.

She looked down at her plate. What was he saying?

"I don't mean that in a bad way, sis. I mean, I was dragging my feet but now that you're back and you need a room, well, it's time."

"Do I get that room, then?" she asked Fancy.

"It's not as big as yours was," her mother answered, looking at Dave. "But maybe Dave might be willing to give up your old room?"

"No way. Her old room has its own entrance from the front door straight up the stairs. I don't want to have to go through a bedroom to get to my room. Uh, uh."

Fancy looked to Gus, who shrugged. "They'll work it out."

Jenny said, "I don't care what room I have as long as it isn't the living room and the couch."

And she meant it, too.

Chapter Eleven

♥

Jere stood beside the market with his hand cupped over his eyes to shield them from the sun. He watched the flatbed as it maneuvered backwards down the side street and turned into the alley behind the businesses. It was a tedious job, and Jere worried that they wouldn't be able to manage it. But after several starts and stops, and one irate driver who didn't like being blocked from coming up the side street, the driver got his load in the right spot.

Jere turned on his heel and hurried back through the shop, going out the back door. The flatbed was loaded with Christmas trees and the sight of them made his heart surge. It was still early in the day and the chill in the air made their breaths appear like small puffs of smoke.

The driver wore heavy gloves and expertly cut the tie downs from the trees. Then he climbed aboard and started shoving them off the trailer to Jere. In a short while, Jere was covered in scratches from the branches. He wiped at the sweat that rolled down his cheeks.

Jenny arrived at work and came out to see what was going on. Once she understood that Jere was not going to be able to man the front until this job was done, she nodded and went back inside. Jere hoped she would know to step back out and ask questions if she needed to.

The last thing to come off the truck was a stack of fresh evergreen wreaths and holiday décor. Jere had purchased a few wooden yard signs of Santa, sleighs, and holiday bell cut-outs.

When everything had been off-loaded, the driver handed Jere a sheet of paper to sign. He did so and smiled at the man as he waved goodbye. He watched the driver pull back out onto the side street and turn toward Court.

Then he gathered up as many of the wreaths and décor as he could carry and went inside.

Jenny was sweeping. He smiled. At least one of his employees didn't have to be told what to do. Joe hated the task and oftentimes didn't do it well.

"Hey, Jenny," he said as he approached. "Got a job for you."

He plopped the items on the counter, and she strolled over. "These wreaths and signs need to be put where people will see them and know we have them for sale. You're a creative kind. Do something with them for me, please. I have to sort trees out back. Yell if you get overwhelmed."

She laughed. "This is fun for me. No overwhelm here."

He nodded and said, "We'll see how you feel at the end of the day."

She waved him off, and he headed back to the task of tree sorting. He found a big problem right away. There was no way to keep the trees standing in a grouping. He didn't want them to lie in the alley. That would be bad for the needles, he felt sure.

How on earth could he keep them upright?

While he stood there trying to figure it out, one of the owners of Abe's Absinthe came out and strolled over.

"Hey, neighbor," the man greeted him. "What on earth is all this?"

"Christmas trees. I'm going to sell them."

"Uh hm. Back here?" The man, whose name was Edwin waved a finger in a circle to indicate the area where they stood.

"Yep. I'm going to keep it on this side, as much as I can," Jere explained.

"Oh, no worries about that. We don't care if you use our side. I just wondered. They sure do smell good," he said.

"Like Christmas," Jere agreed. "Now to figure out how I can get them all standing and not lying down."

Edwin crossed his arms and cupped his chin with one hand. "I'd use rope."

"Rope?" Jere scanned the trees. "And do what?"

Edwin walked to one pile of trees and pulled one upright. "Oh, come here, you beautiful thing." He smelled the branches and then motioned to Jere to come over. "See, tie them all together, loosely. Then, fix the whole bunch of them up against the dumpster. In fact, the city likely won't care if you move the dumpsters together. Make them like a wall."

Jere nodded, considering the idea.

"What're you going to do if it snows?" Edwin asked.

This was the question that Jere had dreaded thinking about the most. "Don't know. Don't have that figured out yet."

"Well, if it was me," Edwin said. "I'd get some kind of tarp. Rig it up from your building across to mine. People won't come out shopping if it's too bad, but a light sprinkling will be okay, and a tarp will keep everyone nice and cozy."

Jere wondered how wide the area was. Might take two tarps, but definitely a workable solution.

"Dude, you're absolutely right. Thank you."

~**~

Jenny was humming one of her favorite Christmas tunes when Jere came back inside. He asked her how many customers had been by.

She tapped her lower lip. "Less than fifty?" She really wasn't certain.

"Got ya." He went to the office. She was curious about the tree situation, so she followed him.

"Did you get those trees all sorted out?"

"Yes and no," he said. "I have to get some rope and figure out a way to tie them together and get them upright before the needles die."

This made her tilt her head. "Why rope?"

"Well, it's the first thing I thought of. Actually, Edwin over at Abe's gave me the idea."

"I bet Joe could make you some stands out of wood. Then you could tie them to the stands with the rope."

He looked at her with wonder. "Now what on earth made you think of that?"

"I just thought about what a Christmas tree needed. I placed the wreaths out on the lattice you have behind the table out front. Hung them with some hangers I found in the stockroom."

He got up and headed outside. "Cool. Let me see."

She had done a good job. The wreaths were at eye-level, and the signs were leaning against the building on the table where customers would see it from the parking slots.

"Excellent," he told her, smiling. "Very eye-catching."

This bit of praise made her blush. He asked her to follow him, and he led the way out back. "Edwin also suggested a tarp rigged up across the alley to cover the trees and allow snow-free shopping. What do you think?"

"Hang up some twinkle lights and you're set," she told him, nodding approval.

"Wonder where we can get the wood? Maybe the co-op?"

"Save money," Jenny said. "Get Will to hunt down someone who has old pallets they want to sell. You can get pallet wood cheap. These stands don't have to be fancy."

"No, they don't," he agreed. Then, out of nowhere, he brought her in for a hug. "You are so smart."

She eased out of his grasp. "Thanks."

"Oh," he stammered. "I'm sorry. Old habits die hard."

"It's fine, but if we're going to maintain a working relationship, it would be better if we didn't have physical contact."

"Right," he said, turning away. "Got it."

She went back inside and started restocking the bins. That hug nearly undid her. Being with Jere felt so easy right now. *Why hadn't she appreciated him when she had the chance?* This question and others sent her into a frenzy of cleaning the storeroom.

When it was almost lunchtime, she stopped working and hunted Jere up. She hadn't brought anything to eat, so she would have to go out.

He stood, looking at her over the desk, and before she could talk to him about lunch, he said, "I don't know what to do about the trees. Now that I have them out there, I feel like they need to be protected from theft. I can't leave them here untended."

She shook her head. "Never even thought about that."

"Me either. Guess I need to call John."

"Why?"

"I'm spending the night here. Maybe every night until they sell."

"Oh, Jere. You can't do that. Why don't you get Dave to spend the night a few nights and maybe even Will, too."

"Not a bad thought," he said. Then he pulled his cell phone out and dialed someone up. He walked back to the door leading out back.

Jere couldn't be serious about spending every night at the market until Christmas. She shook her head and went to the stockroom. Jere's voice floated in.

"Yeah. I could put a tent up out here. It would be like camping."

Jenny swallowed the fear that rose. What if someone decided to attack him? It was an alley, after all. Drunks and kids looking for trouble used the alleys in Mt. Moriah all the time. At least that's what the news media would make one think.

She didn't want Jere to end up a statistic on the news. She intended to talk to her brother as soon as she could get home and find him. And if she had to, she would make a visit to Pandora's and plead Jere's case to Diana about having Will pitch in.

When he got off the phone, she picked up her purse and asked him about lunch.

"Yeah, I'm hanging out here," he told her.

"Did you bring something to eat?"

"No, I didn't. These trees took all my brain space today."

"How about I go and bring something back for both of us?"

"You don't mind?"

"No, of course not. We have to eat. And if you're serious about staying here at night, you really need a good meal."

He agreed and pulled out his wallet. "Let me buy then. No matter what you get, I'll be happy with it. I'm hungry as a bear."

"You still like your burgers well-done with cheese and mustard?"

He nodded. "Yep."

She stuffed the money he handed her down into her purse and told him she'd be back soon.

~**~

When Jenny left, Jere locked the front door and made his way back to the alley. He called Will.

"Yo," he said, when his friend answered.

"Yo, yo," Will answered.

"Okay, so here's the dilemma," Jere said. "One, we have trees and no stands. Gotta have a way to stand them up so people can examine them and get them off the ground."

"Oh, yeah," Will answered. "I see the problem from here, SpaceX."

"Well, see this: we need some sort of tarp covering the alley to give shoppers a chance to get out of snow and rain. Also, I'm sleeping here at night to protect our investment. No way I'm leaving these babies alone in the alley."

"Hm. Yeah, that's a big deal."

"Yeah, so you got any ideas?"

"Let me think about it. I'll call you back this evening. I gotta jet. The counter just got busy."

Jere disconnected, shoved his phone in his pocket and slapped his hands on his hips. Why didn't anything in his life come easy?

He remembered Joe. He needed to call and see how everyone was feeling, anyway. He pulled his cell out again and dialed his brother.

"Hello?" Joe sounded sleepy.

"Did I wake you up?" Jere asked.

"Nope. Just laying here watching television."

"How're you feeling?"

"I'm doing much better. Hope went back to work today. Aunt Maddie only has a small fever and is getting grouchy about us trying to tend to her all the time. I'd say we're about back to normal."

"Are you coming in tomorrow?"

"Yes. I don't see why not."

"Well, I have a problem and you might be able to help me with it."

"What kind of problem?" Joe sounded suspicious.

"Christmas trees were delivered today, and I need some stands made. You got any wood at your place?"

"Nothing you could use for that."

"If I got the wood, could you make some?"

"If you show me what you want, I can probably make it."

"Cool. That's all I need to know. I'll fill you in tomorrow."

"Okay. Was that all you wanted?"

"Yeah, unless you want to loan me your tent."

"Tent? Why? I mean, yeah, you can have it, but what's the deal?" Now Joe really sounded suspicious.

"Ah ... I'm kind of going to sleep at the shop for the Christmas tree thing. No way to protect the trees from theft."

Joe fell silent for a time.

"Joe?" Jere asked.

"Yeah, I'm here. I might have a solution to that dilemma as well. Let's get on it tomorrow. I hear Maddie rustling around in the kitchen. She's hard to let alone in there some days."

"Okay, no worries. Come on in when you can."

Joe thanked him and disconnected.

He stared out at the trees. This had been a good idea when he started the plan. Now? Not so much. He heard knocking on the front door and jogged back to let Jenny in.

She had her arms full of bags from the local burger joint.

"Lunch is served," she told him, brightly.

He grunted. His stomach rumbled and reminded him that he couldn't go without food anymore. Especially when he was busy hauling Christmas trees around the lot.

While he ate, Jenny hunted up the first aid cabinet in the bathroom, which hadn't been used or updated in a long time.

"If you don't mind, I think I'll run over to Union Drugs and get a few things for the medical kit," she said, pulling outa spray bottle of antiseptic. "I need to tend to those scratches first."

He laughed and waved her away. "No. I'm fine."

"You won't think so if that gets infected." She held up the bottle.

"I'll be fine. It's only scratches."

"What about that one?" she asked, pointing at a long, deep one on the underside of his forearm.

"Huh? Oh, yeah. Well, maybe that one," he said, holding it up for her to doctor. "Just don't spray that stuff on my food."

She motioned for him to move his burger and fries to the other side of the desk, and she sprayed the antiseptic on the cut. Then she daubed it with a tissue to keep it from running to his elbow.

His body reacted with a flash of heat from her simple touches. He even felt heat rise in his cheeks.

She stopped, and he lowered his arm. She gave him a strange look and then walked back to the cabinet with the bottle.

He took a deep breath. He should not feel that way about her. Not now. Maybe never again.

What was that look she had on her face? Did she feel it, too?

Chapter Twelve

♥

J enny walked to Sam's studio after work, refusing Jere's offer of a ride. Joe had shown up with some wood, fencing, and a tent and she couldn't ask him to leave when they obviously had work to do. To get to Sam's studio, Jenny had to skirt the courthouse grounds and today, there was a lot going on there as well.

Builders were erecting a platform on the grounds as a part of the Christmas Celebration festivities. A sign advertising the event had been placed nearby. She looked at it closely. Same as what had been in the paper. December 17th would be a big day.

Maybe they would have more information the closer it got. She wanted to go, but she was hesitant. Did she want to endure everyone's gaze and either pity or disgust? Going to church had been hard enough. People who still hadn't found out about her return would certainly know after she paraded herself around at that event.

She remembered Dana and her hurried escape from the grocery store. If it were up to Dana, Jenny would be the town pariah. Dana would do anything to divert attention from herself. Jenny didn't want to be caught up in her sleight-of-hand games, either.

Although as she thought about it, she was still committed to not filling Jere in. It seemed like he had enough on his plate as it was. No sense in creating more turmoil.

Dana would be found out without help. She was like a spider, slinking around, waiting to strike if anyone tried to catch her, but if Jenny trusted in karma, Dana would catch herself in her own web.

Jenny went ahead, down Main Street, past the Inn and as she drew closer to Pandora's had an urge to go inside. She hadn't talked to Diana in a long time, and although she knew that Hope didn't really like her, even less after her defection, it would be nice to visit for a moment. Sam wouldn't care. He lost track of time and was never ready for anything on time.

She pushed open the door to the dress shop, greeted by the scent of warm candle wax, and the sounds of soft Christmas music playing.

The tinkling of the doorbell brought Diana out of the bathroom, drying her hands on paper towels.

"Hey, Jenny! What are you doing here?" she asked, grinning at her.

It was nice of her to be so welcoming. Jenny was certain Will had filled her in by now on what had been going on.

"I was just passing by, really. Wasn't even sure if you would be open this late," Jenny answered. "Wow, y'all have fixed this place up big time for the holidays."

Diana looked around. "Oh yeah, normally we wouldn't be, but we had a meeting with the Chamber of Commerce. But it's Christmas, and we got sales, too. Are you looking for anything special?"

Jenny shook her head. "I don't know. Maybe? I actually came in here the other day to shop, but I wasn't feeling too hot and left before anyone came to see who rang the bell."

Now Diana looked at her closely. "Feeling better now?"

"Yes. Just hadn't had anything to eat and went too long. I'm fine now."

"I heard from Will that you were back in town, and why. No opinions from here, okay?"

Jenny nodded. "Thanks, Diana. I appreciate it."

"So, what were you going to shop for? A dress for the dance?"

"No, but now that you mention it..."

"Here, let me show you the good stuff."

They walked toward the back of the store and Hope came out of the office and said hello. She walked up to Jenny and put a hand on her arm.

"Listen, you don't owe anybody in this town anything, especially not an explanation. You've got friends here, you know."

"Thanks, Hope. It's wonderful to hear that."

The other woman nodded and went back to her desk. Diana led her to a row of dresses that looked to be perfect for a dance event at the courthouse. Long and made of warm thick materials in deep, winter colors, Jenny took a deep breath.

"Party dresses guaranteed to make you forget all your troubles," Diana told her.

Now she expelled the breath she'd been holding. "Thanks Diana, I'll just have to look today. I got a job, but I haven't gotten paid yet."

"You did? That's great, honey! Where?"

Before she could answer, the doorbell tinkled, and Dana Baker swept in. She was like a hurricane, blowing things out of the way as she came. Her face darkened even more once she spotted Jenny.

~**~

Jere wiped sweat from his brow. The outside temps were only in the fifties, but he felt like it was near eighty. Joe had helped him erect fencing around the area where he housed the trees. They had built crosses for the bases of the trees, stood them up, and leaned them against the fencing.

He stepped back and examined their work. It was good. And the best part was he could lock the fencing with a padlock and chain that he wove through the wire. And anyone intent on theft would hurt themselves on the wire that was bent forward at a dangerous angle.

"That'll do for tonight," Joe said, handing Jere a hammer and some other tools they had used. "We can perfect it tomorrow."

Jere grinned and shook his hand. "Thank you so much, bro. No way I could've done this."

"You're welcome. I'm going to go clean up and head out. This cold left me with a terrible cough. If I start coughing, I'll be a mess all the way home. You're right behind me?"

"Yeah, no need to stay tonight. We've got this well-covered."

"You want me to leave the tent?"

"Yeah, just in case. I'll lock it up inside."

Joe nodded and headed inside.

Jere took another look around and shook the fence to make sure it was steady before hauling the boxed tent inside. If things got dicey with people trying to destroy the fencing, he would just set up the tent and spend the night out here.

But for now, he was relieved he was going home to his bed.

He wondered what Maria was making for supper. She'd be glad to have him at her table and not shivering out in the alley, he was sure. As he searched for his truck keys, he felt his phone vibrate.

"Hello?"

"Have you left the shop yet?" Maria asked.

"Not yet."

"Bring home an onion. I forgot."

"No worries, I am almost out the door now. What's for supper?"

"Chicken enchiladas with rice and beans."

His stomach grumbled.

"I'll be there very soon."

She thanked him and disconnected. Joe came out of the bathroom and waved goodbye.

"Tell Hope I said hey," Jere told him.

"Will do. You tell the folks I said hey. We'll get with Maria soon to plan Christmas Eve and all that."

Jere nodded and waved at him as he disappeared through the front door.

The darkness had descended a couple hours ago, so he turned on the white Christmas lights that Jenny had strung over the front of the market. He hauled the displays of fresh vegetables inside from the front. When he pulled down the wreaths, he remembered the proud look on Jenny's face. She'd beamed like a sparkler when he'd given her a little praise.

He took the signs for the front displays into the interior of the shop and then locked up on his way out. All the streetlights and Christmas lights had twinkled into life. The whole town was already awash in red and green, and he smiled.

He saw the platform that had been erected and tried to make out the sign in front of it. Something about the Christmas Celebration. He shook his head. He would keep the market open and sell trees that weekend. He wasn't going to any dance.

Dana flittered through his mind. He wondered if she had planned to go and if she planned for him to take her. He hoped not. She'd be mighty disappointed if she had.

The drive to the house was unremarkable, aside from the fact that the town was already fully arrayed for the holidays. The houses in his neighborhood had lights strung all across their eaves, and some had even decorated their bushes and trees.

It was going to be a colorful holiday. That was for certain.

When he pulled into the driveway, he sat for a moment, making sure he hadn't forgotten anything. Did he lock up? Did he turn out lights? Did he leave anything out that needed to be inside? He picked up the onion he'd brought home and opened his door to go inside.

He heard Jenny as she hurried across the street in flip flops. He wanted to laugh at her choice of shoes in December, but something about the shadows on her face as she came took his breath away.

~**~

Jenny debated and debated on whether to tell Jere what Dana had said at Pandora's. Then she decided that if she didn't tell him, someone else would. Maybe even Will if Diana told him about what happened. It was better for Jenny to come clean than for Jere to find out some other way.

"Jere," she said, teeth chattering. "I had to talk to you. I've been waiting inside the house for you to come home. I was almost afraid you were staying at work overnight after all."

"No," he told her. "We got it all fixed up. Don't think I'll have to."

Now that she stood in front of him, Jenny was hesitant to tell him what she knew. The outside lights illuminated him well enough to tell he was in a good mood. Revealing information to him now might be the best time.

She hated to ruin his good mood, though.

She pulled her sweater tighter around her. "Well, that's good I guess."

"What's wrong?" He used one finger under her chin to tilt her head back, so she had to direct her gaze at him. Heat flared through her body as though he were a heater conducting warmth directly to her soul.

"You haven't been waiting on me all this time to hear about my tree stuff."

"No. I haven't."

"Spill it," he commanded.

"It's Dana," she said, giving him a quick glance.

"Oh, good grief," he countered. "What's she up to now?"

Jenny swallowed hard and said, "She came into Pandora's while I was there this evening after work. I stopped in on my way home." She paused and glanced at him again. He waited patiently. Nothing showed in his face to tell her what he was thinking.

"She came in, and when she saw me, she really unloaded. Accused me of trying to ruin her life, take you away from her, and basically, she was really ugly."

"That's a lie. Ignore her." He ran a hand through his hair, frustration making him tense. "I'm going to have to talk to her. She's got to quit this mess." Then, as an afterthought, "Wonder why she was in Pandora's?"

"She was there to pick up a dress for the Christmas dance, and she was downright horrible to Diana and Hope as well."

"Christmas dance, eh?"

"Yes." She stared at him.

"News to me. Guess she's going with someone else."

"Oh," Jenny said in a small voice. "About that..." She would have to tell him everything about his girlfriend's dishonesty.

"What? You know something?"

"Well, sort of. Remember when I told you about seeing her in the grocery store?"

Jere blew out a breath. "Yeah. I've witnessed her with that guy. She's been friendly with him right in front of me."

"Are you kidding? Is he a friend of y'all's? I mean, I didn't say much, because it wasn't any of my business, but now she's making it personal. If she's going around all cuddly with someone else and blaming me for her situation, well, she's needs to stop. Or you need to have a talk with her."

He thrust his hands on his hips and stared up into the night sky. "What else did she say?"

"She's going to get me back. She laughed all Cruella Deville when she said it."

"She actually said she was going to get you back?" His voice sounded worried.

"She said, and I quote, 'Oh, don't worry little Miss Ballbreaker, you're going to get yours. And sooner than you think.'"

"Well, that doesn't sound good, does it? But if it's any consolation, I've seen her in action. She's a lot of hot air."

"You don't think I should tell the cops?"

He laughed out loud. "No. She's not going to do anything to you. She's just blowing off steam because she's mad that we're working together. Never mind her. I'll talk to her."

Jenny looked up at him and tried to analyze what he said. He was being sincere. He wasn't worried about Dana and what she might have planned.

"Okay, then. I guess I'll just have to wait and see what happens. She makes it hard to feel at home here, though. I didn't have any enemies until now."

"You don't have an enemy now, either. She doesn't count. But you have lots of friends, so like I said, forget her." He smiled.

She shrugged. "Okay. Not like I can do otherwise. I guess I'll see you tomorrow."

He pulled her back to him, his hand like a warm cloth wrapped around her arm. "Listen, I'm really sorry about all this. You don't deserve anything but happiness. Don't let her spoil it."

She smiled at his sweet words. They acted on her rattled nerves like a smooth caress.

Unexpectedly, he leaned down and brushed his lips across hers.

She didn't jerk away. She was too shocked. But when he moved away from her to pull something from the truck, she fled. The scent of him, part-sweat, partly cologne, stayed in her nostrils and filled her heart all the way home.

Chapter Thirteen

♥

Jere stood under the hot water jets for a lot longer than he should
have, but he needed the warmth and unrelenting pounding. He
didn't know what made him feel like kissing Jenny every time she got
near, but he did. The fact that she hadn't pushed him away was as
confusing as her not wanting physical contact.

It was obvious they had to maintain a semi-professional relationship while at work, but outside of that ... he just didn't know.

He got out of the shower and dried off, hanging the towel on a hook
on the side of the shower stall. Maria had a fit if she caught wet towels
hanging anywhere else. Especially on the railing of a bed. He did his
best to follow her instructions. Mostly to keep the peace.

He pulled on pajama pants and a clean tee shirt and slipped his
feet into house shoes. They were terribly ratty and was likely a gift
forthcoming from Trey and Susie. He climbed into bed and pulled his
phone out. No calls. What was Dana up to?

The woman had made him believe she was into him for months.
Now that Jenny showed back up, she was using that fact to pretend to
be on to the next guy. He wanted some answers. He dialed her up.

She didn't answer on the first or second ring. When she finally did
answer, she sounded like a bored housewife.

"Hello?"

"What?"

"What do you mean what? You called me."

"What are you trying to do?" Jere asked, anger flowing out.

"I have no idea what you're talking about."

"Yes, you do, Dana. You practically had a shouting match with Jenny at Pandora's. You threw yourself all over some guy in the grocery store, and you didn't even bother to hide it from Jenny or anyone else looking. You wanted me to find out, I guess?"

"You made it plain we were finished."

"So, what? You decided to try to make everyone in town see you at your worst, so they would tell me about it? I never took you for a game player."

"I'm not playing at anything, Jere. But I'll bet Jenny comes over there every day spreading stories about me, doesn't she? That's how you found out, isn't it?"

"She's not spreading stories. She's telling the truth. Something you wouldn't know how to do if your life depended on it. And by the way, you stay away from her. If you so much as frown in her direction, you'll deal with me."

"Really Jere? Did you defend me to her that way? I'm sure she cried big tears over seeing me at the store, didn't she? She's such the caring, concerned person. Not! She's such a phony."

"Why are you diverting the conversation to her? You haven't denied anything yet, I see."

Silence.

"Well, if there was a doubt before, there certainly isn't now. I hope you enjoy Simon. I hope he doesn't turn out to be something you can't stand in a man, because he's about the only one left that you haven't been with."

"That's mean, and unfair, and ... just wrong!" She disconnected and Jere set his phone aside as if it were too hot to handle. He was officially finished with that whole chapter. She wasn't someone that he needed to be with.

Jenny had been so right about her. He hated to admit that, but he had to. Lying to himself was not something that he was in the habit of doing and he wasn't going to start today.

He picked up his phone and dialed Jenny.

She answered quickly, like she was happy to see him calling her.

"Hey," she answered. "What's up?"

"Just wanted to let you know that well, you were right about Dana. From day one. I was a bone-headed loser to try to make that relationship work. I spoke to her and, well, it's over. For real. For good. And you don't have to worry about her anymore."

Jenny didn't reply. He rushed ahead. "I'm not going to apologize for the kiss tonight, either. I think it means something that I can't stay away from you."

She calmly answered, "The question is not if we still have feelings. The question is, do we act on them?"

He didn't have the answer to that.

~**~

On Wednesday morning when she first woke up, Jenny couldn't keep her thoughts away from Jere and what he'd said. He meant to kiss her, and he wasn't sorry about it. If she was being honest, she felt the same. But she didn't want to act out of rebound, and if he and Dana were truly over, she didn't want him rebounding either.

And that was what this could be for both of them. A rebound.

She decided she wouldn't allow herself to be in a situation with him where another kiss would happen. They had to get a little better at saying no. At least she did.

Until she was better settled in her life and emotions, it had to be at arm's length. Jere had a way of upsetting her carefully planned day with a look, a touch, or a kiss. He always had. His steady, solid lifestyle comforted her. Not like Brandon.

With Brandon, she had been swept away by the promise of glitz and glamour and being in a crowd with other screaming fans. In the beginning, she couldn't believe she had been chosen to be in his life, by his side, in the limelight. Now she knew that being chosen isn't a blessing but a curse, and oftentimes the limelight is so bright it blinds you to the truth.

No, she still had a lot to figure out about her life. She didn't need or want Jere to get into her head and override any decisions she might be about to make. He needed to stay on his side of the street.

She had to work with him. His job offer had been a godsend and no doubt. But everything else had to be halted. She could be platonic. But could he?

She went to the kitchen and poured a cup of coffee, added sugar and creamer, and sat at the kitchen table. It was still fairly early. Nobody else had come into the kitchen yet. Thank goodness her parents loved their coffee and set a timer each night.

The quiet of the dining room, alone with her coffee and her thoughts, put Jenny in a mood. She didn't want to think too far ahead, but she wanted to go to the Christmas Celebration. It was a good way to get out, be seen, reunite friendships, and maybe even have some fun.

She wondered what all had been planned. The sign and the ad in the paper had both been woefully lacking in information. What food would be there? What games? What giveaways?

She had only ever gone to parties at people's homes during the holidays. She didn't remember ever doing more than glancing at the event in town. This memory made her shake her head. Back then, youth and lack of wisdom dictated her life. If it didn't include her friends and social circle, it wasn't done.

She heard someone heading toward the kitchen and got up to put her cup in the sink and get dressed for work. It was Sam.

"Good morning, Jen-Jen," he said, smiling. He pulled a cup from the mug tree and poured a cup. "Do you need a ride today?"

She glanced out at the weather. It was overcast. Maybe rain? "Uh, yeah. Looks like rain."

"Might snow," he told her. "The temps fell overnight."

She frowned. "Ugh. I hope not. I'm not ready for boots and heavy coats yet."

He agreed with her, and she took off for the stairs.

While she dressed, she looked up the weather on an app on her phone. It was definitely colder. She pulled on a pair of knit pants under a sweater in Christmas colors. Might as well look the part, she decided.

The drive to Jere's market was uneventful, and she was glad to get the day started. Jere was already there, of course, and she helped him haul the displays out front. It was fun to put the wreaths and signs out again.

"Hey, Joe," she said to Jere's brother when he arrived. "All the family back in good health?"

"Yes, thank goodness. How are you? Enjoying your new job?"

Heat rose in her cheeks. "If you mean my work here, yes. If you mean working with your brother, then that subject is off-limits."

He laughed and headed toward the stockroom.

~**~

Jere and Joe worked on the Christmas tree plan most of the morning. They made sure the fencing would hold up and arranged the trees by size and price. When that was all done, Jere set about looking for some leftover wood to make a sign directing customers to the back lot.

While they worked, Edwin from Abe's came over and checked out the work.

"Well," he said, arms crossed. "This is much better than what we had talked about. Are you still going to, you know, cover it?" He waved overhead.

"Yep, that's the plan. You know where I can get a tarp or something?"

He laughed. "Of course, silly. I have one I'll bring to you tomorrow, or today, if I can get away. Christmas is our busiest season."

He strolled back to his shop. Then, as an afterthought, shouted, "Do you think this will be an annual thing?"

Jere assumed that this was going to be a loaded question and paused before answering. "Yeah, might be. Depends on how successful it is."

"Okay, well, Paul and I would like to help if so. We could decorate a few trees to showcase what they look like all dolled up. You know, flavor?"

Jere glanced at Joe, who had stopped sweeping up pine needles to witness this exchange. "What do you think?"

Joe grinned at him and yelled across at Edwin. "Bring it on. We're good with that!"

Edwin slipped inside the store. Jere nodded to himself. The decorations of a few trees had never occurred to him. Jenny could hang out back and direct that operation, he decided. She seemed to have a flair for décor, if the wreath project was any indicator.

When they had gotten everything arranged the way they wanted it, and Jere had erected a makeshift sign pointing back to the alley, the two men took a break. It was almost lunch.

"I'm going home for lunch," Joe told him. "Hope'll go tomorrow. We're trying to switch off every other day for checking on Miss Maddie."

"No problem. You ready to take off now? It's fine if so."

Joe looked at his cell. "Yeah, I guess. I'll be back in about an hour."

Jere nodded. "No rush. Do your thing."

Joe pinched Jere's shoulder in passing and headed out. Jere turned to Jenny and lifted an eyebrow.

She said, "I'm going to walk over to the Pizza Emporium."

He frowned. "You know Dana works there, right?"

She wiped the counter with one hand and scooped a few bits of flotsam into her other cupped palm. "I know. But this town is small, and we're bound to run into each other. Besides, I'm not giving up my love of pizza because she works at the only pizza place in town."

He considered what she said and decided that Dana was not to be trusted with Jenny. Not even when she was at work.

"Tell you what," he said. "I'll go along. I think pizza is a good choice today."

She paused and thrust a hand on her hip. "You're not doing this out of worry over Dana and I, are you?"

"No, not at all," he answered, motioning for her to grab her purse. "The sooner we get there, the better. They have a mad lunch crowd."

She lifted her purse and followed him to the front door.

He wasn't kidding when he said the crowd was bad at lunch. He had to park on the side street beside the restaurant.

"I hope there's room to stand inside," Jenny muttered.

He locked the truck, and they walked together up to the door. Jere opened it and the smell of freshly baked dough and roasting veggies struck them in the face. Jere's mouth watered and his stomach grumbled at the delicious aromas.

The people outside must have been patrons who had finished eating. The line wasn't too bad and there were available tables. Jere was immediately glad Jenny had chosen the Pizza Emporium for lunch.

Right up until he looked around and his gaze locked with Dana's. She yelled for someone named Bria to come and relieve her, yanked her apron over her head, and stomped toward the back of the kitchen.

Jere grinned. He knew he had won this round. She wasn't coming back out until the coast was clear.

Today, he was the coast guard.

~**~

Jenny listened to Joe and Jere talking about a schedule for the tree sales. It was already Thursday and two weeks from Christmas. It was now or never.

When they moved outside to talk more about the trees, she turned on a radio under the counter and listened to the weatherperson talk about a cold front that was about to swoop down from the west and bring them increased chances of snow. At the very least, they would get cold temps. She shivered at the thought.

To keep warm and do her part in the tree-selling business, she created a flyer on the computer in the office—while still watching the front of the market. She tried to make it tie in with the Christmas event, which was quickly approaching.

She printed it on the thickest paper they had, almost like cardstock, and stacked about ten copies of it neatly in a pile on the counter. Then, she printed out two extras. One she taped to the front of the counter and the other one she taped to the door, facing out where people coming in would see it.

If she hadn't put the wreaths where she did, she could have placed one on that pegboard, but she hoped the sign the guys had put out would do the trick for outside walkers-by. After she finished that project, she went to find them to tell them about possible bad weather coming through.

She found them talking to a nicely dressed man she had seen working at Abe's. This must be Edwin.

"Hey, y'all," she greeted them.

Edwin did a finger wave and grinned at her. "'Sup?"

She shrugged and pointed at the trees. "That I guess."

Jere turned to her and said, "Slow, huh?"

"A little," she admitted. "But Jere, the weather peeps just said that there is a front moving in. It may snow tonight."

Edwin straightened and did a hands-out gesture. "See? Y'all need this tarp."

That was when Jenny noticed the bundle of black plastic at Jere's feet.

"Yeah, I think he's right. How are you going to hang it?" she asked, looking overhead.

"That's the million-dollar question, Miss Jones," Joe said. "How indeed."

"What about PVC pipe?" she asked. "You could put it in the corners of the fencing, anchor it with rope or heck, even duct tape, and drape the tarp over it."

Three sets of eyes stared at her.

"Duct tape," Jere said. "Southern man's best friend."

"Pipes are cheap at the co-op right now," Joe replied.

Edwin smiled at Jenny. "Well, ain't you just a rose in a field of daisies?"

She laughed and headed back inside. "Not a perfect idea but a good one to get you started."

She could hear their excited voices as they plotted and planned on how to get that tarp overhead to protect the trees and anyone shopping for them. When she got back inside, she grabbed the box of tomatoes, grown locally by a hydroponic farm, and started restocking them.

Once that was done, she was happy to see several people with kids approaching the market. She got behind the counter and waited for the onslaught.

"You got any cucumbers?" the first lady asked. She had a little girl, about three, with her. The child was shy and hid in the folds of her mother's dress when Jenny smiled at her.

"Yes, ma'am. Over to your right on the other side."

The man came in and grabbed a green basket with a handle. That always meant the customer would be buying a lot and didn't want to hand carry it. Jenny smiled and turned the music down a little.

"Oh, don't turn it off," the woman said wistfully. "That's that new *Sarcastix* song. I just love them. I think they got their start in Mt. Moriah if I'm thinking right."

Jenny's good mood evaporated. She turned the music back up and listened to the lyrics.

Oh, baby, you left me out in the cold,
How could you be so bold?
Don't you know what you're doing to me?
I'm so sad I can't even see.

Now that she focused on the song, she could definitely make out Brandon's voice. The words went straight through her heart like a poisoned arrow.

Had he written it about her?

Chapter Fourteen

♥

J ere and Joe spent most of the day working with Edwin, getting the
tarp in place. The wind had begun to pick up, making placement
difficult. When they finished, they stood back and looked at it, trying
to decide if it would be sufficient.

"Well, at the very least, it should afford a dry place for people to
stand." Jere pulled his jacket tighter around him. "I don't know about
getting out of the wind though."

"We don't care if they're in the wind," Edwin said. "Just that they
don't get rained or snowed on."

Joe, ever the tall silent type, said nothing.

Jenny came out of the shop at that moment to let Jere know that
she was leaving for the day. He yanked his phone out of his pocket and
looked at it. It was nearly four o'clock. The day was waning quickly.

"Yeah," he answered. "We're about to go get a bite too."

"Are you going to stay here tonight?" she asked.

"Not all night. Just until about seven. Give some folks a chance to
get by here and see if they want to buy one. People getting off work
need time to get back out after supper."

She nodded and told him he would need to lock the front if he was
going to stay out back.

The men all gave her a warm farewell and turned to their own evening plans. Edwin left to lock up his shop and head out. Joe took cash from Jere to go grab burgers for them.

Jere went to the front of the shop and made sure Jenny had gotten the sawhorses and produce pulled in for the night. When he saw everything had been done, he stuck the key in the door to lock it. Before he could turn the key, Dana's face popped up in the door's window.

Oops.

He'd thought he'd been slick when he avoided her at the restaurant where she worked. He didn't consider she'd come to the market.

He put the key back into his pocket and opened the door.

"Yep." He said it with as little enthusiasm as he could muster.

Her cheeks were pink from the cold. He wondered if she'd walked over.

"Look, I just want to talk to you. I want to explain," she said.

He motioned for her to come inside out of the wind. She did, with a little hop.

She shivered and said, "It's getting so cold."

"Don't need a weather report, Dana. What do you want?"

Her face became crestfallen. "Why are you being so nasty to me? I told you I was schmoozing Simon about a job. I'm not dating him. I wouldn't do that to you."

He laughed derisively. "My ego feels so much better now."

"Jere," she said, coming to him, putting a hand on his arm. "I have to tell you something. I've been keeping a secret."

He gazed down at her hand and then back at her face. "What secret?"

She removed her hand and turned away. "I'm pregnant."

"Congratulations," he said, his heart dancing all the way to his throat. "Whose is it?"

She jerked around, her face incredulous. "It's yours. I haven't slept with anyone else."

He shook his head and tried to find his voice, which had disappeared with all of his saliva. "This ... this ... you can't be."

"Well, I am. I've taken tests three times. It's definite."

He stalked to the door and opened it, letting the cold night air rush in. "Go home, Dana. I don't believe you."

Tears rushed to her eyes. "Jere, it's true!"

He shook his head. "If it is, it isn't mine."

"Yes, it is. Whether you want to admit it or not."

"Go home."

"You can't just dismiss me like some wayward dog, Jere Collins. This is not going to go away."

"Yeah, well, it isn't going to be solved tonight either."

She grabbed his arm and shook it. "You can't hide from this. I don't care if you and Jenny have gotten back together. You're going to be a father. You will have to own up to your responsibilities with me."

He turned his back to her and walked away.

~**~

Sam had been punctual today when he came by the market to pick Jenny up. She was grateful that she didn't have to walk. The wind was blustery, and winter was making itself known. She rubbed her hands together in front of the car's heater vents.

"Wow," she said. "I believe it may snow."

"Nah, not cold enough."

"Bet Dave is cussing a blue streak about being out in it," she mused.

Sam laughed. "Yeah. We're probably going to hear all about his day at dinner tonight."

He slowed the car in front of the courthouse grounds. The workmen had finished putting up the platform and had even added a lectern area where speakers could stand and make announcements. No amplifiers had been placed yet. And no tents or other fixtures were in place either, but Jenny knew that would be coming soon.

"Coming along," Sam said, noting the progress.

"Yep. Guess I better get a move on if I'm going."

"Oh? I didn't think that would be something you would do yet."

She punched his arm playfully. "I'm not widowed, Sammy."

He shrugged as he turned on their street. "I know but, well, there's going to be a lot of people there."

"So?"

He put the car in park and turned to her. "Listen, I didn't want to tell you this, but I heard it from the Chamber of Commerce. They are putting this whole dance thing together. If you remember, dances have to have music." He glanced at her face. The porch's light was enough to see that he was concerned about something.

"What are you saying?"

"*Sarcastix* is playing at the Christmas Celebration."

Her heart fell into her shoes. "No. Oh, please tell me you're kidding."

He shook his head. "No, I'm not. They haven't made it public yet, but they will soon. You might want to just avoid the whole thing."

She opened the door and climbed out. The cold wind dug icy fingers through all the layers of clothes she wore. An even icier layer of frost covered her heart.

She joined him on the way to the front door. The Christmas lights were festive, but she didn't even notice them.

"I'm not going to avoid the whole thing. If Brandon is there, he'll be the one feeling like an odd man out. Not me. I have nothing to be ashamed of. I have nothing to avoid."

Sam put an arm across her shoulders. "I've got your back either way, Jen-Jen."

Together, they went into the house. She loved her family for being so supportive. She would deal with the whole issue of running into Brandon again in her own way.

Dave showed up a few minutes later. He wore a bandana around his head and his jeans were dirty. No one asked him what he'd been doing. Apparently, it was not fun work. But he did have them come outside and see what he brought home.

Tied to the top of his car was a live Christmas tree.

"I just bought it from Jere. Anyone want to decorate this baby tonight?"

They all thanked him for being so thoughtful and everyone agreed tonight would be a great time to do the family holiday decorating.

When Dave had cleaned up a bit, Jenny and her mother served dinner. Tonight, pot roast night, the scent of the food sent everyone's stomach into notable grumbling. They all sat down to eat.

Gus passed the platter of sliced beef, followed by mashed potatoes, and finally a gravy boat. Jenny helped herself to chunky cut carrots that had been sautéed in butter with onions. Dinner rolls were passed around and everyone took one of those.

Jenny listened to her brother's talk about their day. When they fell silent, all that could be heard was the sound of flatware on plates.

"So, Jenny," Dave said. "What's wrong with Jere?"

"What do you mean, what's wrong with him? Nothing that I know about."

Surprise registered on his face. "I figured you would have a handle on it, since you're working over there. I went to get that tree and he hardly had two words to say. He acted like he was plenty mad about something. Yanked the rope off, pulled the tree to the car, and grunted in exasperation over the whole ordeal."

She stopped cutting her meat. "He was fine when I left. I have no idea."

Her mother shot her a petulant look. "I have an idea. It's two words."

They all waited expectantly.

"Dana Baker," she said, looking down at her plate.

~**~

Jere sat in the truck for a moment before going inside his house. He had not allowed the news from Dana to stop him all evening. He'd shoved the entire conversation to the back of his mind and refused to allow it to cloud his thoughts. They had sold three trees tonight, and he felt proud of that fact. If things went on like this, he might have to buy more.

But now, sitting in his truck, tired, and in a weak moment, Dana's news was all he could think about.

Pregnant. With child. A baby.

His baby?

She had done her best to convince him. He didn't know how it could possibly be. They hadn't been intimate in weeks. Why had she chosen now to tell him? Now, when they were as good as broken up. He couldn't help but think it was a last-ditch effort to get him back.

Dana had been voracious in her attempts to get his attention from the beginning. She came to wherever he was, hung all over him, made him notice her. Why she wouldn't continue that trend to keep him was anyone's guess.

She would, he thought. She would do anything to have her way. Even lie about being pregnant. He closed his eyes and tried to think back to when they had been together that way last. Was it even possible?

There was one time ... he remembered. He had too much beer before and after dinner at the Pizza Emporium while he waited for her to get out of work. They had gone to Dana's apartment that she shared with Lori Kitchens. Lori had been out that night on a date of her own, he assumed. They had fooled around some that night. He'd been a little wasted and ended up sleeping over at her house.

He remembered the hangover very well. Had something happened that night?

"No way," he said out loud to the silence in the truck. "No way that happened, and I don't remember it. I wasn't that wasted."

And he always used protection.

But doubts lingered. She'd been curled in his arms naked when he woke up the next day. He remembered that much. He opened his truck's door and stepped out into the biting winter air. He couldn't believe he wouldn't remember having sex with Dana.

He would. No matter how much beer he'd consumed, he would remember that. As he strode to the door, he decided that it never happened. It was easier to believe that Dana, with all her faults, would lie about such a thing to corner him. She wanted him to marry her. That was it.

She'd have to have a paternity test on her baby when it was born to determine who the father was. He was certain it wasn't his. The first flakes of snow fell around him, floating onto his face as he strode to the front door.

His confidence waned as he tossed his keys and wallet in a bowl that Maria had set on the hall table. He felt certain he would never forget an intimate encounter. But he couldn't really prove it. Dana held all the cards in this situation, and he shivered at the thought that his future might be bound up in a game she was playing. Going all in, as far as he could tell.

She was playing to win. His freedom was at stake.

Sounds of the television playing floated in as he strolled into the kitchen. The family had already eaten dinner and Maria had left him a plate already made that he could just pop into the microwave oven and reheat.

Dinner was baked ham, baked beans, and corn, but he wasn't hungry. The burger he'd eaten half of sat heavy in his stomach now. But Maria would be upset with him and fuss if he didn't eat. He set the plate in the small oven and went to let everyone know he was home. They looked up from a program they were watching. Some family drama or other if Maria had her way.

"Dinner is on the counter," Maria told him.

"Okay, thanks," he answered.

"There's potato salad in the fridge," she added.

Jere nodded. "Hey John, you mind coming to the kitchen with me? I need to ask you something."

John took the hint and disentangled himself from Maria and the kids. He sat at the table while Jere retrieved his plate and added a dollop of potato salad to it on his way to sit down.

~**~

Jenny stared at her mother as if she were about to impart important news.

Her mother shrugged. "It's always something with that girl. I remember when y'all were teenagers. Her mother tried to find her every weekend. Dana would go off with kids her parents didn't know and not show up when expected."

"Poor parenting," Gus said.

"Kid looking for trouble, more like." Fancy took a bite of carrots. "If you look hard enough, you'll find it, I say."

"She hasn't been very good to Jere," Jenny agreed. She remembered the gossip between Jenny and the hair stylist in the church bathroom. Dana thought she had Jere tied around her finger. But as far as Jenny could tell, that knot had come untied.

"You must be thinking about the grocery store scenario," Fancy said, cutting a piece of beef. "She acts about as loose as a woman can be."

Dave shrugged. "Yeah. I've heard rumors about her."

Jenny was surprised to hear him say so, but not surprised that she was a conversation subject. Her own mother had taught Jenny that if you don't want to be talked about in a bad way, then don't act in a way to get yourself in trouble.

"Wonder what she's done or said to put Jere in a bad mood?" Jenny mused aloud.

Sam leaned toward her and said, "You don't have to wonder hard. She's trying to keep a man she's already lost."

"Why do you say it that way?" Jenny asked, turning to stare at him.

He leaned away from her and grinned. "You know."

"No, I most certainly don't."

"We ain't blind, Jen-Jen. He's still got a thing for you. He doesn't seem upset at her prancing all over town with another man. He's moved on," Fancy explained.

This took Jenny aback. Jere was not interested in her. Then, like a lightning bolt, his attention and impromptu kisses returned to haunt her. Had that been all there was to it? Was he trying to let her know in gentle ways that the door was still open? Did he still have a light on beckoning her back into his life?

She decided as soon as dinner was over, she would go to Jere's house and lay it all out on the table. She wanted to know what game he was playing if he was playing one. He needed to be plain.

After dinner, she was grateful when her dad offered to help her mother with the dishes. She grabbed her coat and pulled it on. She also added a scarf around her head after looking outside and seeing tiny flakes of snow falling. Without a question, the conversation with Jere would need to be done outside away from eavesdroppers.

She was halfway down the front steps when she realized that Jere's truck was at home, and he would be tired and dirty from the day's work.

"Maybe I should just call," she said out loud, stopping with her hand on the porch rail. She realized that if Dana had come by the shop after Jenny had left, Jere would be angry and in a mood, and likely not wanting to talk about it, especially with her. It would be far easier for him to refuse to discuss it over the phone, too.

She stood there, getting colder by the moment, one foot in heaven and one foot in hell. What should she do?

~**~

"What's up?" John asked when Jere finally joined him at the table.

"Trouble," Jere said. He could feel his cheeks heat at the thought of what he was about to unload on his brother. This would be embarrassing, to say the least.

"With the tree thing? Did something happen?"

Jere chewed on a bite of beans and shook his head. "No."

John fell silent and waited for him to spill his news.

"Dana came to the shop tonight. She told me that she's pregnant."

"What?" John was incredulous.

Jere nodded and cut off a piece of ham. "Yeah, and honestly, John, I'm not sure what to do. I don't think it's mine. She's been sleeping around. I know she has. It wasn't a big deal to me at first, but she's taken to flaunting it around town. Jenny told me—"

"Jenny? What has she got to do with this? Jere, you have got to get this ironed out. Lord, don't let Maria hear us," John whispered. "She's got a real opinion on the subject of Dana."

Jere chewed a moment before answering. "Don't we all? But let me finish. Jenny and her mother saw Dana hanging on this guy, Simon, in the grocery store. He's been the object of her attention for some time. She even ditched me at lunch one day to sit with him."

"Simon? Simon who?"

Jere shrugged. "I don't know. She says she's been trying to get him to hire her at his office. She claimed it was purely platonic. Jenny said it didn't look platonic to her."

"And you think this Simon guy is the father?"

"I don't know. I don't know who else she's slept with. We haven't been together in weeks, and the last time we might have done anything, I was fairly buzzed. Too many beers."

"Don't you practice safe sex?" John asked, frustration lining his face.

"Of course, but that night? Can't say for sure."

"So, you think you're safe, but you don't know?"

"I couldn't swear to it." He pushed the plate away. "I just don't know."

"Jere, you have to try to remember that night and make a decision. If you are the father, things are about to seriously change in your life."

Jere looked up at the ceiling and closed his eyes. "This just cannot be happening."

John stood and started away from the table. He punched Jere's arm in passing. "Call Dana. Make plans to get together and seriously have a conversation. I know you're filled with shock and awe right now, but this isn't something to take lightly. She has to acknowledge her part in this, too. Did she even say if she wanted to keep the baby?"

Jere looked up into John's face. "Didn't have any more talk with her. Shoved her out of the shop, told her to go home. I just couldn't believe it and didn't want to hear any more about it."

"Call her," John instructed. "Do it tonight. I'll tell Maria when the time comes, but not tonight. Get the information. All of it. Good God." He shook his head and left the dining room.

Jere dumped the remains of his dinner plate in the disposal, rinsed the plate and flatware and put them in the dishwasher. Then he pulled the garbage sack out of the can in the kitchen and took it out through the back door.

He didn't put a coat on, thinking he would be right back.

That was before he saw Jenny coming straight toward him, a purposeful stride propelling her across the street.

Another woman with a mission and his name etched in the roster for it.

~**~

Jenny came to a stop in front of Jere, who had watched her cross the street. "Hey," she said,.

"Hey," he answered. "What's up?"

"Where's your coat?" she asked, watching him shiver.

"Inside. I wasn't planning on being out here long. I just happened to see you."

"Oh." Now that she was here, she hesitated to ask her question.

"Did you need me for something?" he asked.

She thrust her hands into her jacket pockets and gave him a pointed look. "Yes. I wanted to ask if you were okay. Dave said you seemed out of sorts when he stopped by and got the tree."

"Oh." Now it was his turn to hesitate. "You know, it's all good."

She shuffled her feet. "No, Jere. I don't know anything. Is it Dana? I mean, it's obvious y'all have hit a rough patch. She's probably giving you grief over hiring me. But I believe, still today, that she's not right for you. I think she's planning something concerning you."

He rubbed his arms and cleared his throat, avoiding eye contact.

"She's a bad influence on you." There, she'd said it. It didn't make her feel any better, though.

"That's what she says about you."

"I never tried to wrap you around my little finger the way she does."

He stiffened, and she realized she'd hit a trigger button.

"You didn't have to try, Jenny. It was just the way it was. And you don't have any room to talk about hurting me."

"You're right. I don't. But I thought you deserved to know that she's planning something."

"What makes you say that? What have you heard?" His teeth chattered, and he tried to gain warmth by shoving his hands into his jean's pockets.

"I overheard her in the ladies' room at church last Sunday talking to one of the girls from Sarah's hair shop. They were gossiping about me, but you were talked about, too."

He looked over her shoulder, contemplating something. "What did she say about me?"

"She said that you wouldn't know what to do when whatever she's planning unfolds. I know it's sketchy, but I was hiding in a stall, eavesdropping. I couldn't hear everything that was said. They were whispering. Then they went out of the bathroom."

"Lori. She was with Lori. That's her roommate." He grew pensive.

"Whoever. She seemed all involved with Dana's plan, even encouraging it maybe."

"Very likely. They are pretty tight."

Jere was too silent, too still. She decided to retreat. "Okay, that's all I came to say. Just be careful. I don't trust her."

"Thanks," he said with no emotion. "Thanks a lot."

She turned and started back across the lawn. He called her name about half-way through the front yard.

"Jenny?"

"Yeah?"

He paused, and she almost didn't hear what he said.

"See you tomorrow."

She waved at him and headed home. Her brothers were hanging lights over the front windows inside and she hurried to help.

Chapter Fifteen

J ere didn't go to sleep right away. After Jenny left, he thought about her words. Things were beginning to make a lot more sense. Lori would egg Dana on in some contrived lie about being pregnant. It was starting to sound like a concoction to trap him into marriage.

He plopped down on his bed and flipped through social media for a long time. He really needed to call Dana and have it out, but he was bone tired. He flopped back, spreadeagle. Would his life be a series of potholes one after another into the grave?

He tried to change his mental quandary and focused on Christmas tree sales. They felt like the only bright spot. He decided to focus on that. Eventually, he crawled under the covers and relaxed, falling soundly asleep.

The next day, he talked to Will over the phone about the sales. He felt like his buddy was his partner in the whole thing. While he had Will on the phone, Jere said, "By the way, you were totally right about Dana. That girl is out to hang me."

Will made a sound of derision. "Man, I told you. She practically broke into my place and almost had Diana and I in a big fight. Thank goodness, Diana is a smart woman and saw right through her tricks. Get away from that one, for real."

Jere didn't tell him that getting away from Dana might be hard now. He didn't want to let anyone else know about the pregnancy thing yet. Not until he had a chance to have a real talk with her and make her see reason. It couldn't be his. Just... couldn't.

He shoved the thought away and dove into work. The bins all needed restocking, and he set to doing that until Joe arrived. Then he turned it over to him. When Jenny came in, he set her at the counter to wait on customers and he went out back to check on the trees.

A chill wind blew down the alley and the tarp fluttered overhead. The snow had only been a brief shower and there was no sign of leftovers, but the day was gray.

The little twinkle lights were turned off since he hadn't stayed overnight. He flipped the switch, and they came to life, giving the alley a festive feel. Edwin over at Abe's had hung colorful lanterns around his back area, and the colors worked well with the lights that had been strung between the businesses.

All in all, Jere felt like it looked good. He unrolled the fencing and pulled the trees upright, leaning them against it. When he had everything in order, he walked around the building to set the sign out.

While he was doing that, a crowd of people gathered in front of the shop. They all cooed over the decorations that Jenny had created and stuck out front. The new wreaths she had brought with her today had everything from Santa to snowmen on them.

He grinned to himself and thought he might need to buy her dinner tonight in appreciation. Those wreaths were selling as well as his Christmas trees. He went back around the building to wait for customers. He didn't have to wait long.

Gus Jones showed up. "Hey Jere," he greeted him.

"Hey Mr. Jones, what's up?"

"Oh, I was just in town and wanted to come by and tell you how much we like our tree. Got it up and sort of decorated last night."

"Excellent," Jere said, smiling.

"Dave told me he invested in this venture. Next year, if you do this again, I want to get in on it."

"Well, sure! I hope it is so good for business this year that we make a lot to put back into it for next year. I'll definitely keep you in mind."

Gus stepped closer and lowered his voice. "I also wanted to come by and thank you for giving Jenny a job. I know that wasn't an easy thing for you to do after what all y'all went through, and you didn't have to do it. But you are a bigger man in my eyes because you did."

Something about the words and the way they were conveyed made Jere stand taller, and he grinned. "Thanks, sir. I think she's going to do really well here. She's selling those wreaths like nobody's business. I needed good people to help me run the shop. She's perfect."

Gus clapped Jere on the shoulder and headed off in the direction from which he had come. The glow that he left behind with just his words of gratitude made Jere smile for a long time.

~**~

That evening, Jenny stayed late to handle shoppers. The visits were growing after dark. When they totaled up the sales from wreaths and trees, they had made a nice profit. Jere was thrilled and even Joe went home with a smile on his face.

Jere grabbed his keys. "Hey Jen, you got plans for this evening?"

She paused in her efforts to pull her coat on and stared at him. "Nothing, why?"

"You're doing a great job. I thought maybe we could grab a bite to eat. I can take you home later."

She struggled to find the right words. "I mean... I guess. Are you sure?"

He gave her a crisp nod.

"Let me call Dave and tell him not to come and get me," she said, pulling her cell out of her pocket.

She caught Dave before he started into town, and after disconnecting, followed Jere out to his truck. She could tell he was brimming with happiness, and she liked seeing him this way. There was only one thing that would spoil it, she thought.

Dana.

Once they were in the truck and Jere had the heat going, he asked her what she was hungry for.

"I think I'd like diner food, if that's okay with you," she told him.

"Sure, sounds good to me too."

He pointed the truck toward the highway leading toward Diago Springs and they listened to Christmas music as it played on the radio.

Eventually, Jere broke the silence. "So, your dad stopped by to see me this evening early. He didn't want much, just stopping in while he was in town."

"Really? She couldn't believe her dad had stopped at Veggie Heaven and hadn't even come in to say hi to her. "He never even popped his head in the store."

"Yeah," Jere said, glancing at her. "I think he just wanted to have a word with me."

"What did he say?" She twisted her rings around on her fingers.

"Not too much. Said the family liked their tree and all that."

"You know, I meant to tell you that myself. It's a lovely tree. We're supposed to do the rest of the decorations this weekend."

"I really don't deserve all this praise. Those trees were grown by a tree farm. I didn't do anything but pay for them and put them up for sale."

She laughed. "Well, it isn't likely we'll be going to thank the farmer, right? You get the praise heaped on your head instead."

"Okay then, I accept." He laughed too, and the sound of it made Jenny feel warm inside. How long had it been since he had laughed in her presence? She hadn't done too much of laughing herself if she was being honest.

"It's really nice to hear you laughing again," she told him.

He glanced over at her and turned into the parking lot of the little diner. "Thanks. It feels good to just let stuff go for a minute and enjoy life. I think I've been wound a little tight lately."

She climbed down from the truck. He had been preoccupied with work and a girlfriend that wasn't worth his time. He joined her in front of the truck, and they walked in together.

"You're not the only one who's had situations going on. I totally understand," she told him as he opened the door and she passed him into the restaurant.

They walked up to the hostess station and waited for the hostess to return. The notice about the Christmas event was on a little placard by the lectern. Jere stared at it for a moment and blinked as if he couldn't believe what he saw. Jenny leaned in and gaped at it.

It listed *Sarcastix* as one of the bands playing the event.

Jere shook his head and crossed his arms. "I guess I'm not the only one with trouble on my shoulders, like you say. You got a fair share, too."

She pulled her jacket around her tighter. "It's fine. We won't even see each other. It'll be fine."

But somehow, the chill she felt dug deep into her bones and a foreboding settled on her like a cape. What was she going to do about Brandon? The town of Mt. Moriah was not big enough for the both of them.

Then she remembered Dana's ominous words. She'd known about *Sarcastix* coming to town. She knew Brandon would be around. She might even have been planning to tell him where to find Jenny.

"*... you'll get yours. And sooner than you think.*"

~**~

Jere sipped on a glass of iced tea and peered at Jenny over the rim of it. "So, what's going through your mind right now? You've been really quiet all through ordering and getting drinks."

She shrugged. "I'm not sure right now. I guess I could say, 'I'll be okay' all day long, but I don't know how it would feel to see him. I'm still hurt over things. Shoot, I'm still in shock over things." She fidgeted with her napkin and lowered her gaze.

He knew her too well to allow her to struggle alone.

"I have a big problem, too. It's overwhelming when you try to figure it out in your head."

She looked at him and he knew she was seeing all the way through.

"What problem? Is it Dana?" Her voice was full of fire now, ready to defend him.

"Yes, but you don't need to worry about it. You have enough things to worry about."

"Focusing on someone else's burden helps make me forget my own. Besides, aren't friends supposed to be there for that? Dividing burdens and increasing joy?"

"I don't think anyone can help lessen this burden if it's true."

She leaned forward and whispered. "Is she pregnant?"

He rolled his shoulders, feeling the tension. "That's what she says."

"And you don't believe her?"

"Not at all."

Jenny fell quiet.

It was hard to tell anyone, but especially her. But as she said, sometimes friends could help you bear up under a burden. If anyone could
help him bear up under this mess, it would be Jenny.

"I don't believe her either. It's possible that this is the very plan that
Dana and Lori were whispering about in the church bathroom. She's
plotting on getting you back by saying she's pregnant," Jenny said.

"But what if she *is* pregnant?" He tore his napkin into tiny pieces.
"What if she is and what if it's mine?"

"I don't believe I'm asking this but, could that be? Is there a possibility that could happen?"

He grinned at her. She shifted in her seat, almost squirming. She
didn't want to ask directly if he had sex with Dana.

He decided to be honest, without going into details. "Not likely,
but maybe possible. One night. One stinking night when I was down-
ing beers, drowning my sorrows over you."

Her shoulders slumped. "Oh."

"Don't mean that as a dig, babe," he told her, patting her hand. "But
no, I don't think so, and I still have to get to the bottom of it all. John
said I needed to have a long talk with Dana. Guess I could go over to
her apartment."

The tall, lanky kid who was waiting tables sauntered over. "Hey,
y'all, can I get you something? Today's special is country fried steak."

Worried about Dana and a possible impending baby, plus seeing
Jenny and how miserable she looked as she gazed at him over the table,
sent Jere straight for comfort food.

"Yeah, give me that special with mashed potatoes and lots of gravy.
Stick some mac and cheese on there too, I guess."

Jenny frowned and then laughed at his food choice. She handed the
menu to the server. "I'd like a bowl of chili, please, and lots of crackers."

"We are a couple of losers," Jere said, shaking his head in mock disappointment.

She bit her upper lip and waved at him. "You started it with that country fried steak business."

He laughed. "True."

After a few moments of silence, they both started to speak at the same time. Jere motioned for her to continue.

"Well, as Mama always says, if you want to get the best load of gossip, go to the beauty shop. I think I need my hair done for the dance." She twirled a strand around her finger and looked at it pointedly.

"Yeah, and I could use a cut, too. Maybe we should both go."

She lifted an eyebrow. "Just not together, right?"

He stretched and his elbow came down hard on the wooden booth. "Ouch! Hellfire and damnation!"

"That's your meanness coming out," she said, sitting back and sipping her tea.

"I don't have a mean bone in my body," he replied. "And no, we should definitely not be seen together at the hair place. I mean, what if Lori is working? She'd tell Dana for sure."

"Is that a bad thing? Maybe Dana would feel rushed to enact her plan even more. Maybe making her think we're together will create some action and we can get to the bottom of this," Jenny said.

He looked at her for a moment and realized she really did have his back. But this was one time when she couldn't do what she wanted to do. This had nothing to do with her, and she shouldn't be in the midst of it.

"Thanks, but I think taking a direct path to Dana and making her tell me everything will be a better plan."

Jenny shrugged. "Okay. But if you want me to start spying on her, I will."

He laughed. Jenny, the spy who came in from the cold.

Chapter Sixteen

♥

J enny hung her coat up on the hall coat tree when she got home. The house was quiet, and the tree had been given lights now. She supposed the family would try to hang ornaments next, and she needed to be there for that. She loved helping decorate, but she needed to be with Jere more. She couldn't help but admit to herself that being with Jere was like wearing her favorite flannel pajamas. It just felt right. Comfortable. *Normal*.

She wandered into the kitchen, but no one was there. She supposed they had all gone to bed. She didn't want to eat or drink anything, so she turned the light out and headed for the living room. She grabbed her night clothes and went into the downstairs bathroom to change. She could put on a movie or something until she got sleepy.

When she got to the couch with the remote in hand, she flipped through a long list of movies, and nothing sounded good to her. She sighed and left the television on the local weather. The droning on and on of the voices soothed her and she could usually sleep to it quite well.

She curled up on the couch and pulled the blanket up to her chin, thinking about Jere and what he might be facing.

A baby. Jere's baby.

A shiver flittered through her.

But what if it wasn't? By the time Dana got married to Jere, she could fake a miscarriage before a DNA test could be taken. Jere would be trapped. He wouldn't quit a marriage without good reason. If she could only prove that Dana was lying...

A woman could have testing done during pregnancy but at a bit of a risk. She was sure Jere wouldn't request Dana to do anything that might endanger the child. So, time was on Dana's side. And if she were faking a pregnancy, faking a miscarriage wouldn't be a stretch.

Rattled at all of these thoughts, the television's monotone noise irritated her now. She turned it off. The Christmas lights from the tree blinked on and off and gave her something to focus on, aside from Jere's troubles. Her mind wanted to go to Brandon and what she might face if she saw him in Mt. Moriah, but she couldn't do it. She wasn't ready to face that possibility yet.

Am I in turmoil because I don't want to see him or because I do?

Exhausted from the anxiety that racked her, sleep crept up.

Her phone vibrated, and she jerked awake.

She lifted it to her face and stared at the number. It was not one she recognized. It was not a local telephone area code, so she didn't answer it. If they wanted to talk to her about her car's warranty, they could talk to her voice mail.

She tossed it over onto the coffee table, pulled the blanket closer, and closed her eyes. In a moment, her phone vibrated again. In utter disgust, she grabbed it and looked at it. The voice mail showed one message.

She had a good mind to hunt the person down who was leaving spam voice mails on her phone. She tapped the button and hit speakerphone to listen.

Brandon's voice sounded low and growly. "Jenny, hey. It's Brandon. I'm sorry I missed you, but I'm just calling to let you know that

I'm coming to Mt. Moriah for a Christmas thing. I would like to see you. I need to say a few things. Things that don't need to be said over the phone, and especially not voice mail. I hope this finds you doing well. Talk soon."

When she took the phone from her ear, she tapped the end button with a shaking hand. Tears rushed to her eyes.

"What do you have to say to me that you couldn't have said in Nashville?"

~**~

Friday dawned bright and chilly. Jere looked at the calendar hanging in the office. It was only a week and a few days until Christmas. He glanced over the tree inventory and decided they would likely be sold out before the holiday weekend, which was fine. Buying more trees would not be necessary. People who would buy would do so this weekend or next and after that, it was a wash.

I just don't want any left-over inventory!

The old office chair squeaked when he leaned back and let his mind wander. The money from the Christmas trees and wreaths would be a nice nest egg to stock away for the coming new year. He considered staying closed from the Friday before Christmas until January 3. Maybe even a week past that.

There generally wasn't much traffic on the courthouse strip through the holidays. The legal eagles who worked at the courthouse would slowly inch their way back to their jobs after the first of the year. That didn't mean his business would pick up much.

He thought about taking a trip. Maybe he would go to Florida. He heard the weather was nice down there in January, while Mt. Moriah would be in its deepest throes of cold. *Who am I kidding? I just don't want to face Dana.* This thought made him shift in his seat.

What am I going to do about the baby? His face grew warm as his heart pounded erratically. This whole situation made him anxious. They needed to talk. Lay it out, hash it out. He hadn't given her much of an opportunity to explain when she'd first told him.

He glanced at his phone. It was only seven thirty in the morning, but he was going to call her, anyway. Get it done and over with. If she didn't answer, he would leave a message.

He tapped her number on the screen. One ring... two...

"Hello?" She sounded sleepy.

"Dana, it's me."

"What time is it?" Sounds of her moving around. "What do you want?"

"I want to talk to you about our situation. I've had time to think about it. Rationally, I mean. Can we meet?"

"I'm off today. Tell me when and where."

"Your apartment, after Lori is gone. I don't relish discussing this with anyone else there. Unless you've already told her."

Silence. Then, "Come around ten, I guess. Give me a chance to get up and get some coffee."

He agreed to that, and they disconnected.

She was so cold, he thought. Now that he could compare her to Jenny, with a new eye, she was a very cold and calculating person. She rarely smiled, laughed, or even had fun. Jenny, on the other hand, could laugh at him and herself all at the same time.

Maybe it was because Dana spent so much time manipulating others. Jenny didn't have a malicious bone in her body.

As he envisioned her laughing green eyes, the front door opened, and Jenny arrived.

"Hey," she greeted him, leaning over behind him to stow her purse beside the filing cabinet.

"Hey," he replied, breathing in the scent of her soft cologne. "I'm going out back in a minute to get the trees situated. Likely be out there a couple of hours. Going to run a few errands around ten and be back so you can go to lunch. Think I'll stay open today. Need to be accessible for people Christmas shopping on their lunch hour."

She clasped her hands in front of her and nodded. "Whatever you say, Boss."

He rose from his chair and stretched. Jenny collected the till and took it to the front, where the cash register was located. Jere heard Joe as he came in through the front, greeted Jenny, and went to the office.

"Little bro," he said, stopping in front of him. "I hate to do this to you, but I need to take the day off. Can I do anything before I split? I need to go to the doctor with Hope. It's Maddie's checkup time."

"Dude," Jere moaned. "You need to warn me about this stuff ahead of time."

"I know," Joe agreed. "I actually forgot about it myself. Hope reminded me over coffee."

Jere waved at him to leave. "Go on, take off. Lucky for you I like you."

Joe grinned. "You have to like me. We share a bloodline." When Jere didn't respond, he strolled away. He said goodbye to Jenny as he was leaving, and Jere heard her joke about going with him.

~**~

Jere stood outside in the tree lot, Joe had left for the day, and business was slow. Jenny didn't know exactly what to do with herself. The market was swept and tidy and fully stocked. She hoped people began flowing through soon, or she would be forced to pull out a notebook and start making Christmas lists.

When the door opened and a man entered, Jenny lifted her eyes to the sky in thanksgiving. The man edged along the row of root vegetables until he stood in front of the cash register. She noticed right away that he wore a hooded jacket and kept his hands in his pockets.

His eyes darted around, and it occurred to Jenny that he might have something aside from vegetables on his mind. There was nothing she could do but stand there staring at him like a deer in someone's headlights. She memorized his eyes, dark and brooding.

She really wished that front door would open. Her heart fell cold in her chest and her body went rigid.

"Give me all your money," the man said.

She got a good look at him. Medium height, medium build, at least from what she could tell under his jacket. A teenager, really, sporting a scraggly beard and mustache. He squinted at her, and she wondered if he was high.

Jere had never told her what to do if a robber came in and tried to rob her. She leaned forward and said, "You really don't want to do this."

He lifted his hands in his jacket pockets as if to indicate he had a weapon. She couldn't make one out, but she shouldn't assume he was faking.

"Yeah, I do wanna do this," he told her. "And I'm telling you, give me all that money."

She sighed like she was done with him and over it all, but she was killing time.

Come on, Jere. Come back inside.

"I don't want to give you the money. We work hard for this money. It's Christmas. What would your mother say?"

This made him frown and fidget and he pulled out a small pistol to point at her. "Ain't got no mother. But I got this. Now do what I said."

Something about the way he said for her to do his bidding struck Jenny right between the eyes. It sounded so much like Brandon when he was drunk.

Everything went gray. She screamed, an unbarring of pent-up trauma from the last few months. She vaulted herself over the counter and plowed into the kid with the gun, his face becoming Brandon Daniels.

The gun skittered away under a bin of cucumbers. She straddled him, slapping him repeatedly and screaming at him about taking her life away and leaving her alone in a big city. The kid's face registered shock, horror, and confusion all at the same time.

He bucked and twisted, trying to get away from her. She came to her senses then and, for the first time since he had entered, saw him. He tried to punch her, and her temper flared anew. But this time, anger at the kid struggling to throw her off so he could escape.

"You little—don't make me hurt you. I've got brothers," she yelled at him. "Jere! Jere! Help!"

The kid yanked her arm sideways, almost managing to get out from under her. Jere came running in, eyes wide with fear.

"Help me!" she yelled.

He pulled her off the would-be robber, grabbed the kid by the hoodie, and snatched him close to his chest. "Don't move, kid. I'm a lot tougher than she is, and you're a lot smaller."

"Man, get me outta here. That woman's crazy."

Jere told Jenny to call 911 and pushed the kid outside where he made him sit on the curb under his watchful eye.

Jenny called as requested but had to sit and put her head between her legs to avoid fainting afterward.

Where did all this bravery come from?

The cops milled around, some outside and some inside. One came up to Jenny and asked her if she was able to make a statement.

She sat back in the chair. The officer took notes as she retold the story.

~**~

Jere re-entered the market when he was freed of the young offender. He nodded to the cop and strolled to stand beside Jenny.

"Why did you decide to attack the kid?" the cop asked.

"It was the only thing I could think to do. I couldn't let him take the money in the till. It was the first and only thing I thought of." Jenny swiped at her cheek, and Jere wanted to replace the trace of a tear with a long kiss.

"Well, next time, think of your safety, little lady. That was brave but stupid, too. Leave the stunts to Hollywood. We'll take him in. Give me your number in case somebody needs more for a report. You know we fill out a ton of paperwork on incidents."

She complied in a shaky voice. Jere placed his hand on her shoulder and squeezed, hoping she knew he was there for her if she needed him.

"By the way, officer, he had a gun."

Now the cop lifted his eyebrows and stared. "Where is it?"

She pointed under the bin with a shaking finger. He stooped and pulled it out with his pencil.

"Guess the kid just got another charge." He took it outside to give to someone.

Jere knelt to pull Jenny into an embrace. "Oh my God, Jenny. A real gun? I thought he was just a punk kid."

"He was. But I'm punkier than he is, apparently." She tried to smile as Jere moved away to stare into her face. His mouth slanted over hers and she held onto him tight. When he leaned away from her, she smiled a wavering smile and he saw tears rush to her eyes and silently fall down her cheeks.

If the cop hadn't re-entered then, he would have taken her into his arms and promised her anything she wanted. He couldn't stand to see her cry.

They answered the rest of his questions, and Jere held Jenny's hand the entire time. Jere could feel the trembles as they shook Jenny's entire body as she relived the moments of horror. Shaken and anxious, he wished the cop would hurry up and finish so he could take her home.

"Guess that'll do for now, Miss Jones. I'm fairly sure someone will call you later about this."

"Fine," Jere said, dismissively. "You have her number. I'm taking her home now if you're done."

The cop shrugged and strolled outside. There were only a couple cops left. The kid had been hauled away in a cruiser.

Jere pulled Jenny to her feet and enveloped her in an embrace.

"I'm so sorry, Jen. I am so, so, sorry."

She held onto him and let the tears come. Soon, it was a soft sob, then became a bit of a hitch in her throat, but she could wipe her eyes and look at him again.

"Thank you," she stammered. "I've never been so scared in my life."

"I swear I never would have put you in danger, Jenny. We've never had anyone come in here looking to rob the place. I guess it's desperation during the holidays. At least that's what they say about Nashville and the bigger cities. Shouldn't happen here. Not in Mt. Moriah."

He pulled her into his arms again and rested his chin on her head.

"Are you okay?" he asked softly.

"Um hm," she replied into his shirt front.

"Want to go home?"

She pulled away. "No." She wiped her eyes again. "I'll just go get cleaned up a bit and then I'll go back to work."

He was flabbergasted. "What? Are you sure?"

She nodded and headed for the restroom. "I'll be fine."

He looked at his phone and noted it was almost ten. He had to be going to Dana's soon. How to leave Jenny now, though? She needed him to stay. She needed him.

"Jenny," he said as she came back to the counter. "I have an appointment somewhere at ten. Are you going to be okay here alone? I swear I'll cancel and stay if you feel even the least bit scared."

She shook her head. "No. Go on. I'll be fine. Like you said, that's not something that should even happen in a small town like this. One in a million shot that he would pick the market."

Jere tilted his head. "You're sure?"

"Sure."

"Okay, well. This won't take long. I'm determined to make it short and sweet. I'll be back soon, and I'll take you to lunch. The least I can do," he said, shaking his head at the incident that still had them both so shaken.

"Thanks Jere, really. I'm going to be fine. I'm tough." This was said with no conviction in her voice at all.

Jere waved as he walked to the front door and wondered what would have happened if Jenny hadn't been so brave. Then, realizing how close they came to a major disaster, he went back and strode around the counter to command another kiss from her.

"Wha ..." she whispered when he released her.

"Please don't ever be that brave," he answered. "I can't lose you again."

He strode out and could feel her stare as she watched him leave.

Chapter Seventeen

When Jere left, Jenny went over the robbery in her mind. She didn't try to stop the gunman to save the money. She had snapped. All of her anger at Brandon poured out on the unsuspecting robber.

That really wasn't fair, but he earned it, coming in here threatening me. And Brandon has a load of that same treatment coming. She'd like to pummel his face for a minute.

But she had made it seem like she was defending the till, even to the detriment of her own life, instead of owning up to her real actions. She couldn't tell the truth of the matter to the cops, and most especially to Jere. Better to be thought of as a crazy brave woman than a crazy woman.

And Jere had been so attentive to her and kissed her like she was treasured. That confused her even more. She wasn't sure she wanted that kind of attention right now. Where did they stand, anyway? He had gotten rather free with his kisses.

"My head is so messed up," she said out loud, sighing. She wandered up and down the rows, aimlessly. "All men can go to the devil!"

The door opened and Sam entered. Except for this one, she mentally added, looking up at her brother.

"Hey Jen-Jen," he greeted her.

"Sam," she said, shoulders slumping. "I'm so glad you're here."

He peered at her, and they walked to the counter. She stood behind it and he leaned on it from the customer's side. "What's up?"

"I was held up today."

Now his eyebrows lifted into his hairline. "What? Like at gunpoint?"

She nodded. "Yes. It was awful."

"Wow, sis. Are you okay?"

She shrugged. "I mean, I am physically. But mentally? Not so sure."

He patted her hand. "I guess not! That's scary. What happened?"

"I mean, he came in with the sole purpose of robbing us. I stood here, right like I am now, and defied him. Then he said some mean thing." Here she paused. Sam was the only one she could trust with the truth.

"All I could see in my mind's eye was Brandon when he got drunk and treated me bad. Next thing I knew, I was flying across this counter and clobbering him. I kept hitting him over and over. It was terrible... and good all at the same time."

"I've been wondering when you were going to break down," Sam said, looking down at his feet. "You went through a lot with that guy, and you haven't shed a tear since you got home. From what I've seen, you haven't even really talked about it."

"Guess we work things out on our own," she told him, swiping at a piece of plastic on the counter.

"Well, I came in here to see if you needed a ride home tonight. I have a kind of thing to go to and wanted to see if I could take you home early."

"A date?"

He shrugged, shuffling his feet. "Maybe."

She was happy about this turn of events. Sam needed to start living a real life with someone to love in it. "Who is it? Anybody I know?"

He tilted his head. "You might. I'm not saying anything else though."

"Okay, then. I could try to guess..."

"No, don't do that. It may or may not turn into anything, and I just don't want to talk about it yet. It's too new and I'm too keyed up about it."

She gave him a long stare. "Is there something about this person that you don't want to share with your family for some reason?"

"Nothing more is coming from my lips. I'll ease y'all into it if there is anything to be made of it. Final answer."

She lifted her palms. "Okay, but don't blame me if a romance between you and someone isn't exactly treated like gold by the family. Especially since you're keeping it a secret."

"So, about that ride..."

"Nope. Take off. I can get a ride from Jere."

Sam laughed out loud at her choice of words. "Oh my!"

"Stop!" she said, slapping at him. "I mean a ride home."

He turned to leave and wiped tears of mirth from his eyes. "I'm leaving. See you later."

She waved at his back and wondered who on earth her brother was seeing that would make him want to hide it from everyone. But he did seem fairly happy.

~**~

Jere knocked on Dana's door and waited, shifting from one foot to the other. She took her sweet time answering.

"I was about to leave," he said when she opened the door.

Her face had pillow wrinkles on it from where she'd been asleep. From the looks of her, she had been sleeping quite hard.

"Come in," she said, opening the door wider. "Don't let the warm air out."

She shivered in her thin dorm shirt and hurried into the bedroom. When she returned, she had donned a robe. She had on fuzzy slippers, too.

"So, what's this all about?" she asked. "I haven't even had coffee yet, so can you talk while I make some?"

"Sure. Make enough for two. I'll help you drink it."

She walked into the kitchen where there was an island dividing it from the sitting room. She could still see and talk to him through the opening over the sink.

He pulled his coat off and sat on the love seat. He didn't really know how to begin the conversation, so he mulled it over while she poured ground coffee into a coffeemaker.

"What do you want to talk about?" she asked, peering at him.

"Um. I ... that is, we ... need to talk about this baby." He tried to find somewhere to focus his attention aside from her face. He didn't want to see whatever look she might be giving him.

"Funny you think we need to talk about it now," she said. "Where were you when I wanted to discuss it?"

This made him stare at her, pretense of avoiding her gaze forgotten. She pursed her lips, waiting for his answer. He uncrossed his legs and leaned forward. "I'm sorry. I know I acted like an idiot. I mean, I'm in shock, I guess. No man ever wants to hear his girlfriend is pregnant."

"It was a shock for me, too. I didn't plan for this to happen, Jere." She pulled cups from the cabinet in front of her, and they clattered when she set them down. "But it did."

He watched her, looking for evidence of a lie.

"Can you come back in here?" he asked, wanting her to stop being so jumpy. It was making him jumpy, too.

She nodded and came back to the sitting room, plopped down on the recliner, and stared at him. "Okay. So, now what? There's a baby growing inside of me, and that's all I know."

"I don't know what now," he answered, lifting his hands in a shrug. "That's why I'm here."

"What do other people do when they're faced with a baby?" she asked, clasping her hands together and putting them in her lap. "Guess there are only a few choices."

"Get married I guess?" It was more of a question. The thought made his blood turn cold. "Marriage, while an unhappy choice, is about the only choice I could live with."

Dana watched his face and said angrily, "To who? Jenny? Because that's who you really love. Why would I marry you when you have nothing to offer us?"

Her words rang true. What about Jenny?

He still loved her. He had always loved her, and nothing that had happened had changed that. But the would-be robbery made him face it finally.

His temper flared. "First, I don't know what you mean when you say *offer us*. Marriage is not a give-me-all-you-got deal. It's a give and take. And second, Jenny has nothing to do with this situation, so keep her out of it."

"Methinks he doth protest too much," she murmured, sitting back in the chair. "There's no room for three in a marriage, Jere. I won't be second place in your life." She paused, then, "You should see how you look right now. It's so obvious that you're in love with her."

He growled low in exasperation. They were getting nowhere. "What do you want, Dana? Do you want to get married? Do you want me to support you and the baby? What?"

She avoided his gaze as if in thought for a moment. He knew she had already figured it all out. She was cunning and purposeful if nothing else.

"I'd like to get married. I'd like to give my baby a decent chance. But, so help me, Jere Collins, you have to get Jenny Jones out of your life."

He cringed. This was what he feared she would say. But he wasn't unprepared for it.

"Fine. I'll marry you, but you'll have to get a DNA test to prove it's mine. If it's not mine, then I'll have the marriage annulled or divorce you."

She stared at him. The wheels were turning. He waited for her answer.

"And what if it is?" she asked, a wicked grin spreading across her face.

~**~

Jenny had a rush of customers while Jere was gone, and she peered closely at each one as if they would come to the counter to rob her. It had been a long day already, and it was only lunchtime. Why didn't she go home when Jere suggested it?

She looked at her phone for the current time. It was past noon, no problem there. Jere would be back soon to relieve her to go to lunch. Not that she was even hungry. How could anyone think of food after all she'd been through?

She rang up a lady who was purchasing one of the wreath's she'd created. She would have to make more soon. They were rather popular, as it turned out.

When every customer had come and gone, and the hour grew late, she thought about calling Jere to see when he might return. She decided against it though, as she didn't want to seem like she needed to leave.

Instead, she went into the stockroom and gathered some greenery and another wreath frame and set to making a very Christmas-like arrangement. Jere had even purchased some wooden cutouts to add to the wreaths, and she hot glued several onto the one she created. Finally, she held it up and inspected it.

"Not bad!" she told herself aloud.

"Not bad at all," a voice replied from the middle aisle.

She knew that voice. A feeling both hot and cold came over her and she set the wreath down on the counter.

Brandon Daniels peeked out from behind a display for gravies and sauces. He strolled up to the counter and gave her his best crooked grin. She must have missed his entrance when she was making the wreath.

She closed her eyes briefly. *Why today? Why on green earth did he have to come in here today?*

"What are you doing here?" Her voice wavered, and she hated how it sounded.

"The band and I came over for the weekend to check out the venue and sound checks and all that."

"A week early? Don't you usually do that a few days early?"

He shrugged. "Depends. This is an outside gig, and winter to boot. Plus, we had nothing going on until tomorrow night. Figured a couple hour drive over from the Ville might be cool. Maybe look up some folks." At these words, he shifted his gaze nervously as if afraid to look at her.

"You mean you came over to Mt. Moriah to see if you could find me, since I didn't answer your call?" Jenny thrust a hand on her hip and stared down her nose at him.

He shrugged again, as if helpless to answer. "Maybe."

"Brandon, what are you doing? Why are you here?"

He casually leaned on the counter. "Do I have to have a reason to come look up my best girl?"

"I'm not your best girl."

The door opened and Jere strolled in. He couldn't see anything but Brandon's back, but Jenny saw the tension in his face as he recognized him, anyway.

"You should go," she said with a lowered voice.

Unaware of Jere's approach, Brandon smiled at her, leaned in, and said, "You miss me, huh?"

Jere slapped Brandon's shoulder, pulling him around.

"Dude!" Brandon yelped.

"Get the hell out of my store," Jere told him, shoving him toward the exit.

"Wait ... whoa! I'm just talking to Jenny."

"Jenny is at work. She isn't allowed to have visitors here."

Jere continued to shove Brandon toward the door. He finally lifted his hands in defeat and stepped out, but he yelled to Jenny, as he did. "I'll see you later!"

When Jere came back to the counter, a thunderhead couldn't have looked more threatening. Whatever he had been doing, whomever he had been meeting with, hadn't gone well for him and now this intrusion had been the last straw.

"You need to go to lunch." It was not a question.

Jenny pulled her purse up from beneath the counter. "Yes," she answered. "I'll go now."

She tried to step past him, but he stopped her with his hand held out. He wouldn't look her in the eyes. "If you're planning to get back together with that jerk, don't come back to work today."

"Jere!" she exclaimed, shocked at his attitude.

Now he pinned her with his gaze. "Not today, not ever. Got me?"

She slapped his hand away and stepped close enough to fit under his chin. "Yes, I got you. And if you think that you have control over my life and what goes on in it because I work for you, then you better think again. Not. Going. To. Happen. Got me?"

He sidestepped her and headed for the office. She strode to the door and slammed her hand against it, making sure it closed behind her as hard as possible.

Chapter Eighteen

J ere didn't stop moving until he was out the back door, panting and huffing the cold air deeply into his lungs.

"What is wrong with me?" he asked aloud, bending at the waist, and trying to get a clear head.

Women! He didn't understand them. He had never understood them. Maybe he never would. That's what happens when you're raised with all brothers, he thought.

He stood straight and found Edwin halfway across the alley, looking at him strangely. When he lifted a hand to wave, the fellow shop owner came all the way over.

"I saw you bend over and thought something was wrong." Edwin had a genuine look of concern on his face. "You ain't sick, are you? Everything okay over here?"

"You know anything about women? How to make them act like they have a lick of sense?"

Edwin laughed and waved his hand across his body. "Um, no. I'm not into that flavor of the human species. I can tell you all about men, though."

"Tell me why I'm such a sap then." Jere crossed his arms and considered the good-looking man. He could be considered something of a guy's guy.

"Women are just tougher than men. They can think things all the way through before a man can even get to first gear. Somebody has you in a mess, I can see that."

"Two. Two somebodies."

"Pal, you need a drink. Wanna go over to the pizza place and grab a brewski after work? I'm not certain I have all the answers, but I'm a real good listener."

Jere grinned and looked down at his feet. "You ain't coming on to me, are you? I'm as straight as the day is long."

"Shoot naw, pal. I'm just offering you a chance to get it out of your system with someone who has no vested interest one way or the other."

Jere really gave him a strong look. "Okay then. Let's make it that dive down the street from your place, though. The Pizza Emporium is the last place I want to be seen at."

Edwin shuddered. "Ew. Okay, then. But if that *dive*, as you call it, is too loud, too smelly, or too loosey-goosey, then I'll be gone. That place needs to be hosed down every night."

Jere laughed at that. "Okay Ed, if it's too much for you, then pick another place. I just don't want to go to the pizza house. One of the girls who wants to kill me works there."

Edwin nodded as understanding came. "I'll bet you that we could get a nice summer blend from a local brewer at that Cajun place out on the highway."

"Oh yeah, I love that place. Let's do it."

"What time?"

"I'm staying here until seven."

"Have you been selling many of our trees?"

"Doing quite well, actually."

"Okay. I can close up tonight a little early, and I'll just come out and give you a hand. Then we can split from here."

"Sounds good."

Edwin stuck his hand out to bump fists. "See you later."

Jere bumped his fist. "Thanks, Ed. I really do need to get this out of my system."

Edwin waved at him and strolled back across the street.

Jere took one last breath of fresh air and went back into the market to man the counter until Jenny got back. He was certain that a paycheck would bring her back, no matter how mad she was.

What do I do about Jenny? What would she say when she found out he had agreed to support Dana until the baby was born and then, if the DNA test showed it was his, marry her? And why did he act like a Yeti when he had seen Daniels? He wasn't ever going to be able to get back together with Jenny now because of the baby. She'd never come between him and his child.

So, what difference did it make if she patched things up with the man that she'd left him for?

Don't you want her to be happy? Not with Daniels. Not with anyone but me.

"My life is so messed up. How am I ever going to live like this?" he asked out loud as he stood at the counter looking out at the vegetables that were his life. They were the only thing he had to offer a woman, any woman. But Dana? This would never be enough for her.

He dropped his head into his hands and let the emotions wash over him.

~**~

Jenny stomped down the sidewalk, her pea coat flapping in the wind, until she made it to Sarah's Head Shop. She pushed on the door and walked to the counter. Lori wasn't there. She was certain Sarah would tell her whatever she wanted to know about Lori. She was going to get the goods on Dana if she could. The only place she could think to start was with Lori.

Loose lips sink ships, she thought.

Sarah wiped her hands on a towel and came over to the counter. "Hey, Jenny, what can I do for you today?"

"Oh, hey, Sarah. I'm looking for Lori. Is she working today?"

"Yep, gone to lunch, though. You want me to take a message?"

Jenny thought hard. "Do you happen to know where she went to eat. I really need to talk to her."

"No honey, I don't. I think she usually goes to the house when she takes lunch. Benefits of living in a small town." She smiled at her little joke.

Jenny nodded. "Okay, thanks. I'll try to catch up to her."

She turned to leave, but the older woman stopped her. "Heard you got a job with Jere Collins. Is that working out okay for you?"

Jenny tilted her head. There was no deceit in Sarah's face. "Yes. Working out fine, thanks."

Sarah smiled and waved at her. "That's great, really happy to hear it."

Jenny left the shop and wandered toward the Inn on Main Street. She could grab a sandwich and a cup of coffee there. After Jere's horrid comments, she wasn't in a hurry to go back to work. Let him sweat.

While she walked, she thought about Sarah. Was she trying to find out if Jenny was managing to work with her old boyfriend, or was she just making conversation? She sure hoped her failed relationship wasn't a topic of conversation with the beautician and her customers now. She really needed things to die down. Jere was besieged with enough trouble already and with Brandon wandering around town, things were certain to get even more difficult.

She pushed open the door to the Coffee Café and walked in. She was almost at the middlemost booth when she saw and heard Lori talking loudly to someone on her phone. She quickly ducked into the booth, hiding. A partition separated the two seating areas.

This is too perfect.

Jenny picked up the menu, pretending to study it.

"Girl, you should have told him that you wanted money from him every month of your pregnancy. He's one of those honorable men. He'd have done it." Lori giggled at her emphasis of honorable.

Oh great. Gossip of the highest order. It had to be Dana.

Jenny listened closely. *Eavesdroppers often hear highly instructive things...*

"Look, girl, you gotta get him to put a ring on it before long. You don't wanna be wearing a pillow, do you?" Lori laughed. "Well, ain't that what the movie stars do?"

Jenny rolled her eyes. Dana Baker was far from movie star material.

"If it gets you more money every month, I'm all for it. That's what I did with my last old man. When things got too hot, I just had a miscarriage. You can do that too."

Jenny took a breath and closed her eyes. *Dana was playing Jere.* She knew it!

The server came up then, and she placed a sandwich, chips, and drink order to go. She had to get back to Jere's Veggie Heaven and let him know what she'd heard. She listened in on the conversation again after the server left, but Lori had stopped talking about Dana and had started talking about herself.

"Are y'all going to the dance? We are, yes. He asked me last week. I think we're going out tonight. Are you going to be home? Just in case he wants to, you know, test my bedsprings."

Lori laughed hard, had a coughing fit, and in a choked voice said, "Oh, he'd be a real catch. I could play the baby card, but I don't know. I think I'd like for a man to want to be with me instead of having to be with me, you know what I mean?"

Jenny sat back. Who was Lori dating? A lump formed in her throat. If it were Sam ... she'd kill him.

~**~

Jere decided the best thing he could do for both him and Jenny was to stay absent. He waited until she returned from lunch, then headed to the office. He had plenty of paperwork that needed to be done, including quarterly taxes. He hadn't even gotten past pulling the ledger book out when Jenny stood in the open doorway and leaned against the frame.

"What?" he asked, looking up at her. The sight of her reddened cheeks and sparkling eyes sent his body into overdrive. He felt like a hungry bear looking at her. Embarrassed by the flush creeping up his body, he looked back at the ledger.

"You and I need to talk, for one thing," she said, pulling out a chair from where it was tucked into a corner of the small room. "And secondly, you need to hear something."

"If it's about Daniels, forget it. I will never like the man, not after the way he treated you."

"It's not about Brandon. Not entirely anyway. It's about Dana and the scam she's pulling on you."

He frowned and felt a headache coming on. "Oh, what now? What scam?"

"I went to the Coffee Café for lunch. Lori was there, right on the other side of my table. She was talking on her phone, and you know she talks a little loud, so I overheard most all of what she said."

"And?" Jere crossed his arms, preparing for a bombshell.

"She was talking to Dana, I'm fairly sure. She said things like, making you pay support every month for the baby. That was bad enough."

"Dana has already laid out her demands. She wants support for the baby, like medical costs, because she has no insurance. Did Lori say my name?"

Jenny crossed her legs. "No. But there's more. She also said for Dana to get you to put a ring on it before too much longer or she'd have to use a pillow like they do in the movies."

Now Jere sat up straighter. "A pillow? Like to make her look pregers?"

Jenny nodded.

He stood and ran his hand through his hair. "That lying little..." He stormed out of the office and into the back alley. He found flotsam from the trees lying around and kicked at it, all the while softly cursing.

Jenny followed him and stood in the doorway, watching him. "Are you finished having a fit and falling in it now?"

He stopped and took a deep breath. "I guess. Not like it's going to do me much good, anyway."

"Why? What did you promise?"

"I told her I'd help her financially as much as I could during the pregnancy and when the baby was born, she'd have to have a DNA test to show it's mine. Then, if it is, I'll take her as my wife and the baby will be raised by both of us."

Jenny looked at her feet. "Oh Jere."

"I didn't sign anything."

"Yeah, but she's probably making up something for you to sign right this minute. Lori seemed mighty happy about Dana getting more money every month. She said that was how she did it with her last man. Said when things got too hot, she just had a miscarriage." She made air quotes over the word miscarriage.

"You mean to tell me, that this is a scam to rook me into marriage and then she'll conveniently have a miscarriage when it's too late for me to get out?"

"I'm afraid so. I really believed this was what she was out to do from the beginning. I'm really sorry."

He shook a tree hard and watched the needles ping onto the ground. "No, no. Don't be sorry. You just saved my freaking life. I should be the one saying I'm sorry. I've been a royal pain in the rear towards you."

He left the tree alone and came to where she stood. He looked down at her and tilted her chin up to meet his gaze. "And I am sorry, Jenny. I'm so deeply sorry for what I said, and how I have acted. You're the only person on the planet who's always had my best interest at heart. Well, the only person who isn't related to me, that is. Man, I sure am glad to find this out now. Can you imagine the fun Joe would have had with me?"

She giggled and he let his hand drop. "You're a special lady, Jenny Jones. Call me if anyone comes by and wants a tree. I've got an errand to run."

He passed her and headed for the desk where he'd dropped his keys. Dana had one more visit coming from him, and it wasn't going to be nice.

~**~

Jere was gone for a long time the second time he left. Jenny knew this time that he was going to see Dana and have it out. She was glad it wasn't her on the receiving end of that anger. She'd seen and heard first-hand what Jere Collins' temper could bring.

While she prepared to lock up the shop, she remembered she needed a ride home. The robbery from the morning had all but been forgotten. At least her knees had stopped shaking.

If Jere remedied his situation with Dana, Jenny wondered if there would ever be a time for them again. He and she just fit together like an ice cream sandwich, and she couldn't deny it any longer. She still had a thing for the market owner, and she couldn't resist giving into the thought of maybe renewing their relationship. The daydream carried her right up until the time when her phone buzzed, and she saw the same Nashville number that had called her the other night.

Brandon, again.

She swiped the phone to answer. "Hello?"

"Jenny?" Brandon asked. "Hey, it's Brandon."

"I know. I recognized your number. Why are you calling me?"

"I thought maybe if you had a few minutes, we could sit and talk."

She considered his offer. She wanted to tell him to leave her alone and never call her again, but she didn't have it in her to be as rude to him as he deserved. Instead, she saw headlights in the place where Jere usually parked and knew he was back.

"I can't talk now. I'm at work. I'll ... I'll call you later." And she disconnected, shoving her phone into her purse where it sat on the shelf near her calf.

Jere came in and gave her a lopsided grin. "That's a wrap. I told Dana that I knew what she was up to, and that it would never work. I told her that she would have to prove to me with a real doctor's test that she was pregnant. She hemmed and hawed, of course. She's not pregnant. Never was."

Jenny held up her hand for him to give her a high five. "That's good, Jere."

"Hey, listen, while we're on the subject of exes, I apologize for my behavior earlier. It's not something that I do, but that guy trips my trigger and not in a good way."

She nodded. "Okay. I get it."

He thrust his thumb over his shoulder. "I need to get out back. Did we have any tree sales?"

"No, surprisingly. But Jere ... I sort of need a ride home."

He nodded. "Sure thing, no worries. I'm going home from here, too. Do you need to leave this minute?"

She shook her head. "Not right this minute." She crossed her arms and asked, "Did she admit to faking the baby?"

"Yes, finally. I screamed at her, and she broke. She's got a weak spot when it comes to confrontation, and she is in the wrong."

Jenny followed him out back while he secured the trees.

"If no one has shown any interest in buying a tree this late, guess it won't happen. I sort of thought we might have a slowdown in sales, but it'll pick back up this weekend."

Then Edwin showed up. "Hey, Jere, you need some help?"

"Sure do," Jere laughed. "But not with trees. I'm about ready to go. I gotta take my lady here to her house and then I can meet you."

Jenny lifted a hand and waved.

"I'm going out for a drink with Edwin," Jere told her.

"You don't have to tell me your business, Jere. You're a grown man," Jenny whispered just before turning and going back into the shop.

The drive to her house was unremarkable, Jenny decided. She didn't ask any more questions about Dana, and he didn't offer any more information. She figured he must have given her ultimatums and waited for her to crack.

When she got out, she paused in the truck's shadow and stuck her head back into the truck. "Thanks for the ride," she told him.

"Thanks for being my friend," he answered with a smile.

Impulsively, she clambered back onto the truck seat and leaned far over to plant a kiss on Jere's lips. "Best friends, forever," she told him, sliding back out again, this time shutting the door.

Chapter Nineteen

♥

J ere drove back to the highway, still feeling the touch of Jenny's kiss. A fire burned between them, and he couldn't deny it any longer. Apparently, neither could she. Maybe the visit from Daniels at the market was not what he thought he saw. Maybe she wasn't going to give that jerk another chance.

He tooled along until he saw the turnoff for the Cajun restaurant, Carl's Crawdaddy Kitchen. He parked in the shadowy parking lot and headed for the door. The noise inside poured through the glass.

The place had new owners, and they had decided Friday nights were made for drinking and music. They didn't disappoint on either score.

Jere stood inside the doorway looking around for Edwin. He strode to the bar and looked down it, finding the entrepreneur seated at the other end, chatting with another man.

Should I interrupt? What if he's trying to get a date?

Jere was uncertain how to approach. Then, Edwin looked up and saw him, waved frantically for him to join him. He plowed through the crowd surrounding the bar and stood at Edwin's elbow.

"Man, I have been waiting for a table like thirty minutes. Don't know what to tell you. This place is hopping."

Jere couldn't disagree. "No worries," he shouted. "I'll just order a beer and wait right here. I don't need to sit down."

Edwin nodded and pointed at the man seated next to him. "This is Tony. Tony, this is my business neighbor, Jeremiah Collins."

Tony stuck his hand out and Jere shook it. Tony was built like a football player. Broad-shouldered and muscle-bound. He wondered if Tony was the type that Edwin found appealing, then felt guilty for even caring. It was none of his business who Edwin liked or how they looked.

The bartender came over and Jere ordered his beer. While he waited for it, he chatted with Edwin.

"Dude, I don't think I've ever even heard your last name."

"Moore," Edwin told him, shouting to be heard. "Everybody wants Moore!"

Jere laughed and took the outstretched beer from the bartender. He had selected a summer ale and tasted the citrus when he took the first drink. He paid the bartender.

"Refreshing," Jere told Edwin, showing the bottle to him.

Edwin glanced at it, then away when a server edged as close as she could and waved at Edwin.

"That's us," he told Jere.

They followed her to a table fairly close to the band and dancefloor, a new addition to the eatery. When they were seated, she handed them menus.

"Are y'all set for drinks, or do you want something else?"

"Just keep bringing these," Jere told her.

"I'm good," Edwin said.

She pulled a pad out of her apron and asked them if they were ready to order food now.

"I am," Jere said, pulling the menu over. "Bring me that seafood boil."

Edwin asked for gumbo and handed the menus over to the server.

"Be right back, y'all," she said.

"Okay," Edwin said. "You needed to pour out your soul. Spill it."

Jere grinned at him and took a long pull from his beer. "Well, you see, it's like an old song. I got women on my mind. One wants to own me, one wants to stone me, and thank God I don't have any more."

Edwin laughed. "I got you, brother. But, why? That is the burning question. What have you done or not done that makes these girls feel this way?"

"The one who wants to own me just pulled the pregnancy card out. Tried to make me think I was her baby daddy."

"Are you?"

"No man. She was playing with me. She wasn't even pregnant."

"Are you sure?"

"Yeah," Jere started peeling the label off his bottle. "She was trying to get me to marry her. I finally got her to confess to lying about it."

"How d'you do that?" Edwin stopped the server with his hand out. "Bring us some of those beignets." She nodded, and he turned back to Jere.

"That's the interesting thing here," Jere answered. "The woman who wants to stone me, found out through eavesdropping on a conversation that the allegedly pregnant woman was playing a game. She dropped that on me, and I hauled butt over to have it out."

"So, she doesn't want to stone you, she wants to own you too."

Jere shook his head, feeling a slight buzz from the beer. "I don't think so. I think she really cares about me. Didn't want to see me hung in marriage ropes needlessly."

"What's in it for her? Everybody wants their piece of flesh in these situations. What does she want?"

Jere thought about his question. What did Jenny want? He held up his empty bottle for the server to bring him another one. "That, my friend, is the million-dollar question."

~**~

The memory of Jere's lips on her own warmed Jenny all the way into the house. Her mother roamed the kitchen, like a pacing tiger.

"Hey, Mom."

Fancy looked up with a worried glance. "Oh, it's you."

"Who'd you think it was?"

"I was hoping it would be Dave. I haven't heard a word or seen him at all today."

Jenny paused beside her mother, who now had her arms crossed and leaned her back against the counter. "And you're worried? Have you asked Sam?"

She shook her head. "He's out on a date or something. This is not like Davy."

"Mom, you're kind of scaring me right now. What's going on in your head?"

"The last time this happened, we ended up at the police station to bail him out."

"Okay, let's talk this through. When was the last time you heard from him? Have you called his cell? Is there anyone else we could call?"

"No answer. That's what's so weird about this."

The front door opened, and someone entered, and Jenny and Fancy both jogged to the family room to see who it was.

"Gus!" Fancy said, breathless.

"Hey, honey. I'm home. Man, traffic was horrible."

"Gus, have you heard from Dave at all? He still isn't home…"

Her husband gave her a pained look. "Not again."

Jenny waved her hand to stop them. "Maybe he's stuck in traffic, too. Try not to blow this out of proportion, y'all."

As they were standing in the family room, turning on the Christmas tree lights, and not saying much, Dave's car lights flashed through the window.

"Oh, thank goodness!" Fancy said, hand over her heart. Gus went to the front door to open it. Dave came in.

"Whew, what a day!" he said. "Did you get in that traffic around the courthouse? I think it must be the Christmas Celebration." He strolled in and hung up his coat on the coat tree in the family room.

"Is that why you're late?" his mother asked.

He turned to face the trio. "Yeah. Are you guys waiting on me for something? I'm sorry I didn't call. This guy wanted me to come by about a possible job. Would be a good thing if it turns out."

"I don't care why," Fancy said, hugging him. "I'm just glad you're home and not in jail."

He winced at her words. "Dang, Mother, harsh much?"

She smiled at him and swatted his backside as she headed to the kitchen. "Let's eat."

Jenny followed them and helped with the meal her mother had left warming in the oven. When they had all served themselves Fancy's tuna casserole, Jenny casually told them about her day.

"So, I had a bit of a wild day, too."

Fancy looked up from her plate. "Really? How so?"

"We got robbed."

Everyone stopped eating and stared at her.

"You what now?" her father asked, shocked.

Jenny looked around the table. Sam was missing, but he already knew, anyway. "Yeah, it was terrible and not so bad all at the same time.

I assaulted the guy, but he isn't likely to press charges considering he was underage with a gun."

"A *gun*?" Fancy asked, her voice rising. "Oh, no. You're not going to work there anymore."

"Now, Mom," Jenny said.

"I think she's right." Gus had the same look of horror that her mother wore.

"Y'all. Jere and I handled it. The police were called, the guy was hauled off. End of story. It's like Jere said ... this was really unusual for Mt. Moriah. The robber was just a kid. It has to be because it's the holidays. Why else would he risk doing such a thing?"

"The world sure is messed up. I punch a guy in the nose and have to serve weeks of community service, and I'll bet that kid gets off scot-free because he's too young to prosecute."

Jenny shrugged. "I don't know, but it turned out fine. I just didn't want any of you to hear this from someone else and be upset with me for not telling you about it."

"Jere Collins is going to have to give some assurances that this won't happen again." Gus took another bite of his food. "And especially to me. I'm with your mother. I don't think you should work at a place that transparent and open."

"That same risk exists everywhere, Dad."

He shook his head. "Still. I'm going to talk to Jere."

Jenny sighed and dug into her food, hoping her father would forget about talking to Jere. It wasn't his fault. The kid was just desperate.

~**~

Jere writhed in his bedsheets, bathed in sweat. Jenny stood in front of him, a robber's arm tight against her throat and a gun aimed at her head. He pleaded with the kid, begging him not to hurt her.

When the gunshot rang out, he bolted upright.

His alarm was going off. It sounded like a gunshot in his dream, but it was just the usual annoying alarm on his phone. He tapped the screen to stop it, then tossed the rest of his covers aside and swung his legs over the side of the bed. A dream. A nasty, realistic dream. A nightmare, really.

The robbery had upset him more than he realized, apparently because he didn't have nightmares often. Maybe more lately than he used to have, but it was because the women in his life were giving him fits.

He strode into the bathroom down the hall and took care of his morning routine. When he came out, he decided he would not go out drinking again for a while. That likely was the culprit of the nightmare.

He got dressed and grabbed a banana for breakfast on his way out. He didn't even stop for coffee, deciding to grab a cup at the gas station around the corner. When he finally made it into the market, he looked around at the place.

What if Jenny had been hurt? He would never forgive himself. This place wasn't worth such a sacrifice. But it was all he had. It hurt him deeply to think he had so much investment in his little business, and it could all go up like a puff of smoke in a moment of someone's bad decision. Even his own.

His thoughts strayed to Dana as he pulled out displays of Christmas wreaths and potpourri packaged with scents of vanilla, cinnamon, and pine. She had definitely been a close call. He would never let a woman get him into that situation again. In fact, he had sworn off women entirely for the time being.

As he acknowledged that thought, Jenny stepped out of Dave's car and slammed the door. She was dressed in knee-high boots, a long coat covering the rest. Her cheeks were red, and he wondered if it was from anger or chill.

She might be the exception, he thought.

"Good morning," he said.

She ducked her head and passed him with a muffled good morning. Anger then, he thought. He finished up his activity in front of the market and went inside. Maybe he shouldn't ask?

Ah, to heck with that.

She came to the counter and began her morning by counting down the till and setting up items on the counter that were considered impulse buys.

"You okay today, Jen?"

She looked up from what she was doing. "Yeah. I guess."

"Seems like you're a little mad or something. Is it Daniels? Because you know I'll—"

"No. It isn't that. My dad's all mad about my working here with a robbery happening and all that. He says he's going to speak to you about your intentions on how to keep me safe from that happening again."

"Keep you safe?"

"Yeah, I know what you're thinking. I thought the same. How can you keep me safe? It's a job where I am face-to-face with the public. Still, he's bent on having a talk with you, he says."

Jere shrugged and hefted a bag of potatoes onto the display. "Okay. I mean, I'll be glad to hear what he has to say, but there really isn't much I can do aside from having Joe or myself work alongside you. Right now, with the other sales outside, it's a little hard to do that."

"Joe's going to be taking off for the holidays soon, so that won't work."

He nodded. "True."

"So, what if you gave Dave a job here temporarily until my dad forgets about this?"

Jere lifted his eyebrows. "Dave? Hm." Dave Jones was an okay sort of guy. A little hot-headed, sometimes, but manageable, Jere thought. "Gee, I haven't given it any thought because, honestly, I haven't really had the funds to hire people. You were the first one, besides Joe, and you have really been a big asset."

She smiled. "Thanks."

"I thought Dave was doing some sort of community service though?"

"He'll be finished with that tomorrow. They take a hiatus during the holidays. I think he'll have another week or so after the new year."

"Okay, sure. I'll think about it and maybe give him a call. Let me ask you this, though," he said. "How do you feel? Do you want to work with your brother? Believe me, I work with mine and some days, ugh."

She bit her lower lip. "I won't lie. That whole scene yesterday really threw me. I didn't sleep well. I think I'd be happier and feel more secure if there was someone else in here with me."

He nodded and headed for the office. "Okay. I'll let your dad know. Is he coming today?"

"Don't know," she said over her shoulder. "Maybe."

"Well, don't let it upset you. We'll figure it out."

~**~

Jenny heard the office chair squeak when Jere sat in it and felt her body physically relax. Why was she so tense today around Jere? Was it because she wanted more than just a friendship now? Was it that she realized what she'd missed all that time in Nashville? Her kiss last night had been out of gratefulness for his friendship. She had thought. But was it really?

She didn't let on to Jere that her anger was not at anyone but herself for being so weak and wanting. If he ever found out that she had anything on her mind except being a good employee to him and the market, it'd send him straight onto the floor, foaming at the mouth.

She was sure that he couldn't stand any more from women for a while. Her desertion and then Dana's pregnancy charade had been too much. If she'd been in Jere's shoes, she couldn't have stood up under all that.

She promised herself to try to be kind and sweet to him today, in spite of everything. He was trying to do that for her, so she had to reciprocate. She owed him that much.

When her father entered the market a few hours later, she stiffened at the sight of him.

"Hey, Dad."

"Hey, Jen. Where's Jere?"

She thrust her thumb over her shoulder. "Out back with the Christmas trees."

He stabbed a hand through his hair. "This is what I mean, Jen. You're in here all by yourself, with no one to help out if anything should happen. Jere knows better than this."

"Dad," she said, placating. "He agreed to hire Dave. He's going to talk to you about it. Don't freak out."

"Good," Gus said, heading back out. "I'll step around back and talk to him. Are you sure you're okay in here?"

She nodded. "Yes sir. I'm fine."

He took a deep breath and breezed out. If Jere played his cards right, he could get Dave for free, she felt certain. Or her father. Either way, someone was going to be her babysitter for the rest of the holidays, and she wanted it that way, yet hated it all at the same time.

Chapter Twenty

That afternoon, Jere called Dave in and had a talk with him. They decided that Dave would work in the Christmas tree lot during the day and Jere would take over at night after Jenny went home. Jere wouldn't mind working alongside Jenny. It would be nice, in fact. She wasn't like Dana, who uttered sarcastic remarks on every subject.

"Dave just left," Jere told Jenny when he came inside later. "He starts on Monday."

"Okay," she said, thrusting her hands into her back pockets.

"Relax," Jere told her. "He'll be out in the lot with the trees during the day. I'll work in here with you, and then he and I will swap out after you leave at five."

"What did my dad say to you?" She wore a worried frown.

"He's just concerned for your safety, Jen. Nothing any father wouldn't say when faced with danger like that robbery. I get it. I hired Dave so I can be in here and help mind the shop."

"I feel like such a baby. I shouldn't have said anything to my family."

Jere tilted his head and stared for a moment. "Why not?"

She pulled her hands out and began motioning with them. "I mean, look at this place? We are right across from a drugstore, a courthouse, the jail, and the police department. So many other places that would keep a kid like that from doing such a thing. It wasn't a normal hold-up. Likely won't ever happen again. Now everyone is worried about nothing."

"No," Jere said. "It's not for nothing. Your dad made good points. I'm not willing to put you or anyone else in that situation again."

"What kind of good points?"

He moved a few steps closer to her and looked into her eyes. "Like, if I had a kid, I would be furious that someone didn't protect her like I would."

"Okay, are we still talking about my dad, because you look like you mean *you*."

He smiled. "If you were my kid, I'd be mad that someone allowed you to be on the front line, too. I need to be more involved with this business, anyway. This is just a good jumping-off spot. I've let managing this place sort of muddle along. Joe has always handled it well, and I didn't need to be very active. Things can change. Things *are* changing."

She fidgeted with the laminated price chart on the register. "Like, what kind of change?"

He put his hand on hers. "What was once between us, maybe?"

She looked up.

"At least we can start from here. See where things go," he added, removing his hand.

A lady looking for winter squash entered, and they had to stop their conversation. The rest of the day was somewhat busy, and Dave sold quite a few trees. Jere said her brother was a natural born salesman. Jenny thought Dave was a natural born hogwash spreader.

Neither of them went back to the former conversation, but the ease between them grew and they found themselves standing too close to each other and occasionally touching each other's hand or leg.

Jere thought it was close to the greatest feeling in the world to have his best friend back. He wasn't going to push for more until she showed signs of being receptive. After the shop closed on Saturday evening, Jere offered to take Jenny home. She looked at Dave, who waved her away.

"Go on," he said. "I'll stay until you get back, Jere."

Jere grinned at him in thanks. They walked around the building toward Jere's truck. He remembered how difficult seeing Jenny had been when she'd first arrived back in town. Had that only been a week? He shook his head.

"What are you shaking your head about?" Jenny asked, climbing up into the truck.

"I just remembered you've only been here about a week. Funny how fast time flies."

She shrugged. "Seems longer than that to me."

"You don't have enough to do to keep you busy," Jere offered. He cranked the truck, and they waited until the heater kicked in, both rubbing their hands.

"And you know that because?"

"Because you spend most of your time with me." This made her pause and grow quiet. "Which is not a bad thing," he added, quickly.

"I think you're right. And I also think I'm at a loss as to how to fix that."

"Maybe you should do a little Christmas shopping?"

She laughed shortly. "Yeah. Right. With what?"

"No funds?" he asked, pulling out of the parking lot.

"Not much," she admitted.

He thought for a moment, an idea growing in his mind. "What if I gave you an advance on your paycheck? Or even better, a bonus?"

"What?" she asked, shocked.

He nodded at the thought. "Yeah. I guess you could call it a sort of early Christmas bonus or something."

She grew pensive. He glanced over at her. "No strings attached, Jen. Don't fret over it. I was going to spread the wealth to you and Joe in a little while, anyway. The trees have really done well, and your wreaths have sold out."

She stared at him. "I don't want charity, Jere."

"No charity. You've earned it. It would help you out with the holidays and help me out with taxes. Ha-ha. See? I'm selfish to the end."

She giggled a little. "Okay. If you're sure."

He took a deep breath. "Yeah. I'm sure. Quite a few things are becoming clear to me now. I'm definitely sure."

~**~

Jenny said goodbye to Jere and walked slowly into the house. She could take what funds she had in the bank and go buy gifts tomorrow. The thought made her excited for Christmas, something she hadn't allowed herself to do since arriving back in Mt. Moriah. The idea put a spring in her step, and she pulled her coat off, hanging it in the hall closet, whistling softly.

Her parents were in the dining room, the newspaper spread out on the table. They were talking animatedly.

"Hey," she greeted them. "What's up?"

"Hey Jenny," her mother answered. "We were just looking at a news story about the old house on Hillside. Apparently, it has been sold to a former movie star."

She strolled to where they sat and stared down at the page. A striking older man with silver hair stared up at her. He seemed familiar, and she peered closer to see what movies were listed as having been his.

Nothing she remembered seeing lately. Maybe old movies? She pulled her phone out of her pants pocket and looked up the actor's name on the Internet.

"Oh, look Mom," she exclaimed. "He was in that old movie Death Falling. Good-looking man, for an old guy."

Her father stared at her.

"No offense, Dad."

He grinned. "None taken. Just watch your tongue about old guys."

"So, we have a celebrity in town now? That's interesting. That house is what...? Three stories? Four?"

Fancy shrugged. "Not sure. It's big though."

Her mother folded the paper together and stood. "Did Dave come in with you? I'm about to put dinner on the table."

"No," Jenny answered. "He stayed over at the market. Christmas tree selling seems to agree with him."

Her mother brushed past her. "Well, so does food. Call him. I'm not holding up our dinner."

Jenny complied. Dave was already on his way home. "Have you seen Sam today?" she asked her mother.

"Yes, he's over at the studio. He's not going to make it for dinner. I suspect he's on another date," she said, looking over at Jenny. "Do you know who he's seeing?"

"Nope. Big mystery. I bet he'll be moving out soon."

"Already started," Gus added. "Helped him today with his bed."

Her mother stirred a bowl of batter for cornbread. "Guess we won't be having him at our table much longer."

She sounded so wistful that Jenny strolled to where she stood and gave her a hug. "It's okay, Mom. You still have me."

Fancy laughed and swiped at a tear. "That's true. I still have you."

Dave came into the kitchen and interrupted the tender moment. "What's for dinner? I'm starved."

Jenny opened the oven while her mother shoved the now filled cast-iron skillet into it. "Food," his sister told him.

"What kind of food?" He slid sideways down the counter and stared over their shoulder at the contents of the pots.

"Shoo," his mother said. "It's food. The kind you eat."

He shrugged and went to join his dad at the table. Jenny gave her mother a conspiratorial wink and her mother smiled. At least two of the kids in the family were still having dinner here. Jenny made a mental note to talk to Sam and find out more about his 'date.' Secretly, she was over-the-moon about the fact that he was spreading his wings, moving out, seeing someone.

The conversation went on its usual track during dinner, and she tried to focus, but her mind went back to shopping for Christmas. She wished she'd thought to ask Jere how much he wanted to give her in a bonus. Having an amount in mind would help decide if she was buying in a specialty store or a discount store.

Oh well, no matter. I'm grateful for anything, she thought.

~**~

Jere had gone back to the market to help Dave close up. He had agreed to give Dave a commission on every tree he sold. That was good for both of them. Dave would sell more, and they all would benefit.

After Dave left, Jere sat at his desk and wrote out a couple of checks. He smiled as he slid them into his wallet. It would feel good to reward Joe for all his patience and work. His brother deserved it.

And Jenny? Giving her a bonus was going to make his entire Christmas. He planned on offering to take her shopping, too. Anything to get more time together. There was nothing that he wouldn't do to make her happy. He hoped that she would accept the bonus and his invitation to shop without worrying. There were no strings attached, as far as he was concerned, and he wanted her to know that, too. Whatever came now would be between them and the time it took. However long that was.

He locked up the market, climbed into his truck, and slowly drove through town. There was only one thing that might put a boulder in his path.

He glanced over at the nearly finished stage on the courthouse grounds. The Christmas Celebration was going to happen next week, and Brandon Daniels and his band would be all over the place. There would be publicity and photo ops on every street corner, or his name wasn't Jeremiah.

If Jenny wanted to be in Daniels' life, he couldn't stop her, but he sure could punch the singer's lights out over it. And he would, too. There was no way he would let Jenny get ripped from his arms twice. Not by that drunken, two-bit player.

Jere accelerated the truck and tore away from the area where the event would be held. Even the event site for the monster music performance to come gave him chills. He wanted to trust Jenny. He wanted to believe that she was over Daniels. But women had a funny way of changing their minds and putting new lines in the romance rulebook.

He drove through Mt. Moriah and stared at all the new decorations.

When had that happened? He'd been so busy that he'd completely forgotten to take the time to enjoy the season. He thought again about the checks in his wallet. If he didn't do anything else toward this holiday, then that would be okay with him. Giving gifts to the two of them would be enough for him.

He smiled as he turned on his street. The way the faces of Joe and Jenny would light up over a bit of extra cash would make all the hard work worth it.

Wasn't that what Christmas was supposed to be all about? Good-will toward men and peace on earth.

God Bless Ye Merry Gentlemen played on the radio, and he continued humming it all the way into his house. When he was about to close the front door, he glanced across the yard and across the street to Jenny's house. Their tree stood in front of the picture window and the lights shone out onto the front lawn.

He was going to enjoy seeing them all at church tomorrow. Maybe he'd get a minute to talk to Jenny and maybe offer the check to her then.

Filled with happiness and warm thoughts, he closed the door and headed for the kitchen where Maria and the family sat at the dinner table laughing about something. Life was definitely good. He joined them and dug into a plate of spaghetti that had been prepared during the day.

~**~

While Jenny got ready for bed, she thought about calling Jere. It was so generous of him to want to give her a bonus. She'd only been there a week. Maybe he was using this as some sort of retribution for the rocky start they'd experienced since she returned. Maybe he was genuinely into the Christmas spirit. Whatever it was, she was grateful for it.

In the end, she didn't call. Instead, she looked up items she thought she'd like to buy for her family online. The pricing didn't thrill her. When had sweaters and gloves gotten so expensive? She placed her phone on the floor next to the couch and closed her eyes. At tomorrow's church service she planned on having a stern word with God over the way people were jacking the price of everything up until no one could afford anything.

She tossed and turned for a while. Her dreams ran the gamut between robbers who held a gun to her head in a discount clothing store and seeing Brandon at the courthouse singing songs she had fallen in love with.

When her mother woke her by opening the curtains in the living room, she was shocked to know it was morning already.

"It sure feels like I just closed my eyes," she said wearily in the way of greeting.

"Me too. Kept thinking about Sammy."

"Did he come home last night?"

"No. I guess he's really out of the house after all."

"Are you upset over that?" Jenny pushed herself into a sitting position. "Because I think it's great, myself."

Her mother turned toward her, crossing her arms. "I hope that's not because you will be the one to get his room."

"No. Of course not. I just think it's a good thing he is going out on his own and making a dent in the world."

Her mother made a sour face and headed to the kitchen. Jenny grabbed her church clothes, a long-sleeved dress and ballet flats, and went upstairs to the bathroom to take a shower. She didn't think any more about Sam and his life until on the way to church. Her mother was speaking her mind about it, and her father said nothing, driving the car in silence.

"He should've had the decency to call us," Fancy said.

"Why didn't you call him?" Jenny asked. "The phone works both ways."

Her mother looked over her shoulder at Jenny in the backseat. "It's a matter of respect."

"It's a case of he's grown and doesn't need to inform you of everything he does any longer, more like."

Jenny saw her father's eyebrows raise, and he glanced at her in the rearview mirror.

"Okay, I'm tabling this discussion. You're full of sass," Fancy said, defeated. "And I'm too tired to argue."

"Sorry, Mom, but that's just the way I see it. Sorry if it doesn't pass muster with you. Maybe you should think about it though."

Silence filled the car, and Jenny wished she'd taken Dave up on his offer to ride with him to church.

~**~

When the family all filed into the pew at First Baptist, Jere looked as far down the row as he could. He found Jenny down there talking to her brother, Sam. He shifted around and shook hands with a man who patted him on the shoulder.

The sanctuary was slanted like an arena. His family always sat in a pew a few rows up from the altar. Stairs went from the top to the bottom and footfalls were silenced by the thick carpeting on the stairs.

Brother Bill stepped to the podium and began speaking. Jere tried hard to focus on what was being said, but he saw Dana slide into a pew with her roommate a few rows below him.

It must be her week off from the nursery. She looked all around and when her gaze scanned those seated behind her, he knew she'd seen him. He felt his face flush. It seemed so wrong for her to be in church. She was a liar and a cheat.

Something that Brother Bill said registered, finally. "For all have sinned and come short of the glory of God."

Jere had to check himself. Who was he to judge? Dana was no saint, but who was? He smiled to himself and promised to let the former antagonistic feelings fall away. Suddenly, he was glad to be in church. Apparently, he needed the ministry more than he even knew.

Later, when everyone had tithed, been prayed over, walked the aisle to salvation, and shaken hands with their neighbor, church let out. Jere couldn't wait to rush down to speak to Dana.

He jogged down the steps two at a time before she could disappear into the crowd. When he found her, he pulled her by the arm to turn her around.

"Dana," he said, a little out of breath.

She yanked her arm away. "What? Don't you dare touch me, Jeremiah Collins."

He held up a hand palm-out. "Whoa! I didn't mean anything by that. I was just trying to grab you before you left."

She thrust a hand on a hip. "What do you want? I thought we'd said all that was needed."

He realized slowly that she was never going to be a forgiving person who could bury the hatchet with a short conversation. "Fine. Never mind. I hope you have a nice Sunday." And he turned sharply around and went back up the stairs to the landing where everyone gathered to go out into the atrium of the sanctuary.

He never looked back. He forgave her. Someday she would forgive him, he hoped. Until then, she didn't have to interact with him ever again. And that gave him all the freedom to forget all about her as well.

When he caught up to his family, John and Maria stood talking to Gus and Fancy. Jenny, Dave, and Sammy were all missing.

"Mrs. Jones," he said. "Where did Jenny and the boys go?"

Dave and Sam had been known as the boys all of his life.

Fancy turned. "Oh, they went over to see Sam's studio. He's ... moved out now."

Jere could tell this was news that hadn't gone over well with Mrs. Jones. "Think they'd care if I popped in?"

She shook her head. "No, go ahead."

He nodded and took off for the doorway to church.

~**~

Jenny grinned when Jere appeared at the door to Sam's studio.

"Your mom told me where you were," he explained as she let him inside.

"Oh okay. No worries. Sammy was just showing us his new digs. He got the apartment over this place," she pointed overhead.

"Wow, that's cool."

Dave and Sam came through the doorway that led to the back of the studio.

"Hey Collins," Dave said, coming forward to grasp his hand. "You lookin' for us?"

"Well, to be honest," he said, cutting his eyes toward Jenny. "I have some business with your sister here."

Sam stifled a grin and pushed Jenny toward Jere. "Go on, then. You heard the man. You're in trouble and you have to face the music."

"Oh, no!" Jere exclaimed, thrusting his hands out. "She's not in trouble, dude."

"Stop shoving me, Samuel," Jenny said in a threatening tone. "I will beat you down."

He laughed, and the others joined in.

She sauntered away, following Jere through the studio's door, turning at the last moment to stick her tongue out at her brothers.

Jere opened his truck's passenger door for her, and she climbed up into the vehicle.

"I've been trying to pry out of Sam who he's been seeing, but no dice. Do you know?"

He stood beside the open door. "Nope. He's being the pillar of privacy."

She shrugged. "Oh, well. What did you want to talk to me about?"

"I wondered if you had thought any more about the bonus."

"Well, yeah. What woman wouldn't love to have free money to shop with? But you didn't tell me how much it would be, so I was a little limited in my dream spending."

"Aw. Shoot. I'm an idiot." He hauled out his wallet. "Here," he said, pulling out a check and handing it to her. "This is for you."

Jenny took the check and stared at it. "Five hundred dollars? Jere! No, that's way too much."

He laughed. "You can't tell me how much money to gift my employee."

She tried to give it back. "Jere, you can't. This is too much. I'm not worth that much. Those wreaths didn't bring in that much."

He gently pushed her hand back toward her. "Yes, you *are* worth it. Every penny. And in addition to that, I'm offering my services to run you around to shop with it and buy Christmas for your family."

She stared at him, her mouth slightly open in amazement. "But ... but ..."

"No buts. You're keeping that money, and if you don't have a checking account yet, I can take you on your lunch hour to open one."

"Jere, you're too good to me." She shook her head and stared down at the check.

He gazed at his feet for a moment before lifting his eyes to meet hers. She swiped at a tear that escaped.

"I want your Christmas to be good, Jen. You've earned it with all you've gone through. I hope you'll relax and enjoy the holidays. I might even have an ulterior motive."

"Like what?"

"Would you go to the Christmas Celebration with me?"

She grinned at him through the tears that fell down her cheeks in fat drops.

"I will," she said. "It would be my pleasure."

"This is all my pleasure and I feel absolutely wonderful about it."

From her elevated position, Jenny bent down, and he met her lips with his own.

"Merry Christmas!" they said in unison.

Chapter
Twenty-One

♥

The next day, Monday, Jere arrived at the market early. Workmen hammered and sawed and generally made a massive noise at the courthouse grounds. The event site was thoroughly coming together now. Jere stood and stared for a few moments, cupping his hand over his eyes to shield them from the rising sun.

It appeared there would be booths there as well. He supposed that would be for food and drinks. Maybe for crafts and fun stuff too. They would all have to wait to find out, he mused.

He got the store open, the cash register ready, and went to prop open the back door. He was surprised to see Dave already out there.

"Hey, man," Jere said. "Didn't see your vehicle out front, didn't know you were here."

"Slept over at Sam's place. Had a few beers and didn't want to drive. Also, didn't want my mama to smell booze on me on a Sunday. I walked to work today, left the car at Sam's for Jenny if she wanted to have it today."

"Cool."

Jere heard Joe rustling around in the market. "I'll check back with you in a few," he told Dave as he turned back inside. Joe was in the stockroom, moving boxes around.

"What's up?" Jere asked, poking his head into the small space.

"The sky?" Joe asked with a grin.

Jere shook his head. "Lame, man, real lame."

Joe shrugged and carried a box of summer squash into the shop. Before he could start unloading it, Jere stopped him.

"Hey, I have something for you. Come on back to the office."

Joe straightened and followed him silently.

Jere pulled the check from his wallet and handed it to his brother. "And do not say you don't want it either."

Joe tilted his head. "Why are you giving me this?"

"So, you and Hope and Mrs. Maddie can have a nice Christmas. It's your bonus."

"Jere, this is likely all you made in profit this whole year. You sure you know what you're doing?"

"Yes, I do. Take it and shut up."

Joe pulled his own wallet out and carefully put in inside. "It is greatly appreciated and will be used, for sure."

Jere stepped closer to his brother and clapped him on the shoulder. "I love you, man."

Joe laughed, and they hugged. "Love you too, little brother. Merry Christmas."

"Merry Christmas, and Happy New Year."

They separated, and Jere heard Jenny arrive at her place in front of the register.

"Let the day begin," he said to Joe, who had already headed back to his squash.

There were plenty of people coming and going in and out of the market that day. Many were looking for food for their Christmas feast. Jere was happy he'd brought in extra vegetables and fruits to handle the holidays. No one left disappointed.

When they had a break, Jenny said, "Next year, I want to make some baskets to sell. You know, with fruit and jams and jellies and so forth in them."

He grinned at her, pulling out a stack of brown bags. "Next year, I'll let you."

~**~

The rest of the week went by like a blur to Jenny. There was work to do and decorating to finish, and the big meal to plan. If she wasn't at work, she was sitting with her mother elbow-deep in cookbooks and recipes.

She promised Jere that Thursday she would be ready to go shopping. He'd been true to his word and taken her to open a checking account. She still didn't have a debit card, but she had checks and most stores would accept those.

"Okay," Jere had said. "I'll close up early for a few hours. We can go shopping over in Diago Springs if you want to."

"No," she told him. "I think everything I want to buy is in town."

When Thursday rolled around, she couldn't wait to get off work and get into the stores. She could imagine how crowded they would be. Jere told Dave they were going to knock off early and he could have an afternoon to do something fun.

He drove Jenny into Mt. Moriah's business district and parked in one of the slots along Main Street. She was so excited, her feet fairly danced on the truck's floor. She didn't even wait for him to open her door, shoving it aside and leaping to the ground on her own.

"Where to?" Jere asked.

She tapped her lower lip with her forefinger and thought. "Let's start with Pandora's. I need to find something nice to wear for Christmas. And I'll bet they have a nice scarf or gloves that I can get Mama."

He grinned and waved for her to go forth, and she did. She breezed into Pandora's Boutique and greeted Diana and Hope, who were both in the showroom.

"Hey Jere, hey Jenny," Diana greeted them, smiling. "Good to see y'all. What're you doing in here, Jenny Marie?"

"Christmas shopping," Jenny answered, her face unable to contain her happiness.

"For you or for Mrs. Fancy?"

"Both."

Hope said, "Oh, I bet I know something that your Mama will like, Jenny." And she led her to the back of the store to a rack where pretty sweaters were hanging.

"Wow, Hope," Jenny exclaimed. "I didn't know you were selling other garments aside from formalwear and the like."

"Thank Diana," Hope told her in a conspiratorial whisper. "She's really gotten good at judging the market. These items sell like nobody's business."

"Well, I sure want one." Jenny browsed through the sweaters. "I like this blue one."

She held it out, and Hope nodded. "That will go so well with Mrs. Fancy's blue eyes."

Jenny giggled. "Okay, put that one aside for me. Now to find something that matches my eyes."

Hope looked over her head at two more customers who came in. "Excuse me, Jenny. Diana, will you help Jenny for me?" And she switched places with Diana.

"What's your pleasure?" Diana asked Jenny. "A dressy dress or something that will go over into the next year?"

"Show me both."

Jere wandered around the front of the store while Jenny shopped. She told him he could leave if he wanted to. He just smiled and shook his head.

She found a nice dress, long-sleeved with a lace overlay that fitted her perfectly. Both of the shop employees agreed it was exactly what she should wear.

She made her purchases and grinned at Jere as they left the store.

"I am so excited. I wanted to buy just the right dress."

He nodded. "I think you did it."

That made her smile all the way to the truck.

~**~

Jere decided that if the stores that Jenny wanted to shop in were located around the Main Street area, he would just leave the truck parked where it was, and they could walk to the various spots. It was a fun afternoon already. Jenny had purchased a dress that accentuated her figure in ways that all men would appreciate. He would be so proud for everyone to see her as his date. He figured his gray suit that he wore for holiday church gatherings would go nicely with it.

They walked past the Head Shop, and he looked in the window as they passed. Sarah was sitting in one of the chairs, looking back. Her face spoke of loneliness and loss. He waved to her.

Jenny saw him wave and followed his gaze. She also waved.

Sarah didn't move, but only lifted her hand and gave them a slow smile.

"Wonder what's wrong with her?" Jere asked.

"Not sure. Maybe she's having a slow day?"

Jere tilted his head. "Did you know she owes like a gazillion dollars in back taxes?"

"What?" Jenny turned and stared at him. "Really?"

He nodded. "Yeah. I overheard her talking to one of the tax guys at the place I use for Veggie Heaven."

They continued on, and eventually, Jenny made all the purchases she'd planned for gifts for the rest of her family. She assured him that the money he'd given her was plenty, and she even had a tidy sum left over.

He took her home and helped her inside with all her bags. Mrs. Jones came into the foyer to see who had arrived. She wiped her hand on a kitchen towel.

"Did y'all eat dinner yet?"

Jenny shook her head. "No. Too much shopping to do. What're you having?"

"I made some fresh French bread and a pot of spaghetti. Our men folks have already eaten, but I'll be happy to heat it up for you and Jere."

Jenny looked askance. Jere thought about the cold sandwich he would have at home. "Sure! I love spaghetti."

Jenny grinned. "Yeah, I guess we'll have some."

Her mother waved at them and headed for the kitchen. Jere waited while Jenny went upstairs to stow her gifts from prying eyes until she could get them wrapped. She left the dress for herself downstairs to show her mother.

When she came downstairs, he watched her descend. He thought she was probably going to be the prettiest woman at the event. Her green eyes sparkled with excitement. They strolled through the hallway and entered the kitchen. His stomach immediately growled at the scent of basil and oregano and baking bread.

They sat at the table and Fancy brought them iced teas with lemon slices, as well as their plates. Jere's was piled high. The loaf of Italian bread enticed him from its basket when she placed it in front of him.

"Wow," he said, admiration tinging his voice. "You know me too well, Mrs. Jones."

Jenny laughed. "If she knows anything, she knows that a hungry man is a pliable man. What are you trying to get out of Jere? You know he'll be weak and easy after all that food."

Fancy shrugged and crossed her arms. "Nothing. Just loving my people. That's all."

Jere didn't hear any of the following exchange between Jenny and her mom. He was in spaghetti nirvana.

~*~

Jenny woke on Friday and felt the surge of energy that fun events always brought. She looked forward to going to the Christmas Celebration with Jere. It had turned off warm for December in the hills. Today was expected to be in the sixties and not much lower than fifty tonight. Perfect weather for being outside.

She was grateful that Jere had given her the day off. He was going to try to be open for tree sales through the noon hour, but then would go home and be ready to take her to the dance. She stood in front of the mirror on the old dresser in the bedroom she now occupied. It wasn't as large as the one she used to have, but it would do for now.

She pulled her hair up and observed the effect. It might be nice to just wear it loose. She let her hair fall and shook her head for it to settle into place. It would be much warmer on her neck, too.

Oh well. Don't have to decide this second. She sighed and pulled the belt of her robe tighter. *Nothing a cup of coffee and a few moments with pins and hair spray won't fix.*

With that, she went downstairs and into the kitchen. No one was up yet, aside from her mother, who she felt certain never slept.

"Good morning," Fancy greeted her.

"Good morning. What on earth gets you up so early? Dad doesn't work today, does he? Most people are off for the celebration in town."

"No, he's off."

Jenny went to the coffee pot and lifted an eyebrow as she poured a cup.

Her mother sighed. "I don't know. I think I may have to get some sort of sleep aid. I just cannot stay asleep for more than a few hours. It's so aggravating."

"Have you talked to your doctor about it?"

"Yes, but she says I should try over-the-counter things first. I really don't want to take anything. It seems so silly. I should be able to sleep for goodness' sakes."

Jenny carried her cup to the table. "I don't know, Mom. I've heard that Melatonin works okay, and it's all natural. Maybe she has a point. How do you know if you don't try?"

Fancy nodded. "True. I guess I just hate pills."

"Ha. Don't we all."

Her mother made a new cup of coffee and joined her. "How are things going with your job? Is working with Jere okay? Y'all seemed kind of cozy last night."

Jenny shrugged. "Yeah. I mean, I believe we've buried the hatchet. Whatever that means. We had fun shopping and all. He asked me to be his date for the celebration in the park today."

Fancy smiled. "Did he now?"

"Yes, he did. Stop with the cat-who-ate-the-canary grin. It's a casual thing. No strings."

"If you say so," her mother murmured.

It wasn't long before Dave came into the kitchen, hungry as usual. Fancy got up and started frying bacon. The aroma filled the house and Gus joined them in a little while.

Jenny helped her mother make a nice big breakfast so that everyone could go awhile without getting hungry, since they were all going to be at the event. She was anxious to get upstairs and get dressed.

Today she would *not* be late for anything.

Chapter
Twenty-Two

♥

J ere stared at Jenny. The dress that she'd picked out at Pandora's fit her body like a glove. Her hair glistened like a copper penny, and she wore it loose and flowing around her shoulders, and that perfume she wore made him want to gather her in his arms and never let go.

He grinned wordlessly and extended his elbow for her to take so that he could escort her to his truck. She giggled a little at his gallantry.

The sun beamed down overhead and promised to make them all wish they were not wearing winter-weight clothing.

Once Jenny was inside, he strode around the truck and climbed in.

"I think I'm going to park out back of Veggie Heaven and we can walk from there. I'm sure the courthouse parking areas will be full or marked off as no parking.

"You may find others have had that same idea," she replied.

He gave her another appreciative stare. "Ready?"

She nodded and smoothed the wrinkles that tried to form in the dress as it folded into her lap. "I wanted to tell you thanks again for all you've done for me."

"No thanks needed. You've been a great asset to me and my business. As well as a really nice diversion. I'm glad you're back in Mt. Moriah in case I forgot to tell you."

"Well, looking back, I think you were too mad at me to say anything like that, but cool. I'm glad you're happy about it. I'm glad to be back. I realize I have a lot of things to do to rise above my life as it stands, like getting a car, and maybe even finding a place to live. I mean, I don't want to keep living at home. Since Sam moved out, it's made me open my eyes a little."

"I've been thinking a lot about that, too. I guess I'm just lazy. Living with John and Maria has been so easy. But they might like to have the house to themselves, just them and the kids. So, yeah, me too."

They turned into the opening to the alley behind Veggie Heaven and nestled his truck into a tight spot. It blocked anyone else from doing likewise and also protected his Christmas tree inventory.

In a few moments, they were hand-in-hand strolling around the courthouse grounds looking at the vendor tents that had been set up. It was not quite two yet, but it seemed as if most of the town had decided to show up.

Jenny stopped at the Park Commission's tent to pick up a listing of the day's activities. Jere leaned over her shoulder and scanned the page. There would be face-painting for the kids, and free balloons in Christmas colors. Then, food vendors would open soon. He noted several had already opened and had small lines forming.

"Are you hungry?" he asked.

"Not yet," she told him. "My mother made a massive breakfast."

He looked around. "Nothing exciting going on yet. You want to walk over to Sam's studio and see him for a while?"

She nodded and folded the itinerary. "Yeah, let's go. The main event is the music, and the first band doesn't come on until four."

"What time does Daniels' band come on stage?"

She blinked a few times and answered, "Tonight. *Sarcastix* is the headliner."

He tilted his head and caught her gaze. "Are you going to be okay with this? It's still new and maybe still a little painful. We do not have to be here for that."

The instrumental strains of a familiar Christmas tune wafted to his ears. He watched her struggle mentally with his question. When she answered, it was an honest assessment that he respected.

"It is still new and still painful, and I might be harboring a lot of resentment, but I still want to come for the dance. I don't care if he *is* the headliner. I don't care about anything but having fun with you tonight."

This made Jere's heart swell with love. This might not be the best time to tell her how he felt, but sometime within these 24 hours, he would. She would be a captive audience and would have to hear him out. No matter what her reply was, he would tell her he was still in love with her and maybe had never stopped.

~*~

Jenny couldn't believe how much she enjoyed being with Jere. They had walked over to Sam's studio and found him painting an oil of the courthouse. The colors were vibrant and depicted summer in all of its glory.

"Commissioned for the gallery in the courthouse," Sam told them shyly. "What do you think?"

"Think it's about the most beautiful picture I've ever seen," Jere told him, staring at the painting as if it were a museum piece.

"It's really good, Sammy." Jenny grinned at her brother before punching him playfully in the arm. "I think you've been holding out on us."

"It's amazing what you can do when you are being paid to do it," he said.

They joined him in a cup of coffee and stood out on his balcony overlooking the parking lot of his studio and small apartment.

"Are you going to the dance tonight?" Jenny asked him.

"Yep. Planning on it."

"Are you going to be with anyone?"

"Maybe," he answered, softly.

"When are you going to introduce this person to us? Who the heck are you dating, anyway?"

He laughed. "It's killing you and David. He's been bugging me for a week."

She shrugged. "We're all curious."

Jere leaned against the railing. "I bet I know. Lori?"

"Kitchens?" Sam asked, shock on his face "Oh heck no."

"That was my only guess," Jere said. "I give. Who?"

Sam stared into his coffee mug. "I promised I wouldn't tell but let everyone find out tonight when we show up together."

Jenny sighed. "Fine. Be mysterious. I don't care. She better treat you right. That's all I'm saying."

In a short while, they said goodbye and left, walking back to the event site. Things were in full swing. Jere picked up a flyer at a local insurance agent's booth and folded it into a fan for Jenny, who regretted the choice of material her dress was made of.

They strolled around the courthouse and walked together to the local community garden that was on the park grounds. It was not in any shape to speak of, but the promise of vegetables to come murmured from its depth.

"Won't be long before squash and carrots and tomatoes will be all over this place," Jere said, musing at the grounds.

Jenny watched him and felt pride swell in her chest at his knowledge of the food stuff in the garden that was literally within walking distance of his market.

"Do you ever come here and harvest anything?" she asked as the question occurred to her.

"No," he answered quickly. "I wouldn't do that. This garden is for the people of Mt. Moriah and their families. Lord knows we need better food choices."

She couldn't disagree with that.

The sounds of merriment came from the other side of the courthouse, faint yet distinct.

"Let's get back," Jere suggested, turning to go. He took her hand, and they walked away from the area. As they walked, Jenny thought about how far they had come in the repair of their relationship or friendship over the span of a week. She was utterly grateful.

~*~

At the event site, Jere lost any thought of time. There was so much to do and see. He and Jenny walked a lot. They visited every booth and taste-tested everything from scones to salted nuts. When they had seen it all and made their way back around the courthouse a second time. They decided to take a break and sit down on one of the benches situated for that purpose around the grounds.

He put his arm loosely around Jenny's back. They fell quiet for a time, taking in the sights and sounds of the celebration. The town leaders of Mt. Moriah had gone out of their way to make this event one that everyone would remember.

Jenny looked at the itinerary and said, "It's almost three. The magic act happens on the stage then. Do you want to go see it?"

He smiled at her. "I want to do whatever you want to do."

She nodded. "Okay then. Let's check it out."

They got up and walked to the area in front of the stage. Metal folding chairs were lined up. Enough to fit fifty to one hundred people. They found what they thought were good seats where they could watch the magician at work.

When the Great Sari appeared on stage, dressed in flowing garments and a head wrap, no one would imagine that he manned the co-op as a manager nearly six days a week.

Jere laughed and looked around for Will Birmingham, his friend. Will worked at the co-op with James, the Great Sari. He didn't see Will or Diana anywhere.

"I hope Will is around somewhere. He's gotta see this," he said to Jenny.

The Great Sari's magic act lasted about a half-hour and drew quite a good crowd. When he finished with his last feat, those gathered clapped loudly and whistled their approval.

"That was fun," Jere said. "What's next on your list?"

Jenny pulled out the itinerary and looked. "A reading of poetry at four."

"Uh. Do you want to stay for that?"

"Not if you don't."

"Actually, I'm getting hungry. Thought maybe we could find something to eat with more sustenance than nuts."

"Where to?"

"How about splitting a pizza?"

"Is Dana working?"

He hadn't thought of Dana since church on Sunday. He didn't know and didn't care if she was there or not, but the look on Jenny's face said that she *did* care.

"Don't know. We can go somewhere else."

"There was a food truck over on the far side," she reminded him. "What if we go see what they have?"

"Good enough," he agreed.

While they walked to the place where the food truck was located, he looked around for people they knew. He saw her family seated in the stage area. Dave was missing as was Sam, but he already knew they wouldn't be here until nighttime so they could imbibe. Loads of beer and wine coolers had already been delivered and bars were being erected even as he had the thought of them.

The event was transitioning from a daytime event into an evening one already. He looked at the sky and realized that nightfall wasn't far away, thanks to the shortness of the wintry days. He took Jenny's hand and hummed a Christmas song that he heard playing somewhere.

She joined in and soon they were singing out loud, oblivious to the stares they gained as they went. When they arrived at the food truck, they discovered, to their delight, tacos, and burritos.

"You want one or two tacos?" Jere asked Jenny.

"How did you know I would want tacos?" she asked, giggling.

"Oh, I know, never you mind." He laughed at her and stepped up to the window. He ordered two tacos for both of them and a couple of sodas.

When he finished, he led her to a picnic bench nearby to sit and eat. There were not a great number of people over on this side of the event. They had picked the perfect time to eat.

While they sat there, chatting, and joking with one another, Dana strolled through the area, practically ironed onto the dark swarthy man she'd been seeing. When she spied Jere and his date, she flipped her middle finger up to let him know how she felt.

"Classy," Jere yelled at Dana's disappearing back. "Very classy."

"Oh, don't let her ruin your night," Jenny said, waving at him to ignore the rudeness Dana seemed to spread everywhere she went. "She's really an awful person. I cannot believe you didn't see through all that."

He didn't reply but went to the window to collect their food which was even served on a plastic tray.

He set it all down on the table and handed Jenny a napkin. "I did see through her. I just was too hurt over you to do anything about it."

Jenny chewed for a moment and then answered. "You've hinted at being really hurt by me before. I'd like to drop it. Can we forget about Nashville?"

He wiped at taco sauce running down his hand, before staring at her. "I don't know, Jen. Can we?"

"What are you asking me, really?"

"I mean, he's in town. He's going to be up on stage. Do I need to worry about you changing your mind and disappearing?"

The look on her face told him immediately that he had gone too far.

Chapter Twenty-Three

♥

J enny sat dumbstruck. Had Jere really just said that? Did he seriously mean that he thought she would repeat her stupid mistake
with Brandon again? Angry tears rushed to her eyes. She wiped her
mouth and stood.

"Thank you for the tacos and the time together," she said coldly.
There was no way she would sit here and be insulted again. Jere had
taken liberties in that area far too much over the last week or so.

"Wait," he said, rising to hold out a hand. "I'm sorry. I was out of
line by saying that. I guess I'm still rankled by your choice back then.
I may be a little hungry-angry."

She stared at his hand. He moved to lift her chin so that her eyes
were on his.

"Jenny. I'm sorry, really."

She shrugged and sidestepped his hand. "Guess you'll have to spend
the evening with yourself and your guilt, huh?"

And she turned and walked away. It stung so much to hear him
suggest that she might repeat her fatal flaw again. Was everyone in

Mt. Moriah watching her to see what she would do when Brandon appeared?

She had seen him a few times, and even when he had come face-to-face with her at her job, she had felt nothing more than remorse for being so naïve. Brandon was her past. She had begun to believe that Jere might be her true future and lifelong love, but now that was in question. If he couldn't trust her, there was no future.

She hurried around the walkway leading back to the Christmas dance. Music could be heard even now from the warm-up band. She looked around for someone, anyone to talk to, to be busy with, so that if Jere came looking for her, she wouldn't be sitting alone looking pitiful.

Seated in the back row of the chairs facing the stage, Sarah Greene had one arm draped over the back of the seat next to her. She would be the perfect distraction, Jenny thought. She plopped down on the opposite side and thrust thoughts of men behind her.

"Hey, Sarah," she said, smiling.

"Hey there, Jenny," she replied, returning the smile. Her pale hair glistened in the last vestiges of the day's sun. "Where's your date?"

Jenny shrugged. "Oh, you know men. They don't always have us in the center of their day." She tried to sound dismissive, but Sarah wasn't fooled.

She pinioned Jenny with serious green eyes. "Nope. Not believing that for one second, Miss."

Jenny allowed her gaze to fall to her folded hands in her lap. "That obvious, huh?"

"Well, now, I'm not saying that you two are joined at the hip these days, but it would take a mighty powerful wind to separate you."

Jenny nodded. "I guess it would seem that way. I don't know. He says things sometimes that make me think he hasn't forgiven the past. I just want to move on, you know?"

"Is that so?" Sarah asked, jutting her chin at the stage. "You might want to prove it to all involved by telling that guitar man a final goodbye."

Jenny caught on to what she meant right away. "Has he been going around town saying something?"

Sarah winked at her. "A few things. Mostly, a song he's written for you. It'll be the thing that brings you back, he thinks."

"Ew! I hope it's not that one that's been playing on the stations around here."

"It is."

Jenny slumped. "You're right, Sarah. I need to cut all ties and make it stick. No wonder Jere is still trying to settle things in his mind."

Sarah patted her hand. "I'm no role model for love, my lady. But I do have a smidge of wisdom. Clean break, fresh start."

Jenny nodded and thanked her as she stood to go and find the man who had broken her heart and couldn't ever mend it.

~*~

Jere gave Jenny a few minutes before following her. *What a bone-headed move!* No wonder women gave him so much grief. Apparently, he could open his mouth and stick his foot in it at a pin drop.

He strolled around the courthouse, mentally beating himself up. Once he was on the event side, he looked for Jenny. She wasn't at any of the booths or sitting in the staged area for the dance and music.

"Where is she?" he asked under his breath. Had she gone home? She could have gotten a ride with anyone.

He wouldn't have blamed her if she had. He deserved to be ditched for such a terrible suggestion as he had made. Of course, she wouldn't hook back up with Daniels. The jerk had broken her heart, and she was not one to forgive easily.

This thought made him quicken his steps. He found Mr. and Mrs. Jones again and asked them if they had seen Jenny.

"Not since breakfast," Fancy said, then added jokingly, "Have you lost my daughter?"

"I guess so," Jere replied, turning to leave. He couldn't stand the thought of how close to the truth her question had hit. Acting like a jerk to Jenny was a quick way to lose her forever.

"We'll tell her you're looking for her if we see her," Fancy called after him. He lifted a hand and waved over his shoulder without looking back.

Once he had searched every place Jenny might have gone, Jere finally sat down in one of the folding chairs and tried to think where she could be. The darkness was descending quickly and if he didn't find her soon, he might as well give up. It would be easy to hide.

As he had these thoughts, the event people flipped a switch and big spotlights came on, illuminating the crowd which had grown in the last half-hour as he'd sought Jenny. In fact, a band came on stage and began tuning their instruments.

The music would begin soon, and he wanted to have this bad feeling between him and Jenny over and done with by then. He wanted the two of them to be able to spend this time together having fun, not in a battle.

He stood once again and looked over the heads behind him. He would totally lose his seat if he left now. He looked at the empty chair next to him.

I have to find her and soon.

He strode toward the booths again. He brushed shoulders with Sarah Greene. She turned and smiled at him.

"Hey Jere."

He returned the smile. "Hey yourself."

The crowd pooled around them. "You lookin' for Jenny?"

Surprise must have registered on his face because she grinned. "I saw her earlier. I think she's looking for you, too."

He nodded and asked, "Where do I find her?"

She pointed behind him. "Not sure, but maybe up closer to the stage. Hard to tell from here."

This made him turn and squint at the milling crowd in front of the stage. "Okay, thanks," he said, plowing through the crowd. Sarah was lost somewhere behind him.

Strains of an old tune came through the speakers on the stage as he hurried forward, skirting the rows of chairs. People were on their feet now screaming for the band, which was doing a great job of covering an old Bryan Adams song that had lyrics that struck him to his very core.

Baby, you're all that I want...

He squeezed past a few people dancing in front of the stage and finally caught sight of Jenny standing on the very edge of the stage on the far side.

She wasn't alone, either. He stopped in his tracks. She stood talking to Brandon Daniels who had a guitar low-slung around his body. They were laughing and talking like long-lost friends.

Had he been wrong—again?

~*~

Jenny felt her face flush with excitement. There was something about a music event that made her feel alive. She sought everywhere for Brandon and found nothing. Finally, she spied one of the band members lounging behind the stage, smoking.

"Steve!" she yelled, hurrying toward him.

The drummer's faced registered recognition and a slow smile spread across his face. He ground out the cigarette and opened his arms for her to be embraced.

"Jenny," he said, hugging her hard and lifting her off the ground. "I wondered if you would show up here."

She straightened her clothes as he set her down. "Wouldn't miss it. But, hey, where is Bee? I'm looking for him."

Steve Nicholson stared at her a moment. "You sure you want to do that?"

She nodded. "Yes. It's a sort of farewell meetup. We're done, Steve. But I want to wish him well. No hard feelings."

He took a deep breath. "Come on then."

He led her behind the stage, past the glaring eyes of security. When had *Sarcastix* gotten so powerful that they merited security people? Jenny did a finger-wave to the burly man and hurried past.

Steve led her to the band's van, parked in a secluded location across from the event site.

Brandon was climbing down as they walked up. He jumped to the ground from the stairs and grinned. "Jenny!"

"Yep. It's me."

"I'm shoving off," Steve said. "Y'all don't need me."

Brandon gave him a grateful smile and waved for Jenny to come inside.

"No, thanks. I just wanted to talk to you for a minute. Likely best that we're not seen together." She glanced around for paparazzi.

"What's on your mind? I wanted to talk to you too, but you gave me the heave-ho the last time, and well, I wasn't going to push it." He crossed his arms and stared at her.

The man was such eye-candy, it was hard to focus. Jenny felt the same tug of her heart now as she had before.

Be careful, girl.

"I wanted to tell you that I don't have any hard feelings about what we had and how it ended. I believe the whole experience made me grow up. I'll always be grateful for what we had, even if it didn't last."

He walked to her and draped his arm over her shoulder, walking her away from the van. "I gotta get going, but I really am glad to hear that. You're a special woman, Jenny. I guess you taught me a few things too."

When they got to the backstage area, he grabbed his guitar, and they walked together to where he would race onto the stage in a few moments. The warm-up band was finishing their last song. The ensuing silence from the music, followed by the applause, signaled it was almost time.

"I hope you know that I really am trying to kick the booze." Steve smiled down at her from where he stood on the second step. "I owe that to you. You probably saved my life."

She laughed at this, and he joined in.

"Brandon, thank you so much for being a good guy. I could have ended up far worse than being kicked out of a hotel. I hope you find happiness with someone someday. I won't forget you."

He stepped down to where she stood and gingerly swung the guitar behind him to give her a hug.

They were both enjoying the farewell embrace when Jere stepped up to them.

"Guess no answer is still an answer," he said to Jenny, who turned from Brandon to gape at him.

~*~

Jere turned and strode away as fast as he could. He felt so stupid. Jenny hadn't answered his question before because he'd hit home. She *was* planning on reconciling with Daniels.

"Good riddance," he muttered as he stormed toward where he'd parked the truck. She'd have to find a way home alone.

His heart hurt like never before.

How had he gotten so thickheaded?

Dana was a user for certain, but Jenny? He could hardly believe what he'd just witnessed. Was everyone laughing behind their hands, just waiting for this to unfold? He looked around at the couples walking down the sidewalk.

Christmas was the time to get with loved ones. Why was he the only person in Mt. Moriah who was getting dumped on? This thought made the hurt wane and the anger take over.

He slammed the truck door hard. Harder than necessary. And he remembered this same anger that had taken him over when he'd witnessed Jenny's desertion the first time. He got the truck running and allowed the heater to warm.

He pounded the dashboard with his fist. *What a big fat steaming pile of manure this day has turned into! Jenny the Destroyer has done it again!*

Then, as if a light had come on in his head, he recalled all the things he'd done for her over the last week. She'd not argued at any of it enough to matter. He'd given her a job, hired her brother, given her money, taken her places.

All that he'd done out of love for her came back to smite him in the face.

"What a fool I am," he moaned, throwing his head back into the headrest and closing his eyes against the injustice he felt. He opened his eyes and decided to wait before driving. In his current frame of mind, he'd only end up running someone over or plowing into a tree.

The longer he allowed himself to cool down, the more he wanted to rush back to find Jenny to tell her off. She earned a good cussing in his book. How on earth could she do this to him? Hadn't he been the pinnacle of kindness? Hadn't he done everything he could to make sure she was cared for and happy?

Some people don't deserve it.

Even as he thought this, he looked heavenward and knew he was wrong for thinking such a thing. But he'd been good to Dana too and look where that had gotten him.

"When is it my turn, God?" he yelled. His voice reverberated inside the truck. "Don't I deserve kindness and love?"

He closed his eyes and let his head drop. Maybe he'd been wrong about both women. They were not the ones he needed, or he wasn't the one they needed.

Either way, he lost. He lost the long-held notion that he would find a true love, a soulmate who would be his forever and ever and share his love, and give it back, wholly, unfettered.

Just as he determined to quit trying to find love, the passenger side door opened, and Jenny climbed in.

Chapter
Twenty-Four

♥

"Jere," she said, closing the door. "Let me explain—"

"Explain what?" he asked, anger splotching his cheeks. "What do you have to say, Jenny? That you lied to me, that what we had meant nothing ... again?" Big shot music man, Daniels wins the last round, eh?"

"It's not what you think?" she answered, putting her palm out. "What you saw was—"

"Was what? The two of you obviously enjoyed whatever you were plotting. Get out, Jenny. I have nothing left to give you."

He turned away and stared out the driver's door window.

She didn't know what to do. She decided to explain it calmly and rationally to him and hope he would listen and not bolt out of the truck.

"Jere, you have to believe me. This was not what it looked like. Brandon and I were not plotting anything. We were making sure that each of us understood how things ended was not what either of us wanted."

He jerked around, fury rippling through him. "So, you admit it? The two of you didn't want to break up ... it was a mistake? Is that what you're saying? Well, I hope you'll both be very happy."

He leaned across her and opened her door. "Get out."

"You can throw me out, but you have to listen to the whole story first."

"I don't have to do anything. I can't believe you're sitting there trying to make me hear about a reconciliation between you and someone who did you wrong in Nashville and won't hesitate to do it again in some other city." He sat back in his seat and crossed his arms. "I don't want to hear anything else. Just go."

She closed the door. "Jere, listen. Do you hear that song?"

He chewed on his cheek. "Yeah so?"

"He wrote that song for me ... about me. That's why I went to find him tonight. To let him know that he needs to move on, find someone else to write songs for."

Jere didn't look at her, but he was listening.

"I told him that what we had was over but that I didn't bear him any ill will."

"Had to hug it out to seal the deal?" His anger simmered in his words.

She reached over and pulled on his arm to shake him out of the funk. "Jere, I swear that what you saw was an official goodbye."

First, he looked at her hand on his arm. Then, his gaze traveled to her eyes to test her sincerity. "Goodbye?"

"Farewell, adios, arrivederci, goodbye."

"You swear?"

His pout reminded her of Dave when he was a young kid. Pouting was a fine art, and some men could do it better than others.

She made a cross over her heart with her hand. "Cross my heart and hope to croak."

He sat there, thinking it over. She pulled on his arm until she could take his hand.

"Jere, if I've learned anything over the last week, it's this: there is no one for me but you. You care for me in ways I never understand but am so grateful for. Like, working in the market with me and letting Dave be outside. I know you'd prefer to be out there, but you want me to feel safe. You want to keep me safe."

He nodded. "I do. I promised your dad."

"Nobody else has ever done that for me except my dad. You show how you feel with every word and deed."

These words made him turn to her and squeeze her hand. "I love you, Jen. I think I always have. I think that's why it hurt so much when you left Mt. Moriah with Daniels last summer. When you came back, I was so scared ... sometimes I couldn't breathe. Even when I was with Dana, something was missing. You ... you were missing."

She smiled. "I love you Jeremiah Collins. I've been an idiot chasing after a dream man when he was beside me all along."

He leaned over and kissed her gently.

"You forgive me?" she asked when he drew away.

"I guess. If you will promise me one thing."

"What?"

"You'll marry me in the spring when all the flowers are blooming, and everything is fresh and growing."

She caught her breath. "Are you proposing?"

He nodded, lifting her hand to his lips. "What do you say?"

"Yes," she answered. "A thousand yeses forever."

~*~

They walked back to the venue, hand-in-hand. They reached the chairs facing the stage, and suddenly, Jenny spied Sam with his date. They held hands and laughed together. Jere bent down and whispered in her ear.

"Sam is dating Edwin?"

"Yeah, I'm as surprised as you are."

"Ed's a good guy. I'm happy for them."

She smiled over at him. "Me too. Wanna go give them a hug?"

He shrugged, and she pulled him along. They stood next to the couple, and Jenny hugged her brother. Jere shook Edwin's hand. The music was too loud to speak and be heard, so they all just grinned and swayed to the song the band was playing. Each content with the other's company.

Sarcastix had been entertaining the crowd for a while and seemed to be wrapping it up. Jere stood with Jenny wrapped in his arms, right in front of the stage, so Daniels would never miss the sight of possession. It was the epitome of males squaring off for a female's affection.

Brandon stepped to the mic and told the crowd goodnight. He didn't stop there, though.

"It's been a great night, y'all. I just want to thank the organizers and the officials in Mt. Moriah for making it possible. And for those of you out there hugging your girl tight—" Here he paused and gave Jere a strong stare. "Be good to her, man. She's the best part of your life." Then, he held up his guitar in salute to the crowd which went wild with appreciation.

Jere grinned at his words.

"Good night and Merry Christmas!" Brandon yelled.

Jere turned Jenny around and kissed her until she was out of breath. When they strolled away from the Christmas party and headed for his truck, small snowflakes began to fall.

They were thinking of warmer days ahead. A wedding in the spring rang through the air on the heels of every holiday song they could remember, and they sang at the top of their voices all the way home.

~~~*~*

**Keep reading for a sneak peek at the next book in the
MT. MORIAH series**
The Little Theater
By bestselling author
Kim Smith

The Little Theater

♥

"Don't make me do this," Sarah Greene said.

"But Mom," Tony answered, wheedling. "You have experience."

"Not in a long time," his mother told him, putting his peanut butter and jelly sandwich into his lunch bag. "Besides, an assistant director has to have time to devote to the theater."

"You own your own business," he said. "You could take off any time you needed."

She grimaced and shook her head. "No, way. The Head Shop needs a lot more of my time, not less of it."

Her fourteen-year-old son shrugged. "Fine. But I told Mrs. Dunkin, and she said she was going to call you."

Sarah looked at him with chagrin. "Tony Greene. Please tell me you're kidding."

The look on his face said he was not kidding.

She let out an exasperated breath. "I really wish you would talk to me about this sort of thing before you recruit me. Now I'm sort of enlisted to it whether I want to be or not."

"Why?" He stared at her over the breakfast bar.

"I mean, I can't exactly tell your teacher no now, can I? It would be rude, especially after you have built me up to be this famous actress."

"Wait. I didn't tell her *that*," he said, miffed. "I just told her you had been in drama when you went to high school."

A loud beep sounded outside their modular home.

"That's the bus!" he yelled, grabbing his lunch and backpack. He gave her a quick peck, then jogged out of the kitchen and out of the house altogether. She sighed. The roar from the bus sounded loud as it took off down their gravel road.

Sarah and Tony lived on a patch of land right off the highway that led to the high school. It was postage-sized, but it was theirs. She and her husband, Adam, had bought the trailer and put it on the land when Tony was still young. Little by little, they had built a life on the periphery of Mt. Moriah.

He'd worked for the small accounting firm, LaRoux and LaRoux, near the courthouse. Life had been good right up until he left town with all of their money and the blond secretary that he worked with.

Adam left a massive tax debt, thanks to his ability to toggle money from one account into another, and his inability to say no to the small casino in Diego Springs.

Now, she lived with a shy teenager and owned a hair salon whose books were in the red as bright as blood. She stared out of the back door at the big Victorian on the hill behind the house. The local news reported that some movie star was moving into it, and she'd seen moving vans pulling in and out for the last two days.

Sarah couldn't imagine what someone with that kind of money wanted in the small town of Mt. Moriah. She daydreamed about it all the way into town.

~*~

"Don't make me do this," Asher said. "Mary, If I have to, I'll beg. You've got to help me out here. I'm standing in the middle of my living room with furniture and boxes everywhere. The last of the movers just left, and I don't have a clue how to set a house up. You have always done it for me every time I moved around LA," Asher pleaded.

Asher Shelton had lived in various places in and around Los Angeles, and the final spot in Beverly Hills had been his favorite, mostly due to the loving care Mary O'Neal had given him.

"Sorry Ash, you're on your own now. I tried to talk you out of ditching the easy life for some backwater, out-in-the-sticks town no one ever heard of. You were adamant you wanted the calm life away from all the cameras and limelight. You got what you asked for."

Asher paced among the boxes, all labeled with the room the contents belonged in.

"So, figure it out on your own from here on out, Ash," Mary continued. "My days of doing your bidding are over. I'm sure there has to be an interior decorator around there somewhere. If not, try Nashville. I'm not your personal assistant anymore, remember? You gave that up when you announced to the world on national TV you wanted to leave the hectic life of Tinseltown for the quiet life in Tinytown, Tennessee."

Here she paused to see if he would say anything. He let her go on. "Seriously, Ash, did you not think about it for one second? You know those late-night talk show hosts make their reputation out of getting famous people like you to blurt out something you shouldn't. You let him bait you right into it," Mary said, a hint of frustration in her voice.

"Mary, I grew up in that lifestyle with both of my parents acting in Soap Operas. I've seen what it's done to too many people over the years. It started to consume me, too, to the point I couldn't live my life like I wanted to anymore. I lost all my privacy. I couldn't even go

to a burger joint for a quick snack without being mobbed by fans and
two-bit paparazzi. Conmen always looking for a fast buck for some
lucky photo taken at the worst possible second," Asher replied, a shiver
of distaste going through him.

"Ash, you sound like the mob boss you played in that last movie.
No one says two-bit," she said, aggrieved. "That's always been a
made-for-movie line. You have a lot to learn about real life. Good luck,
you're going to need it. You're in for a rude awakening, but you'll find
that out on your own. I have to go, I have a dinner appointment with
Dave—"

"Dave who?" Asher cut her off.

"Heston," Mary answered.

"Heston? Honey, you know he doesn't have a future in film. He
barely made it through the filming we did in Romania five years ago,"
Asher shot back. "Book a plane and come save me instead."

"Hey, you didn't leave me much of a choice. I have to have a client
since you jumped ship. I'm hoping *he* has the fortitude to stay in the
business."

Those words stung as they echoed in his head, and she disconnected
the call. "Great. Just great. Looks like I'll be sleeping on mattresses on
the floor tonight. I have no idea how to even put the bed together."
He strolled to a box that was marked storage. "And no tools to do it
with even if I did know how."

His thoughts swirled through his head as he talked out loud. "Guess
I have to go into town tomorrow to see if there's anyone around here
I can hire to put this furniture together for me. I remember seeing
a small local furniture store in town. Maybe they'd be interested. Or
maybe they'll know someone with a sense of Feng Shui to get this place
in order."

He wandered to the big window that looked down over the town. "Well, assuming anyone here has ever heard of Feng Shui. I can't believe Mary refused to help me out." He sighed with resignation. "Not like she could have gotten here tonight anyway though."

~*~

Business was slow. Sarah wandered the shop picking up towels and sweeping up hair until her back ached. She had let the two girls that worked for her go home early. Nothing was going to happen at the Head Shop she couldn't handle alone. It was mid-January, and most Mt. Moriah folks were hurrying home in the late afternoon, not stopping along Main Street for a haircut.

She swiped at a strand of her own hair and walked to the door to look out. No one doing much out there. She stepped outside into the wintry air and enjoyed the cold that freeze-dried the sweat on her body. She had always loved winter. Especially in this picturesque town where snow fell in overnight clumps, turning everything into a glistening white wonderland.

An expensive-looking black car inched along Main Street, whipping into the parking spot across the street at the Hamblin Furniture store. The Hamblin family had sold to someone else, but they kept the name. She watched as a medium height man climbed out and straightened his clothes before heading inside. From the back, he wasn't familiar, and he had out-of-town plates on his car.

Her curiosity was piqued, but she heard her cell phone ringing and hurried back inside.

"Hello?"

"Is this Sarah Greene?"

"Yes," she acknowledged. "May I ask who's calling?"

The woman cleared her throat. "Yes, you may. I'm Kathleen Dunkin. Your son, Tony, is in my theater class at the high school."

"Oh, yes, Mrs. Dunkin. He told me you would be calling." Sarah tried hard to keep the chagrin out of her voice. "It's about the play for this semester?"

"Yes," Kathleen replied. "I hesitate to make such a monstrous request, Mrs. Greene, but I am in a real pickle. Tony told me you were in drama in high school. Perhaps on this very stage?"

"I was," Sarah told her, waiting for the request to come.

"Would it be possible for you to come see me one afternoon at the school? Maybe this week?"

Sarah let out her held breath. "I suppose I can plan to come. I would need to make it late afternoon. I have a business."

"Yes, Tony told me. I live over in Diego Springs, so am not too familiar with all the places in town, but I'm learning. So, would you like to make it at 4:00 on Thursday?"

Sarah could imagine her bent over her desk with a pencil hovering over her teacher planner. "Yes. That sounds fine."

"Good," Kathleen answered. "I've got you in my book."

They disconnected, and Sarah felt trepidation at the thought of helping with the school play. She wandered back out to the front of her shop and watched for the man to reappear. At least there was something to distract her.

Click here to buy In the Holler, Book One of the Mt. Moriah Series

Click here to buy The Inn on Main Street, Book Two of the Mt. Moriah Series

~~*~~

If you enjoyed reading this book, I would hugely appreciate a review. It only takes a moment, and it means a whole lot to me.

Thank you!

Made in United States
Orlando, FL
19 November 2024

54004174R00143